without a word

Also by Kate McQuaile

What She Never Told Me

KATE McQUAILE

without a word

Quercus

First published in Great Britain in 2017 by

Quercus Editions Ltd
Carmelite House
50 Victoria Embankment
London EC4Y 0DZ

An Hachette UK company

A CIP catalogue record for this book is available
from the British Library

TPB ISBN 978 1 78429 675 9
EBOOK ISBN 978 1 78429 676 6

10 9 8 7 6 5 4 3 2 1

Typeset by CC Book Production

Printed and bound in Great Britain by Clays Ltd, St Ives plc

Edward and Martha McQuaile.
Never Forgotten.

Prologue

That shot was the one I'd been waiting for. The canal had frozen over. It was as if one day the water was flowing and the boats were moving and the next everything was trapped in the ice. Under the ice, too. I wondered what would rise to the top once the thaw came – supermarket trolleys, dead ducks. Bodies, even. There was always going to be some fool who thought he could walk on the ice, and maybe one did, in the dead of night, when no one was watching. It had me thinking I could do something different. I'd been up to my eyes in politicians you wouldn't let into your garden shed, Z-list celebs you wouldn't inflict on each other, let alone on the newspaper-buying public. I'd always had the urge just to wander around with a camera and no agenda and all the time in the world to wait for the perfect shot, but I didn't have too many hours left for that kind of thing after marathon stints waiting for some shabby politician to emerge from the love nest where he had been shagging some pretty waitress half his age. The great thing about the snow and the ice was that London came to a complete stop and left me with sod all to do. So, when the snow looked like it was going to stay on the ground, I wasn't really thinking about anything. I didn't have a plan. I just started taking shots as I walked around. The one I liked best had a couple in it. Random couple. I had no idea who they were. I still don't. They probably never saw it. They certainly couldn't have had any idea I was taking the shot; they were too wrapped up in each other. Even though I say it myself, it was terrific. The pair of them, looking into each other's eyes as if nothing and no one else existed. And nothing else did exist because there was just the white snow covering everything. Her red coat was the only bit of colour in the whole scene. It was a picture waiting to be taken. I felt as if they were my creation somehow, as if they only existed in the lens of my camera. I often wonder what they're doing, how their story is turning out. Are they still together a few months on, or has love's young dream perished?

Extract from a profile of photographer Danny Beresford
in *The Sunday Times Magazine*

November 2006

Chapter One

The screen has gone dead, the connection broken. But I can still see those terrible images in my mind, flashing up in front of me like scenes from a movie trailer. I see her get up from the red sofa and walk towards the door. I see the glass she has left on the low table, the amber liquid inside it glowing in the low light. And then my eyes are drawn to the open door and the darkness beyond. I can hear the sounds of the storm that's raging outside: the heavy beat of the rain, the eerie howl of the wind. I can also hear the sound of the logs crackling in the grate and I can see the flames leaping and dancing around them. But the flames are moving now, spreading beyond the fireplace, burning orange and red, consuming everything in front of them. Amid the roar of the flames, I hear the whiskey glass shatter. I am frozen in front of the moving wall of fire. And then my hands rise involuntarily to my face as I see something take shape inside the flames. It's a moving, blazing form and it screams an unearthly scream. That's when the screen goes blank. That's when I start to scream.

*

Lillian had phoned. She told me to turn on the computer and get Skype up and running. 'We've got the broadband going at last! I have so much to tell you,' she said.

It was Saturday night. We could have been in some wine bar or pub, but I was in London, in the flat we used to share in Maida Vale, and Lillian was in Ardgreeney, where we'd both grown up.

I remember thinking, as we talked, that if anyone had suggested to Lillian, just a year before, that she might end up leaving London and returning to live back home in Ardgreeney, she would have laughed her head off. But there she was, delighted with herself and her new life, and snuggled up on a big crimson sofa with her legs curled up under her, drinking a hot whiskey with lemon and cloves. There was the mother and father of a storm raging outside, Lillian said: the perfect night to be in by the fire.

She was wearing a white bathrobe and had a towelling turban on her head. Her face looked shiny from the cream she'd lathered all over it. She was in for the evening. She wasn't expecting anyone and she wasn't going anywhere.

I told all this to the guards. Over and over. Over and over. I could remember every word of the conversation.

'I have so much to tell you, but let me give you the tour first. You've just got to see this place. It's amazing. Aidan's builders have done a brilliant job,' Lillian said, adjusting her headset, and picking up her laptop and then walking through the cottage, making sure the camera was angled so that I could see the transformation. What had been little more than a semi-derelict hovel was now the kind of place they could probably rent out to tourists for a small fortune, if they ever moved into the big house.

'Fabulous,' I repeated time and time again as she pointed out one feature after another: the gleaming state-of-the-art kitchen in the extension that ran seamlessly off the original structure of the cottage; the master bedroom, painted a dark teal, against which the enormous bed, with its cream and white coverings, stood out. 'I can see you in *House & Garden* any day now,' I said.

'Yeah, all the dust over the past few months has been worth it. But it's a pity it's dark. We'll have to have another Skype chat in the daytime so you can see the view over the sea from the back. It's absolutely incredible. And – wait for this – we have our own private access to the strand! Wooden steps, all the way down.'

She looked like the cat that had got the cream. I felt a little twinge of envy, but quickly dismissed it, reminding myself that Lillian had known what she wanted and had made it work for herself. It wasn't that I wanted to go back to Ardgreeney – that hadn't been her goal, either. But I think that maybe, in some deep part of myself, I wanted the kind of certainty that Lillian had found, and I had no certainty with James.

The tour finished, she sank back into the huge sofa.

'What's Aidan up to?' I asked.

'Out with the lads. There's a stag night for one of his pals and he couldn't get out of it. And, anyway, if he was here I couldn't tell you all the gossip.'

'Well, crack on with it. I'm all ears,' I said.

'You have to promise to keep this to yourself, but do you remember what I told you about our plans for Eaglewood? Well, he talked to his mother this morning and she's more or less agreed.'

'Are you serious? Just like that?'

'Well, maybe a bit less than more. He said she was a bit taken aback at first, but that she was okay with it by the time he left her. I hope she really is up for it, because we need her to keep the riding school going. For a while, anyway.'

'I suppose congratulations are in order, then,' I said.

As I raised my glass of wine, I became conscious of how grudging I must have sounded with my 'I suppose'. So I quickly added, 'Congratulations are *definitely* in order!'

Lillian beamed. She started to raise her own glass, but put it down again before she had a chance to drink from it. She frowned.

'Sorry, Orla; someone at the door. I'd better see who it is. Give me a sec,' she said, getting up from the sofa.

As she walked towards the door, my landline rang and I turned to pick it up. A wrong number. I looked back at the screen. There was no sign of Lillian. I looked away again, this time at my mobile phone to check whether there had been a text from James that I hadn't heard ping as it landed. Nothing. I looked back at the laptop screen, which still showed the empty sofa, the open door and the blackness beyond it. I could hear the noises picked up by the microphone on Lillian's laptop: the wind blowing down through the chimney, the crackling of the leaping flames in the grate. Somewhere in the background was the roar of the sea.

Later, when I tried to dig into my memories of that night, I thought I might have heard other sounds that I couldn't quite make out then: the sound of words carried on the wind, the hum of a car that could have been distant or could have been just down the road.

Was it just the wind? When I was a child, my grandmother told me that the howl of the wind was the sound of the banshee, and that, when you heard the banshee, it meant that someone was going to die. I told this to my mother, who laughed, said there was no such thing as the banshee and told me that my grandmother was just trying to frighten me.

I lost track of myself for a while as I waited for Lillian to come back. She was probably having some necessary conversation with whoever was at the door – a neighbour, maybe, although the nearest house was several fields away. I wasn't worried. Not then. I was even a bit annoyed. You don't arrange to talk to someone on Skype and then disappear to talk to a neighbour for God knows how long.

But that wasn't the only reason I was irritated. Until she had gone to answer the door, the conversation had been all about her and Aidan and that wonderful house of theirs. She hadn't asked about me. I had things of my own I wanted to talk to her about – James, for a start. He and I were going through a difficult patch. He had become distant, unreachable, and I didn't know why. I realised that it must have been building up for a while, but I had no idea what was behind it. The fact that he lived in Edinburgh wasn't helping. I wanted Lillian's advice.

I looked at the screen again. The hot whiskey, still on the coffee table where she had put it, glowed amber and gold in the changing light thrown by the fire, which still burned brightly in the grate. I could still see the flames dancing and hear them crackling. I could still hear the wind, shrieking and howling away. But there was no sign of Lillian.

Give me a sec, she'd said. That second had long passed. Where was she? I listened, beginning to grow anxious now. I stared at the screen, staring at its borders for any sign that she was just beyond them, within reach. But there was nothing.

And at some point I realised that something was terribly wrong.

I called her name into the microphone.

'Lillian! Lillian! Are you there? Are you all right?'

But there was no answer. There was nothing I could do but wait. I sipped my wine. And then the crackling of the flames seemed to grow louder and I watched in shock as I saw them catch the rug and then the sofa. I heard the sound of the glass exploding as the flames swallowed it up. And then, through the moving wall of fire, I saw, to my horror, a human shape bending and falling, and it was screaming a long, unearthly scream.

I heard another scream as the screen went dead, but this time the scream was coming from inside me.

I grabbed my mobile and pressed Aidan's number, but he didn't pick up. I tried it again. Same thing: 'Leave a message and I'll get back to you as soon as I can.' I didn't have time for that. Dad, I thought. I'll call him and ask him to get the emergency services out. But the phone in my parents' house rang unanswered, and neither Dad nor Ma had mobiles. I called Lillian's mother but she didn't pick up. She was probably out for the count after downing God-knows-how-much vodka or gin. So I called directory enquiries, got the number for Ardgreeney Garda station and dialled it. I blurted out that I was afraid something terrible had happened to my friend.

The guard who answered the phone told me to calm down and speak slowly. I took several deep breaths and started again.

'My friend – she lives – at Oriel Cottage. It's off the Seapoint Road. I was talking to her and – she went to answer the door, but she didn't come back! And now the house is on fire! I think – I saw someone burning! I think it's her!'

'Where are you calling from, miss?'

'London.'

'London?'

'Yes. We were talking on Skype – it's like a phone call, but it's a video thing. You do it on a computer. But, please – the house is on fire now!'

'Just a moment, miss,' he said.

I waited, frantic, for what seemed a very long time.

'Are you still there, miss?' the guard said when he picked up the phone again. 'The fire brigade is on its way out to the cottage. We have Garda officers going there too. Now, I'll need your name and all your details.'

'My name is Orla Breslin,' I said. I gave him my landline and mobile phone numbers, and my address in Maida Vale. I told him my friend was called Lillian Murray and that she had recently moved back to Ardgreeney to live with her boyfriend, Aidan McManus.

'I know Aidan well,' he said.

Of course he did. Everyone knew Aidan.

'Do you know where he is now?' the Garda asked. 'Have you talked to him?'

'He's out. That's what Lillian said when we were talking. She said there was a stag night.'

'Have you called him?'

'I've tried, but he isn't answering.'

'Can you stay where you are, where we can get hold of you, Orla? And try not to worry too much.'

The guard ended the call, promising to call me back. And while I waited for the phone to ring, I dialled Lillian's number over and over again. And, over and over again, I got her voicemail.

'Hello, this is Lillian,' it said. 'Please leave a message and I'll get back to you.'

But there was no point in leaving a message, because I knew somehow that Lillian would never get it.

I shivered. And even though the flat was as warm as toast, I couldn't stop shaking.

Chapter Two

Ned Moynihan hadn't been long home when the call came. The drive from the station had been an exercise in avoiding hazards as the worsening storm sent tiles flying off rooftops and debris skittering through the air. He could tell as he closed the door behind him that the new double-glazed windows were no match for the roar of the wind and the explosions of thunder that followed the flashes of lightning. Still, the one good thing about weather as bad as this was that it tended to keep the villains indoors. He was looking forward to his glass of Bushmills and then the lamb casserole that Eily had told him earlier she was going to make.

The first challenge to his expectation of a quiet, relaxing evening came in the form of Annie, his bolshie twelve-year-old daughter, who immediately drew him into an argument she was having with Eily about her status as an almost-teenager, which, she said, meant that she should be allowed to stay up later.

'We'll talk about this tomorrow,' he said, ruffling her mop of brown hair. 'But now, bed.'

Ned waited as Annie stormed out of the kitchen, banging the door behind her.

'She's becoming a right little madam,' he laughed, turning to Eily. He had intended to kiss her, as he usually did when he came home, but he held back when he saw the angry expression on her face and the blaze in her eyes.

'You shouldn't have given in to her,' Eily said, her voice sharp.

'But I didn't give in to her!' Ned protested.

'You did. You said you'd talk about it tomorrow. That means you'll give in to her. And you won't be here most of the extra hours she's up. I'm the eejit you're inflicting a later bedtime on,' she said. 'Anyway, let's eat. I'm starving. I nearly ate with the kids.'

It took him just a fraction of a second to decide that he would leave the decision on the rules governing Annie's bedtime entirely to his wife. Her 'I nearly ate with the kids' came across less as a statement than as a warning, and he was taking it on board. They had gone through a bad patch a few years before and he didn't want to risk upsetting the equilibrium they'd managed to regain. It had been his fault entirely – he accepted that. He had been ambitious, climbing up the ranks faster than he had ever imagined and maybe even believing he was on a trajectory that would take him all the way to Phoenix Park and the Office of the Commissioner. He had taken Eily for granted, assuming that, despite being a young mother with a small child, she was okay with him working long days and nights.

He wasn't going to make that mistake again. As well as Annie, they had Tom now, and he was determined to keep his family on a higher footing than his job.

Funny, though, he thought, how his and Eily's troubles had kicked off during his first posting here. Sure, he had been a bit of a workaholic, but maybe being posted to the town where they had both grown up hadn't helped, either. It certainly hadn't been great for him, but he had had no problem staying away from his father and visiting only when he had to. It was different for Eily. She was close to her parents and having them nearby had been convenient when she needed help with the kids. Even so, maybe it had all been a bit too claustrophobic for her.

That posting had lasted just a few years and had ended with his move to a detective unit in Dublin. Now they were back, and he had to admit that he had been apprehensive about it. But the past few months had been smooth. They'd bought a lovely old detached house, with a huge garden and high stone walls, on the outskirts of Ardgreeney, the kids were settling well into school and Eily was thinking of returning to nursing. She'd taken up again with some of her old school friends and was getting involved in all sorts of social stuff – a book club, a choir, bridge classes.

Jack and Winnie, her parents, had retired and moved up to Cavan, Winnie's home county, to live beside a lake. The bit of distance between them was a good thing.

Eily seemed to be happy generally, but her tetchiness tonight bothered him. He hoped it wasn't a portent of things to come.

'You're the boss and I defer to you in all things,' he said, making eyes at her and pulling her close. He buried his nose in her dark hair, which smelled of shampoo. 'If I wasn't so hungry, I'd be tempted to ravage you.'

She pulled away, smiling now and nodding her head towards the ceiling. 'Not with Little Miss Antichrist's ears on high alert upstairs,' she said. 'But there's always later.'

'Promises, promises,' Ned said.

After dinner, they watched the news. The big story was the weather, with reports of gale-force winds across the country blowing down trees and damaging buildings. He was glad to be inside with his family.

The call came shortly before half nine. Out of the corner of his eye, he saw a cloud of annoyance pass over Eily's face as he picked up his phone. She got up off the sofa and went to the kitchen, leaving him to listen. A minute later, he followed her. She glared at him.

'Sorry, Eily,' he said. 'That was Fergus. There's a fire at Aidan McManus's place, where he's living with his girlfriend. She can't be found.'

Her look of annoyance disappeared, to be replaced by one of shock.

'Jesus! What about Aidan?'

'He's okay. Seems he was over at his mother's and the girl-friend – her name's Lillian Murray – was on a video call to someone in London and went out of the house during the call. The friend in London was waiting for Lillian to come back in and saw the house catch fire. She thinks she saw someone in the flames. Anyway, Matty Walsh got the emergency services out. The fire's under control, but no one knows whether Lillian is inside the house. There's no sign of her anywhere. I'll know more when I get out there.'

'What, you're going there now? At this time of night? And in this weather? Can't someone else handle it? Why does it always have to be you?'

'Because it's my job. And the press will be all over it because of Aidan. I have to go out, Eily; I really do. I'm sorry.'

'No, it's all right,' she conceded. 'You have to. I know that.'

He grabbed his coat and kissed her.

'Don't wait up,' he said. 'I have a feeling this might be an all-nighter.'

He expected her to respond with her usual, 'Don't worry, I won't.' But she didn't. She asked him to call her when he knew more about what had happened. She looked worried – which wasn't surprising, of course, because she'd known the McManuses all her life.

He drove back through the town along Main Street and down on to the Seapoint Road. As the gaps between the houses grew bigger, the street lights became fewer, to the point where the darkness was absolute and he had to switch his beams on full. In the distance, an eerie light formed a break in the darkness. As he turned into the lane that led to Oriel Cottage, he saw that, despite the heavy, driving rain and the efforts of the firefighters, the cottage was still ablaze, the flames soaring into the sky.

He pulled up a short distance from the blazing house. As he got out of his car, he heard a strange cacophony of sounds: the roaring flames, the banshee-like keening of the wind, the fast, thunderous beat of the sea.

He saw Superintendent Fergus Gallagher's car arrive. They'd already spoken on the phone as they drove towards the cottage, and Fergus had suggested that, because Aidan might feel more comfortable talking to someone he knew, even vaguely, Ned should be the one to speak to him.

'He's in the car, over there,' a uniformed Garda told them.

Ned glanced towards the patrol car and saw a face staring out at the blazing house. It looked ghostly, devoid of features and expression.

'Any idea yet whether the girlfriend is in there?' Ned asked the young officer.

'No, sir. But we've looked around outside and there's no sign of her anywhere.'

Ned walked to the car and got in beside Aidan McManus. He hardly recognised the rain-sodden man who sat there, shrivelled and shrunken, wrapped in the blanket that someone had put around him.

'Aidan,' Ned said, making his voice and tone as gentle as possible, 'I don't know if you remember me. Ned Moynihan.'

He watched Aidan's head turn slowly to look at him. The man seemed almost surprised to see that someone had materialised inside the car. He said nothing, but nodded.

'We'll need you to help us try to find out what happened. Will you be able to do that?'

Another nod. Then, 'I . . . I can't think straight . . .'

'Take your time.'

After a few seconds, Aidan began to speak in a mechanical voice. He had left the cottage around seven o'clock to join a group of friends for a stag do. Lillian, already in her bathrobe and planning to have a quiet evening, had told him not to drink too much and not to get back into the car if he did get plastered, but to get a taxi home.

'I was in Clarke's,' he said, mentioning a pub that Ned knew was popular with Ardgreeney's well-heeled, rugby-playing crowd. 'That's where we were meeting up. All the lads were there.

'We were drinking away when I felt my phone buzz in my pocket. I didn't look at it there and then. And then it buzzed again, so I looked at it and saw there was a missed call from my mother and a voice message. I wasn't going to call her back or listen to the message, because she calls me all the time, but then I thought I'd better, just in case there was something wrong . . . The storm, you know . . .'

His voice trailed off and, as if to stem a new flood of tears, he screwed his eyes shut. Ned waited.

'I went outside to listen to the message, because the pub was too noisy to hear anything. My mother wanted me to call her. She said it was urgent. So I called her and she said a big branch had fallen through the roof of one of the stables and there were slates flying off and crashing all over the place. The horses were panicking and she needed me to help her. So I went straight away.'

'Did you go back inside the pub to tell your friends where you were going?' Ned asked.

'Yes. I ran inside and told them I had to go and help my mother, and then I got into the car and went straight to Eaglewood – that's my mother's house. She was in the yard. The wind was bad. We were afraid it would blow the doors off the stables. So I told her to keep trying to calm the horses while I strengthened the doors and bolts. I went to get a hammer and when I came back . . . my mother . . . she was on the ground. I thought she'd just slipped, but when I saw her face . . . You know those things they tell you to look out for . . . I knew she'd had a stroke, so I dialled nine-nine-nine.'

He looked at Ned, his eyes suddenly filled with a new expression of anxiety. 'Do you know how she is, my mother?'

'We'll get you to the hospital shortly,' Ned said. 'And then?' he asked gently. 'How did you find out about the fire?'

'The guards arrived at the same time as the ambulance. They told me Lillian had been talking to Orla – that's her friend in London – and that . . . Orla said Lillian went to answer the door and . . . then she saw the fire . . . That's all I know.'

He screwed his eyes closed again, but the effort couldn't stop the tears that began to flow freely. He bent his head into his hands and started to sob.

By the time Ned drove home to have a shower and a short sleep the following morning, the fire at Aidan McManus's cottage had made it on to the national news. So far, the press hadn't got wind of the girlfriend going missing, but that would be the next big revelation in the story if she didn't show up in the next couple of hours. Several journalists he knew had already called his mobile, but he had chosen not to answer. Eily, who had never pressed him for details of even the big cases he had worked on in the past, was anxious for information. It wasn't surprising – she had known the McManus family for as long as she could remember. And, although she didn't really know

Aidan all that well, since he was younger than her by a good few years, she was horrified by what had happened.

'Do you think the fire was started deliberately? Do you think that girl's body could be lying in there?' she asked. 'Jesus – it's too horrible for words.'

'Well, we haven't been able to find her yet. And if the friend in London really did see someone in there . . . well, it has to be a possibility.'

'Did Aidan recognise you?' Eily asked.

'I think so. I told him who I was and he seemed to recognise me, but it wasn't as if we were having a social conversation.'

Aidan and his mother had been at Ned and Eily's wedding, invited by her builder father, who had done a lot of work for the McManuses over the years. Malcolm, Aidan's father, had been dead a few years, at that point. Aidan, who must have been about seventeen or eighteen at the time and still at whichever expensive boarding school he had been packed off to when he was still in short pants, was already being tipped as a young rugby player to watch.

But Ned could hardly remember him having been at the wedding. That day, the best of his life, Ned's head and his eyes and his heart had had room for nothing but Eily. He had asked the band to play Dexys' 'Come on Eileen', and he had sung the chorus at the top of his voice, substituting 'Eily' for 'Eileen'. And all the wedding guests joined in, singing, 'Come on, Eily,' and Eily herself had laughed and laughed. And then, without any prompting from him, they had played Van Morrison's 'Brown Eyed Girl', and he must have looked a right eejit as he danced

21

around Eily, making pointy signs at her dark chocolate-brown eyes with his fingers.

Beyond cheering him on in key international rugby matches over the years, Ned hadn't had much contact with Aidan. They were too many years apart and didn't mix in the same social circles. But, thanks to Eily's family and the kind of local knowledge he had absorbed without even being aware of it, he knew a fair amount about the McManuses.

Aidan's grandfather, Phelim McManus, had been an unskilled labourer with brains and ambition. He had made a load of money in America – it wasn't quite clear exactly how – and had returned to Ardgreeney in the early nineteen thirties. Eaglewood was already derelict, having been burned down in the twenties, and Phelim bought it for a song from its owners – an Anglo-Irish family that had lived there for generations, but had moved to England after the fire.

With good looks and enough money to make him attractive even to the landed gentry in the area, Phelim married Alice Downes, the daughter of a wealthy farmer, and established himself as one of the most prominent men in the locality. Phelim and Alice produced Malcolm, Aidan's father.

Ned had heard all sorts of stories about Malcolm over the years. Like his father, Malcolm had prospered and had married well; his wedding to Kathleen Butler-Lacey, a leading fashion model whose father was one of Irish racing's top trainers at the time, had made the front pages of the national papers. Malcolm's name appeared frequently on the business pages of the national newspapers, too, due to his talent for buying and selling land and property. What had never appeared in the papers were the rumours that he was a Republican sympathiser and had regularly provided a hiding place for men on the run. Indeed, according to some of these rumours, he had been a gunrunner during the nineteen seventies and had even taken up arms himself. The rumours also had it that Malcolm's father, Phelim, had been involved in the border campaign of the nineteen fifties.

Whether the stories were true or not, Ned had no idea. He had never met Malcolm, but he remembered Jack O'Donnell describing him as a bowsie and a scoundrel, and saying more than once that he wouldn't have trusted him as far as he could throw him and that he could never understand what a fine woman like Kathleen had ever seen in him.

Ned stood in the shower for ten minutes and then went to bed, asking Eily to wake him after an hour. He hadn't been asleep for more than a few minutes when he felt his wife shaking him.

'Sorry, Ned, but you'd better take this. It's Fergus. He said it was urgent.' Eily handed him the mobile phone he had left in the kitchen.

He held the phone to his ear and listened.

'Okay, give me ten minutes,' he said, and got out of the bed.

'What's happened?' Eily asked.

'They've found a body.'

'In the cottage?'

Ned nodded.

'The girlfriend?'

'They don't know yet. But I suppose it has to be.'

He started pulling on his clothes.

'You wouldn't make me some tea and a bit of toast while I get my clothes on?' he asked her. 'Fergus wants me back over there, fast.'

Chapter Three

I was half crazed with worry as I waited for the guard to call me back. I tried to convince myself that I hadn't really seen the burning shape and that my eyes had played tricks on me. I had imagined the scream too, I told myself – that eerie, unearthly scream. What I had heard was only the scream that came from my own body.

The guard would tell me that Lillian was safe, that she had gone to help a neighbour with something urgent and that she had stayed with the neighbour as the fire blazed. She had left her phone in the cottage; that was why she hadn't called me to tell me she was all right.

But I couldn't get those horrible images of the flames consuming everything in their way out of my mind. It was as if they were on a continuous loop that I was doomed to watch over and over again.

When the phone rang, I jumped, hoping it was Lillian. But

it was the guard calling back, and I held my breath as he told me that the fire was under control.

'Thank you for alerting us so quickly,' he said.

'What about Lillian? Is she okay?'

'I have no news of Lillian. All I've been told is that the fire is under control. Now, Orla, can you give me any contact details you have for Lillian's family?'

My stomach lurched. 'Does that mean . . . you think Lillian's in there? In the house? But I saw her go outside before the fire started . . . She can't be inside! She can't!'

'I'm not saying that at all, now. It would just be helpful if you could give me any useful addresses and phone numbers, including Lillian's.'

I gave him all the details. I told him I had called Lillian's number over and over and that it had gone to voicemail.

'What about Aidan?' I asked. 'Have you talked to him?'

'I can't really tell you any more than I've told you already,' the guard said. 'I'm sorry. I'll call you back when I have more news.'

I tried Aidan's phone again. My heart was pounding. What would I say to him? What *could* I say? His voicemail came on. He must know by now that I'd raised the alarm. Surely he would want to talk to me?

I called James, in Edinburgh, but he didn't pick up. I remembered then that he was getting together with some old friends from university that evening. I tried his mobile, but the call went through to voicemail.

'Please call me,' I said. 'It's urgent.'

I tried him again several times and each time his voicemail

came on. I gave up around two in the morning. I didn't want to tell him such terrible news in a voice message.

I stayed up all night, hoping desperately for good news. But it didn't come.

By morning, the fire was all over the television and radio news, in the UK as well as in Ireland. The focus was on Aidan. He was safe, the reports said. He hadn't been in the house when the fire broke out. There was no mention of Lillian. And there was no mention of anyone having been injured or having died in the fire. I heaved a sigh of relief. This must mean Lillian was safe; I had imagined the shape in the flames.

When my phone rang, around eight, I rushed to answer it, certain it was Lillian. But it was a different guard. He asked questions about the fire. At what point had I noticed the flames? Was I sure the fire had begun after Lillian went outside? Was it possible it started while she was still inside? Could she have come back in without my having noticed?

'Can you tell me if Lillian is all right?' I asked, my anxiety returning.

'Sorry; I have no information. I've just been asked to talk to you. I can get someone who knows more to give you a ring,' he said.

A couple of hours later, my phone rang again.

'Is that Orla Breslin? My name is Ned Moynihan. I'm a detective inspector with the Garda in Ardgreeney. I just want to give you an update on what's been happening.'

'Is Lillian safe?' I asked.

I sensed him hesitate and my heart began to thump so loudly in my chest – *boom, boom, boom, boom* – that it was all I could hear as I waited for him to speak.

'I'm afraid we have no definite news of Lillian,' he said.

Don't panic, I told myself. No news is good news. She ran down on to the strand to get away from the fire. She went to her mother's. Yes, that's where she is now: at her mother's. She's in shock. She hasn't thought of calling anyone.

There was another moment of hesitation at the other end of the phone.

'Orla, I have to tell you that we found a body in the house. We don't know that it's Lillian's, however,' the detective said.

I felt myself slipping from the sofa on to the floor. The images rolled through my head again, vivid and terrifying. I saw the flames, gobbling up everything in their path. I heard the whiskey glass shatter. I saw the human form take shape among the flames, only now it began to take on Lillian's features. I had watched her burn to death.

No! No! No! I howled silently. I couldn't speak. Every part of me was in terrible agony.

'Orla?'

The detective was still at the other end of the phone.

'I'm sorry . . . I can't . . . take this in . . .' I said.

'And I'm sorry I haven't been able to give you any good news,' he said. 'I understand how you must be feeling. Is there anyone you can go to or who can come to you? A friend or a neighbour, maybe?'

'Yes . . . No . . . I'll be fine . . . I'll stay here. Will you let me know . . . whether it's . . . ?'

I couldn't finish what I was asking him, but he understood.

'Of course,' he said. 'In the meantime, can I ask you not to tell anyone about the body? We aren't releasing that information yet.'

He didn't tell me to try not to worry. In a strange way, I was glad of that.

My parents called. The news was all over Ardgreeney. They were calling to tell me that there had been a fire at Oriel Cottage, but that none of the news reports had mentioned Lillian.

'Do you know if she's all right?' Dad asked.

'No,' I said, choking. 'No one knows where she is.'

I told them about the Skype call and how she had gone to answer the door, but hadn't come back, how I had seen the flames spread and about the human shape I had seen inside the flames.

'The guards found a body, Dad,' I sobbed. 'I'm not supposed to say that to anyone. They asked me to keep it to myself. They don't know whether it's Lillian.'

'It's all right; I won't say a word about it. But maybe it's not her. Have you talked to Nancy?' he asked, referring to Lillian's mother, who lived on the same estate as my parents.

'No,' I said. 'I called but she didn't answer. She was probably in one of her alcoholic stupors. And now . . . I don't know what to say to her. I'm sure the guards will have been to see her.'

'Would you like us to go and talk to her?' he asked.

'Oh, Dad, would you? I can't face having to talk to her on the phone. And . . . do you think I should come over?'

'Only if you want to and you're up to it. Why don't you try to rest now and then make a decision tomorrow?'

'Yeah . . . Sorry, Dad; I just can't talk about this any more. Do you mind?'

'No, of course not. Now, go and rest. And if I hear anything, I'll call you.'

I crawled into my bed and pulled the covers up around me. I closed my eyes and prayed that the terrible images would go away for long enough to allow me to fall asleep.

I woke to the sound of the phone ringing. At first, my head was empty of everything but the sound that reverberated around it. But only for a second. The memories of what I had seen the night before exploded in my head and in front of my eyes. The room was dark. I must have slept for hours, all through the morning and afternoon.

I picked up the phone.

'Hello?' I croaked.

'Orla?'

I recognised the voice. It was Inspector Moynihan again.

'Sorry. I was asleep. Is there news?'

'The body in the house isn't Lillian.'

'Oh, thank God!' I gasped in relief. 'She's all right, then? She's not injured or anything?'

'We haven't been able to find her.'

'But . . . she must be somewhere!'

'We're trying to find her. We need you to help us,' the inspector said. 'You told us last night that she heard someone at the door and went to see who it was.'

'Yes.'

'And you said she was gone for a long time and didn't come back.'

'Yes . . . I waited. The door was open. I thought she must have been talking to someone she knew. She didn't come back. And then, the fire started . . . It was horrible . . .'

'Can you tell me everything you saw? I'm sorry to have to ask you to go through it all again. It must be very distressing for you.'

I told him everything. How Lillian was so excited to give me a video tour of the cottage after living through months of renovation and building work; how, just as she sat down on the sofa, she heard someone at the door and went to open it; how I could see the darkness and hear the storm through the open door; how I waited for her to come back and, then, how I saw the flames creep across the room from the grate.

'Did you see or hear the person who came to the door?'

'No,' I said.

'But you heard the knock on the door?'

'No, I didn't hear that either. But Lillian said there was someone at the door. She seemed . . . surprised. She didn't seem to be expecting anyone. And Aidan was out. If it had been him, he wouldn't have knocked. He would have used his key.'

'Unless he had forgotten his key, maybe?'

'But, if it had been Aidan, she would have just let him in. I'd have seen him. And I'd have heard him,' I said. 'Have you not talked to Aidan? I thought the television said he was all right . . . The body . . . Was it him?'

'Aidan is fine. He's at his mother's house. We haven't identified the person in the cottage yet,' the inspector said. 'And, in the meantime, the most important thing is to find Lillian. Are you, by any chance, planning to come over to Ardgreeney?'

'Should I?'

'It would be helpful.'

'I'll have to clear it with work ... there's a lot going on at the moment.'

'What do you do?'

'I'm a journalist. But I don't think there'll be a problem. I'll try to get a flight tomorrow morning.'

'Good. One more question for now – was it a PC or laptop you were using to talk to Lillian?'

'A laptop.'

'Can you bring it with you? We'll need to look at it.'

'Okay.'

He gave me his mobile number and said, 'Send me a text when you know which flight you're going to be on and I'll have someone pick you up. Look out for a guard in uniform, with your name on a big piece of card.'

When we finished speaking, I called James. I wanted – needed – to tell him what had happened. But I got his voicemail again.

I called my editor and told him what had happened. 'Take as much time as you need,' he said.

I lay back on the bed and stared into the darkness. The knowledge that Lillian hadn't died in the fire had brought great relief. But I was still frantic. Where was she? And who was the person I had seen burn to death in the flames?

Chapter Four

They hadn't yet had a formal identification of the body found in Oriel Cottage – or what was left of it. But it was a man's body, not a woman's. The pathologist had verified that straight away. And a local man called Patsy McLennan had been reported missing. In all likelihood, the body was his.

Ned drove to the man's address on Quay Street, one of the oldest streets in Ardgreeney and the main conduit between the centre of town and the strand and small harbour. As he opened the door of the car, he felt a wet blast of ice-cold air and pulled the collar of his coat up around his neck, wishing he'd worn a scarf. The wind had died down, but it was still strong, especially down here, sweeping the sea with it as well as the rain, and it was loud enough to drown out the roar of the waves. He bent his head into the wind and walked towards the squad car that was parked a few yards ahead of him. Already, he was drawing an imaginary straight line between the missing man's house and Oriel Cottage. Patsy wouldn't have had to walk up to Main Street and then on to the Seapoint Road to get to the cottage. He could have walked down to the strand, turned right and kept walking until he reached the wooden steps leading up to the cottage. Even on a wild, dark night, it wouldn't have taken McLennan very long to get there using that route.

Patsy McLennan's house was the only one in the street that appeared to have seen no change; the thatched roof was still in place and the two small windows either side of the front door looked old and rickety enough to be the original frames, inserted when the house was built. The other houses had been upgraded and extended to varying degrees, in some cases to the extent that the original structures were only hinted at.

It was a sign of the times. Ardgreeney had always been a relatively prosperous little town, within easy enough reach of Dublin, but not close enough to become one of those commuter towns where most people got on the train first thing in the morning and came back last thing at night.

But things were changing. The town was expanding fast and the small nucleus of streets that formed the town centre belied the size of the population living in the new estates to the north, south and west – estates that couldn't be built fast enough to accommodate the demand of a population that had increased by nearly forty per cent, to twenty thousand, in just a decade.

Ned remembered one young Garda complaining that, when he and his family had first moved into their tiny estate, they'd had a clear view across the fields to the sea, but that almost overnight the fields had been filled with shoebox houses that blocked their lovely view.

There was still a core sense of community in Ardgreeney, but only just, and it was under pressure as the provision of services and amenities failed to keep up with the huge influx of people into the estates.

The population explosion had, however, been reflected in Ardgreeney Garda station's move from an old house on the Dublin Road to a huge state-of-the-art building, sprawled over half an acre, on the northern edge of the town, and an upgrading of its status to district HQ level.

Here, on the eastern side, by the coast, the odd new house was being built, but there was nothing like the huge development that the big builders went in for. Not yet, anyway, Ned thought, but it was only a matter of time, what with house prices going through the roof.

He had never quite understood the property craze. It was all very well to see your house soar in value, but it didn't mean you were rich, unless you were able to buy somewhere else at a fraction of the price. And, he wondered, why would you want to go through the hassle of it all, settling into a house and then selling it and having to do the same all over again?

He looked around, trying to stretch his line of sight as far as he could into the grey mass of cloud and sky. You couldn't see the burned-out shell of Oriel Cottage from here, but you could smell it on the wind, mixed in with the saltiness of the sea.

A few people had come out of their houses. They stood around, huddled into their coats, curious about the extraordinary things that were happening in their quiet little part of Ardgreeney.

Ned thought they looked like black Lowry figures against the sky, which, despite being low and threatening, seemed to emit a light against which everything stood in high relief.

Based on what he now knew about Patsy, Ned had expected the cottage to be half derelict, both inside and out. But it wasn't. Sure, the thatch looked as though it needed some attention and the whitewash was a bit on the grubby side, but these were the jobs you got done in the summer. When he ventured inside, Ned noticed that it smelled a bit musty, but the place was surprisingly clean. He had expected a hovel.

After looking over the cottage, Ned spoke again to the officer who was first on the scene, now keeping watch on the street outside. 'Run it all by me again,' he said.

The young guard repeated his account. He and another guard had done a house-to-house, in hope of finding someone who might have seen Lillian Murray or could give them any information that might throw light on what had happened to her. No one had been able to offer anything. But when they knocked on the door of Patsy McLennan's cottage, a worried-looking woman had come running out to tell them Patsy was missing and that she was concerned about him.

'Who is she?' Ned asked.

'Her name is Moira Daly. She's a relative of some kind.'

'Where is she now?'

'In there,' the guard said, pointing towards a small house with pebble-dashed walls, about fifty yards away.

Ned knocked on Moira Daly's door and a thin woman, who looked to be somewhere in her seventies, opened it, her face a mixture of hope and despair.

'Have you found him?' she asked, before he could introduce himself.

'Not yet,' Ned said. 'But, if you don't mind, Mrs Daly, I'd like to ask you a few questions.'

'Of course,' she said, standing back from the door to let him in. She led him into the kitchen, where they both sat down at the table.

'When did you last see Patsy?' Ned asked.

'I think it was about six o'clock yesterday evening. I took him in his tea. I do that every day,' she said.

'That's very generous of you,' Ned said.

'He's my cousin – the only one left on that side of the family. He's not what you'd call "all there". I keep an eye on him – you know, I give him a hot meal every day and make sure the house doesn't fall down around him. You have to look after your own.'

Ned nodded. He thought of all the people whose deaths he had been called out to investigate down the years: elderly people who had lain dead for days and even weeks because they had had no one to watch out for them. He wished there were more people like Moira Daly.

'What makes you think he's gone missing?'

'I went in this morning, at seven, to check he was all right – you know, after the storm – but he wasn't there.'

'Could he just have gone out for a walk?'

'Ah, no; he never gets up early. Patsy goes to bed very late, if he goes to bed at all. He's a bit of a night wanderer. I don't think he came in last night. I'm worried he might be lying in a ditch somewhere.'

'Maybe he took shelter somewhere and fell asleep,' Ned offered.

He tried to sound positive. And, indeed, under normal cir-cumstances there would be every reason to be hopeful that a man described by his cousin as 'not all there', who went out wandering by night – even while one of the worst storms ever was raging – would turn up safe and sound. But, in this case, his conviction was weak. Two people in the same town and on the same night seemed to have disappeared off the face of the earth. More often than not, coincidence counted for a lot of things. But, this time . . . well, he wasn't so sure.

Nor was he sure he should tell Moira about the body found in Oriel Cottage. They hadn't released that information yet, because this was now looking like a criminal investigation – though exactly what kind of a crime, or crimes, they were going to be investigating wasn't clear. And, after all, the body might not be that of her cousin. Still, he felt like a cruel fraudster as he left her. He had given her hope – hope that was almost certain to be snatched away from her. Sometimes he hated this fucking job.

Chapter Five

I spotted the young guard immediately as I walked into the arrivals hall. He was holding up a big sheet of paper with my name scrawled on it in capital letters, and he was scanning the people coming through. He shook my hand, introducing himself as Garda Michael Keane and asking me to follow him to the car.

There was no conversation after that. He seemed jumpy and didn't make any effort to talk to me, as if he was afraid to engage in conversation in case I asked him questions he couldn't or wouldn't answer. I sat in the back of the car, looking out of the window, but barely registering where we were or when we came off the motorway.

At one point, I caught sight of myself in the driver's mirror and was shocked to see how terrible I looked. I had washed my curly blonde hair quickly in the shower that morning, but now it looked dull and lank, as if I hadn't washed it for a week. My eyes looked big and staring, as if the skin around them had shrunk away. There was no colour in my face.

When we arrived at the Garda station, I was led to an office where a man I assumed to be Inspector Moynihan was on the phone. He looked up as the guard knocked and entered, nodded a silent greeting to me and signalled that I should sit down. He held up an index finger, indicating that he would end the call shortly. While I waited, I tried to form an impression of him. He was somewhere in his forties, quite good looking, with dark hair and deep blue eyes. A kind face. I closed my eyes for a few moments, listening as he spoke into the telephone. He had a low, dark-brown kind of voice. A voice I had already decided I could trust.

After a minute or so, he put the phone down, stood up and walked over to me, holding out his hand.

'Orla. Sorry about that. I'm Ned Moynihan,' he said. 'Now, I'm sure you haven't had anything to eat, so let's sort that out first. Would a cheese sandwich be all right? Tea?'

'Yes, please,' I said, realising that I couldn't quite remember when I'd last had a meal. I was beginning to feel faint from hunger.

He picked up the phone again and asked someone to bring the sandwich and a mug of tea. Then he brought his chair from behind his desk and placed it so that he was sitting just a couple of feet from me. He leaned forward, his elbows on his knees and his hands clasped loosely in front of them. Maybe detectives were encouraged to do that kind of thing when they were talking to witnesses, to get the best out of them. But I didn't feel I was being manipulated. He was, I felt, on my side.

'First,' he said, 'is there anything you'd like to ask me? I can't promise that I'll be able to tell you everything, but I'll try.'

'Do you think she's . . . dead?'

'At the moment, Orla, we don't know anything. We've found nothing inside or outside the cottage to suggest that there's been any kind of physical attack or struggle. We haven't found anything that shouldn't be there. Of course, it was a terrible night, so it isn't impossible that the rain wiped out any evidence of anything like that having happened. But, beyond the fact that Lillian is nowhere to be found, we can't be sure of anything at all.'

I nodded, my eyes filling up.

'And the person who died in the fire?'

'It was a man. We haven't named him yet.'

He looked at me in a kindly way. 'I think you need to eat. Let me hurry that sandwich up,' he said, getting up and leaving the office. When he came back, he was carrying a tray.

'Here you are,' he said. 'Not Michelin-star quality but it should fill the gap. I'll leave you alone for a few minutes while you eat it.'

'It's okay,' I said, shaking my head. But he was already closing the door behind him.

The sandwich didn't look unappetising, but my insides were churning with anguish and every mouthful was a struggle. I managed to eat only half of it.

Inspector Moynihan came back, glancing at the plate.

'Not great?' he asked.

'It helped.'

'Are you sure you're all right to talk?'

'Yes. I'm sure. I want to help.'

He sat down in front of me, this time leaning back against the chair.

'Why don't you tell me a little bit about yourself? What you do for a living, how long you've known Lillian. That sort of thing,' he said.

So I told him I worked as a journalist on the business pages of the *Tribune* newspaper in London and that Lillian and I had known each other all our lives.

'You appear to be the last person to have spoken to Lillian,' he said.

And then, he added, 'You're also the only person who has been able to say there was someone at the door.'

'But there *was* someone at the door!' I said, raising my voice. 'We were talking. She went to answer the door and I waited and she didn't come back. I saw her go to the door. I saw her ... disappear!'

'I'm not doubting you, Orla. I'm just trying to make sure that we have every single bit of information that will help us to find her. So, for example, if I ask you a question in several different ways, it's not because I don't believe you; it's because I need you to be absolutely certain that you haven't left anything out, no matter how insignificant you might think it is. It's important that you try to remember as much as possible from the conversation you had with Lillian. So, are you sure she had no idea who was at the door?'

'I ... Well, she looked puzzled. She said there was someone at the door. She was surprised; I saw it on her face. I took that to mean she didn't know who it was.'

'Is it possible that you misheard what she said?'

Despite what he had said about repeating questions, I began to get upset. I even began to doubt myself for a moment. But I *hadn't* misheard her.

'No. I didn't mishear anything. What she said is what I told you she said!'

Inspector Moynihan seemed to move closer. His eyes, though still kind, bored into me.

'Orla, we *are* very worried about Lillian, although we're not excluding the possibility – indeed, we're hoping – that she hasn't come to any harm. I know these questions are difficult for you, but can you think of any reason – any reason at all – that might have made her go out last night? Is it possible that she *wanted* you to think that someone had arrived at the door?'

'What are you saying? That she set this up? That's . . . That's ridiculous. Why would she have done that? She only moved over from London a few months ago. She was really happy with Aidan. I know she was. And the fire – someone died in that fire! I've known Lillian all my life. She would never have done such a dreadful thing!'

'People sometimes do set things up,' the inspector said gently, 'and for all sorts of reasons. Sometimes they're involved with someone else. We have to consider that possibility. I'm not saying Lillian has done anything like that, but I have to ask you – because I know from her mother that you're her closest friend – whether she might have been involved with anyone other than Aidan?'

I hesitated. Lillian had been involved with a series of unsuitable men – mostly older and married – over the years. The affairs had usually ended in tears, and the tears were usually hers. You

42

didn't have to be a shrink to work out why she went for men who weren't available. My take was that she saw her father, by dying, as having effectively abandoned her, so she had repeated, over and over, the pattern of abandonment by taking up with men who wouldn't stay with her. Maybe she thought subconsciously that some day one of these unsuitable and unavailable men would stay, and then she would have made things right with her father.

But I didn't tell any of that to the inspector. And there wasn't much I could have told him, anyway, because she'd stopped talking to me about these liaisons of hers. She knew I didn't approve of them and that I thought she was, at best, wasting her time.

'No,' I said. 'Not really . . . not since she met Aidan.'

'What about before?'

'I think she may have been seeing someone in London before Aidan. But I'm not sure.'

'Can you give me a name and any contact details? Just so that we can check him out.'

I shook my head. 'I'm sorry. I don't know anything about him. The only reason I thought there might have been someone was because I once saw a text land on her mobile. We were in a wine bar and she had her phone on the table. It said something like *I'm desperate to see you*, and when I asked her about it she said there was a married guy at work who was obsessed with her and kept pestering her. She said she'd made the mistake of being nice to him one evening when they were all out drinking and that he wouldn't leave her alone.'

'Was there a name on this text?'

'I just saw an initial. I think it was R.'

The inspector handed me a piece of paper with a mobile phone number on it – a UK mobile phone number.

'Do you recognise that number?' he asked.

'No, I don't think so.'

'Why don't you tap it into your phone and see if a name comes up?'

I tapped in the number. It produced no name from my contacts list. I looked at him, waiting for him to tell me why it might be significant.

'This number showed up on Lillian's mobile,' he said. 'The call was made the Sunday before Lillian went missing and it lasted about ten minutes. We don't know who called her, because it's a prepaid mobile. But we do know that the call was made from London. The Met are helping us with this. They're looking at her UK mobile records. Do you have any idea who might have been calling her from London?'

'I don't know . . .'

I felt faint. The room was beginning to spin. I gripped on to the edges of the chair and tried to stop myself keeling over. Inspector Moynihan was saying something, but I couldn't hear his voice because my ears were filled with a rushing sound.

'I'm sorry. I don't feel very well. What did you say?'

Inspector Moynihan shook his head and raised his hand, his palm facing towards me as if putting a physical stop to any further questioning.

'We can talk later, when you've had some rest,' the inspector said. 'You have family here, don't you? How about we get you to them now and see how you're feeling later this evening or tomorrow?'

I nodded.

My hands were growing clammy and I was beginning to feel faint again. I held a hand up to my forehead and, when I drew it away and looked at it, it was wet.

'The man who died . . . Who was he? Did he set the house on fire?'

The inspector shook his head. 'I can't tell you because we don't know.'

It was evening when I woke up. I looked at the clock, which showed that I'd been asleep for hours. I hadn't dreamed of anything. I grabbed the dressing gown my mother had hung on the back of the door and stumbled down the stairs and along to the sitting room, the door of which was closed. I could hear the television, but the sound was turned low. I pushed open the door and the face that met me, filling up the screen, was Lillian's. My parents swung around, surprised by my entrance. They both looked guilty, as if they felt they were doing something behind my back. Dad reached quickly for the remote control and turned the television off.

'It's all right,' I said. 'I want to know what's happening. I want to hear what they're saying about her.'

But when Dad turned the television on again, the topic had shifted to the economy.

'Sorry,' he said. 'I thought it would upset you.'

'How could it upset me more than I'm upset already?' I snapped.

My father's face was filled with hurt. He began to apologise again.

'Oh, Dad, don't. I shouldn't have spoken to you like that. It's just that . . . seeing her on the telly just now . . . it makes it much more real now that everyone knows. Before it was about Aidan and now . . .'

I sat down beside Ma and she took my hand and cradled it in hers.

'Your phone has been ringing,' she said. 'I tried to answer it, but it's locked.'

I scrabbled around in my bag for my mobile and took it to the kitchen. There were several missed calls and texts from James, and two voice messages, all saying much the same thing in different combinations of words and sentences: *I've been trying to call you. Where are you? Please call me.*

He answered immediately when I rang.

'Orla, what's going on? What's happened to Lillian? I've seen the news.'

'I don't know. She disappeared. We were talking on Skype and she went to answer the door and that was it – she didn't come back. And then the place was on fire.'

I spoke dully, trotting out the events I had been replaying in my head so many times that they had become embedded there, like one of those poems I had learned by heart at primary school and could still recite without having to think. I didn't want to think.

And then I remembered the anguish I had endured two nights before, when, frantic with worry and powerless to do anything but wait for the guards to call me back, I had needed to talk to him.

46

'I called you. Loads of times. You didn't answer.'

'I'm sorry. I was at the reunion and . . . I was drunk.'

'For two days?' I asked, accusingly.

'It was a bit of a lost weekend. I'm sorry. I should have been in touch,' he said. He sounded embarrassed. 'Orla, where are you? I've been ringing the landline as well as the mobile.'

'I'm in Ireland. I came over to talk to the guards.'

'What are they telling you about Lillian? Do they think she's . . . ?'

He didn't finish the sentence, but I knew the word he wasn't able to utter. I couldn't say it either.

'They're not saying anything very much,' I said.

'Do you think Aidan did something?'

'Jesus, James, how do you expect me to know? How can you ask me that? I don't know what happened to her and it's doing my head in!'

He was silent for a few seconds. When I heard his voice again, it sounded strangled. 'Do you want me to come over?' he asked.

I would have been glad to see him and have his support. But something about his tone made me think that coming to Ardgreeney was the last thing he wanted to do, so I lashed out.

'What would be the point?' I asked, and, as I heard my own voice, laden with scorn and anger, I instantly regretted it. But it was too late to take it back.

Chapter Six

Ned had to consider whether Aidan McManus had killed Lillian Murray. Perhaps they'd had an argument that turned violent. But the timings of the calls between Aidan and his mother, and his eventual call to the emergency services, seemed to put him in the clear. And although Ned knew well that murderers were often accomplished actors, Aidan's grief at the disappearance of his girlfriend had come across as overwhelming and genuine.

He talked to Aidan's friends, who confirmed that he had told them his mother was having a spot of bother with the horses in the storm and that he was going to shoot over to Eaglewood to see what needed to be done and then try to rejoin them later. They hadn't heard from him again that evening. He had been in good form, they said, only showing signs of anything like anxiety or agitation after he had spoken to his mother.

Records of the calls from Aidan's mobile phone and his

mother's landline backed up what he had told the team. The phone call from his mother came at 8:11 p.m. and he called her back at 8:16 p.m. He called for an ambulance at 8:52 p.m. In between, there were missed calls from Orla Breslin. His voicemail also showed that Orla had begun to leave him a message much later that night, but had abandoned it. Aidan had already left the cottage before Lillian began her Skype conversation with Orla Breslin. If they'd had even a minor argument, Lillian had given Orla no sense of it. Indeed, Orla had painted a picture of something akin to domestic bliss at Oriel Cottage. And, Ned thought, if Aidan *had* killed his girlfriend, he wouldn't have had time to get rid of her body. For once, it looked as if the nearest and dearest was in the clear.

The team was trying to trace the UK mobile number that had shown up on Lillian's phone a week before she disappeared, and had asked for assistance from the Metropolitan Police in London. The Met would look at Lillian's UK mobile records and would also talk to her former colleagues about the married man who, according to what Orla said she'd been told, had been pestering her.

Apart from the brief call she had made to Orla in London ahead of their Skype conversation, Lillian had made no calls during the entire day. Indeed, her call history seemed to have no story to tell. Nor was there was a record of anyone else having called her that evening or earlier in the day. An examination of the data handed over by Lillian's telephone provider in Ireland had thrown up nothing.

Lillian Juliet Murray had vanished. The forensics team had found parts of her mobile phone in the debris inside the cottage, which suggested that her departure hadn't been planned. Unless, of course, she *had* planned to leave and had set everything up to look as if she had been abducted. Lillian's mother, thin as a rake and reeking of alcohol, had been little help in providing any real insight into her daughter's life and personality. Her response to most questions had been a bewildered headshake and 'Orla will know, they're very close.' Ned had asked her to consider the possibility that Lillian had planned to disappear and she had stared at him, all comprehension drained from her face. Orla Breslin had ridiculed that idea, but Ned knew that people often kept secrets from those closest to them.

What didn't make sense, if Lillian *had* planned to leave, was the fire, but that could have been a tragic accident. And, at the moment, there was no evidence to support the idea that the fire had been started deliberately.

In the meantime, the team was knocking on doors, visiting pubs, stopping cars and asking people to look at a recent photograph of Lillian.

The only person they hadn't spoken to was Kathleen McManus. They'd listened to the message she had left on her son's phone, but hadn't been able to speak to her because of the stroke. The doctors at the hospital said that, because of her strong constitution and previously good health, there was a chance that she would recover, but it would be a while before she got all her faculties back, if she ever did.

The media were like vultures, circling and swooping. The fire at the cottage had been big news and the immediate question for journalists had been whether Aidan McManus was dead or alive. The subsequent discovery of a man's charred body and the disclosure that Aidan McManus's girlfriend had disappeared brought a luridness to the story, and the coverage was relentless. But beyond those facts, there was little news that Fergus and Ned could provide. Already, just three days on, the newspapers were beginning to run features rather than news, turning the disappearance of a young woman from an isolated cottage on a stormy night into the second biggest tragedy of Aidan McManus's life – the first being the injury that had ended his days of international rugby stardom.

Scanning the latest such piece, Ned shook his head and sighed. He turned his attention to the sheets of paper one of the team had put in front of him – details of calls from members of the public reporting sightings of Lillian. One caller had reported seeing her on Valentia Island in the very early hours of the morning after she had gone missing. For fuck's sake. Someone would have had to beam her down there.

He looked at his watch and saw that it was already well into the afternoon. Where had the hours gone? He wanted to talk to Orla Breslin again but that would have to wait until tomorrow. There was a more immediate task he had to deal with, and it was one he was dreading. He had left Moira Daly hoping against hope that her cousin would turn up safe and well. Now, he was going to have to dash those hopes of hers, because the body in the cottage had been identified as that of Patsy McLennan.

As he walked along Quay Street towards Moira Daly's house, he saw a few curtains twitch.

He didn't have to say a word when she opened the door. The sight of him standing there must have told her everything she had been dreading. She led him inside, where he gave her the news that Patsy was dead and informed her of how he had died. She wept, and then apologised. People often did that, apologised for their grief, and it always moved him.

'I'm sorry, I can't get it out of my mind, him dying like that,' she said. 'Do you think it was quick? Would he have suffered?'

Ned thought of the image described by Orla Breslin, of a human shape ablaze, stumbling and falling through the flames. He thought of the scream she said she'd heard, but he wouldn't tell this to Moira Daly. Sometimes the right thing to do was to lie.

'It would have been very quick,' he said. 'The fumes would have made him unconscious. He wouldn't have felt anything.'

He patted her arm. It seemed like an inadequate gesture, but there was nothing else he could say that would offer her even the tiniest shred of comfort.

'Why don't we make a cup of tea,' he suggested, thinking that even a small task like boiling a kettle and making a pot of tea would give her a short break from the contemplation of her cousin's lonely end.

The tea was strong and brown, the kind of tea Irene, his stepmother, made. As they sat drinking it, Ned asked Moira whether Patsy had had any connection with Lillian Murray.

'Connection? You mean, were they friends?' she asked, frowning. 'Sure, what kind of friendship could Patsy have had with anyone? He hadn't a clue what friendship meant. He never had a friend in all his life!'

She started to weep again, the sobs coming thick and fast. Ned waited for her to become calm.

'No, they weren't friends or anything like that,' Moira said.

'Sure, she only came to live in that house a few months ago. But I often saw her on Quay Street because she used to walk along the strand to come into the town. You know what it's like – everyone around here knows who everyone else is, even if they don't talk to each other. Though she did talk to Patsy. I think she knew he wasn't all there. He took to standing outside the house, waiting for her to walk by, and his face would light up when he saw her.'

Ned watched her expression change suddenly as she realised the import of what she had.

'Oh, God,' she said. 'Are you thinking that Patsy started that fire? Oh, Lord almighty, surely not . . .'

'I'm not thinking anything of the kind, Moira,' he said firmly. 'And you're not to think it, either.'

He didn't go straight back to his car, but walked down to the strand. He needed a few minutes to stand back and think. No, not think. Just stand back and let his mind open to the thoughts and sounds that rushed to fill it. On a fine day in summer, this was a perfect little curve of a beach, with the town behind it, the harbour south of it and a stretch of parkland on higher ground to its north. On that kind of a day, you could close your eyes and hear that soft hissing of the sea. But, today, his ears were filled with the shrieking of the seagulls and the thunderous sound of the waves crashing into the shore. His eyes became gritty and his eyelids blinked furiously, trying in vain to keep out the sand that the wind was lifting and sweeping in every direction. Rubbing his eyes, he turned away from the strand towards the harbour, where it seemed that the entire fishing fleet was taking shelter. The wind was raw and biting, cutting through him, making him shiver. It was dark now. It was time to go home to Eily and the kids.

A few old men sat bent over their mugs of tea in the grim dump of a café that sat at the bottom of Quay Street. The scene reminded him of an Edward Hopper painting in which lonely figures stood out against the harsh electric light. At some point, some canny entrepreneur would see the potential of a place like this and then the lonely old men would have nowhere to go except the pub, and it was getting harder and harder to find the kind of pub where you could just go for a quiet drink and not have to endure loud music.

His eyes were still stinging as he started the engine, and it wasn't just because of the sand. He had tried to put a small bit of distance between his job and his return home, but the sea had offered no comfort, no distraction. Moira Daly's plight had touched him deeply. In his first encounter with her, he had given her false hope. Now he had tried to allay her fears again by dismissing any suggestion that Patsy might be blamed for starting the fire. He hoped he wasn't going to be letting her down for a second time.

At home that night, he and Eily talked about Patsy McLennan, who had been a fixture of her life during her years of growing up in that part of Ardgreeney. She was genuinely upset.

'He really was harmless,' she said, tearfully. 'He used to hang around the shop and ask everyone who went in or out to buy him sweets. And we were horrible kids. We used to tease him and call him dreadful names, and he never seemed to mind. He used to just smile.'

She blew her nose.

'How old was he?' she asked, and then, with a sad laugh, said, 'He always looked old.'

'Seventy-six. And not a good seventy-six, according to what we've been told. Looked at least ten years older. He had arthritis, apparently. Sleeping in damp ditches wouldn't have done him much good.'

'What was he doing in the cottage? Did he set fire to it, do you think?'

'That's what Moira asked me, and I said no. But I honestly don't know what to think. Everyone we've talked to says he wouldn't have harmed a fly.'

'He wouldn't,' Eily said, shaking her head. 'Is there any more on that girl? Do you not think it's very odd that, just as she goes outside, poor Patsy goes in and the place goes up in flames?'

'It *is* odd. But there's nothing on the girl. She seems to have disappeared into the ether. Aidan isn't aware of any connection between Lillian and Patsy, and, to his knowledge, Patsy had never visited the cottage. It may be as simple as Patsy wandering around in the storm, noticing the cottage on fire and foolishly going in to see if he could put the flames out.'

'Do you really think that?' Eily asked.

'What else can I think at the moment?'

Later, he lay awake listening to Eily's regular breathing, which was interrupted every few minutes by a series of gentle snores. The scenario he had half-heartedly suggested to Eily had to be possible. Patsy had had a childlike admiration for Lillian – Moira told him that. He had been out and about in the storm and had seen the cottage ablaze. His instinct had been to rush inside to find Lillian. But that would suggest he hadn't seen Lillian outside.

It all came back to Lillian and whether she had planned to disappear or whether she had been abducted. He looked at the clock, which showed that it was already three o'clock. He groaned and turned on to his side, determined to get at least a few hours of sleep before it was time to start all over again.

Chapter Seven

The man who died in the fire was called Patsy McLennan. I hadn't known him, but I'd watched him die horribly. When Inspector Moynihan called me to tell me he had been identified, I wept.

It appeared that Lillian had known the man, the inspector said.

'Did she ever mention him to you?' he asked.

'I don't think so. No, I'm sure she didn't,' I said. 'Inspector, is there any news of Lillian? Anything at all? I know you can't tell me everything, but . . . I just need to know whether there's any point in hoping.'

He seemed to give my question some thought before he answered.

'There's always a point in hoping,' he said slowly. 'But I'm not saying that because I have reason to think she's all right. It's just that I don't have any reason at the moment to think otherwise. I'm sorry I can't give you anything better than that.'

'Do you think the man – Patsy – had anything to do with Lillian disappearing?'

'Sorry, Orla, but I really can't go into any detail about any of this.'

None of it made sense. When I saw the human shape in the flames, I thought it was Lillian. Now, I knew that Lillian hadn't died in the fire. But where was she?

Maybe the idea Inspector Moynihan had put forward – that she had staged her own disappearance – wasn't so outrageous. Maybe she was already on her way to wherever she was going before that poor old man, alerted by the flames, arrived on the scene. But that was impossible, I told myself. Lillian was happy. I had seen how happy she was. She would never have done anything like that. And why would she have duped me in such a horrible way? We'd been best friends all our lives. She would never have set me up as an unwitting accomplice in a plan to disappear.

And why would she have gone to such lengths? If she had wanted to disappear, she could have disappeared in London. Why go to the trouble of moving back to her hometown to stage a vanishing act? And if it had been the case that she wasn't as happy with her new life as she'd hoped she would be, surely she would have simply told Aidan she'd made a mistake and ended the relationship?

Conflicting thoughts like these plagued me. Lillian was in my mind all the time. I kept seeing her. She was standing on the kerb, waiting for a break in the traffic. She was walking past my parents' house. I knew it couldn't be her, but my heart still raced and my stomach still tied itself up in knots.

I desperately wanted to see Aidan and couldn't understand why he seemed to be avoiding me.

I'd tried his mobile countless times since the night of Lillian's disappearance, but my calls went unanswered. They didn't even go to voicemail. Maybe he didn't have my number on his phone and was declining calls from a UK number he didn't recognise. Maybe he couldn't face all the calls he must be getting from journalists and had bought himself a new phone.

There was only one way to speak to him. I would go to Eaglewood. I put on a pair of trainers and told my parents I was going for a walk.

'In this rain?' Dad asked.

'I just need to walk,' I said. 'I'll take a brolly.'

Why did it always rain when I came home? But this wasn't even proper rain, the kind that lashed and pummelled and pounded, the kind of rain that Lillian had gone out into. This was a dirty, pathetic and depressing drizzle that was going to go on for most of the day.

The town was quiet. The rain seemed to have kept most people inside. For once, I was half glad of it, because I could pull the hood on my anorak forward and hide behind it, instead of having to cope with people bathing me in sympathy and then ghoulishly asking me for details of what I had witnessed.

I turned into Quay Street, where I saw a Garda car parked. It was easy to tell which house Patsy McLennan had lived in, because all the blinds were down. I stopped for a few seconds outside, the words of a prayer coming silently into my mind. When I reached the strand, I turned to walk south, with the sea to my left and the Seapoint Road running more or less parallel, to my right. The dampness of the sand made walking more difficult than I had expected, and it was a long time before I was standing at the bottom of the rough wooden steps that Lillian had told me led from Oriel Cottage to the beach.

The steps were damp and slippery, and there was no rail, so I had to concentrate on the climb. I wasn't prepared for the sight of the burned-out, blackened house that loomed in front of me, and I had to stop for a moment to close my eyes and wait for the vice that was squeezing my stomach to release its grip.

The cottage and its immediate surroundings were off-limits, cordoned off by Garda tape, but there were no guards in sight. I slipped under the tape and walked around to the front of the house and the empty space that would have been the front door.

I had expected the house to be a ruin, but the exterior walls and the internal supporting walls were still standing. I walked inside and looked up towards the roof, mostly open to the skies, through which the rain poured. The ground was wet and filthy, strewn with debris. The awful, pungent smell filled my nostrils. The image of Patsy McLennan stumbling through the flames flared up in front of me and I had to close my eyes and catch my breath.

I stood in front of the big stone fireplace and then shifted away a few feet to mark the place where the sofa would have been, with the now burned-out window behind it. I began to imagine Lillian there now, the way she was that night, sitting with her legs curled up beneath her, her laptop on the coffee table in front of the sofa.

And then a chill spread through me, and I began to imagine someone else that neither of us had been aware of. Perhaps someone had stood outside the window that night, watching Lillian, staring in at her, then knocking at the door. Another thought came then, and it made me shiver. If whoever had taken Lillian had watched her through the window, he might have seen me, too, on the screen. And he might be wondering, even now, whether I had seen him. He might be here now. He might have followed me. I swung around, suddenly afraid, and ran outside, half expecting whoever had taken Lillian to be waiting there for me.

I no longer wanted to go on to Eaglewood. All I wanted to do at that moment was to get away from Oriel Cottage, away from the chill that was enveloping me. I didn't go back down the steps to the beach. I was too afraid. So I ran up the lane to the Seapoint Road and continued to run until I was back in the centre of Ardgreeney. There was no way Lillian had planned to disappear. She had been taken. And she was dead. I was sure of that now.

My visit to the cottage seemed to have stirred up all my nerve endings. I felt as if every hair on my head, every one of the light, downy hairs on my arms, was crackling with electricity. I was afraid. That night, I had the falling dream for the first time in months.

Grey stone steps stretched away from me, down, down, so far down that I couldn't see where they ended. I stood at the top of the steps, as if on a mountain peak, perched precariously with nothing to hold on to, trying to keep my balance and stay still, but knowing that I had to give in to what was pulling me down. I stood like that for a long time, but eventually I couldn't stand any longer and I began to fall – slowly, at first, but then picking up speed and spiralling downwards so fast that I was blind with dizziness.

As usual, I didn't reach the bottom. I woke myself up, shaking at the intensity of the nightmare.

I couldn't risk going back to sleep immediately, for fear I would fall back into the dream, so I went downstairs to the kitchen and made tea. I moved quietly and closed the kitchen door behind me, not wanting to disturb my parents. But it wasn't long before I heard Dad's footsteps on the stairs.

'Are you all right?' he asked.

'I couldn't sleep.'

'You were screaming,' he said.

'Oh! I'm sorry – I had a nightmare. Did I wake Ma as well?'

'Only for a couple of seconds. She's dead to the world again. Now, why don't you talk to me about everything that's been going on? And I don't just mean Lillian. You haven't been yourself for a while.'

I had always been closer to Dad than to Ma, who was closer to Fidelma, my older sister. It was Dad who had got up during the night when I had nightmares as a child. It was Dad I'd tended to confide in when things were bothering me. Moving away from home, to university and then to London, had diluted that closeness, as I became more independent, but it was still there and I felt it now as I watched Dad bring the kettle back to the boil and make a mug of tea for himself.

So we sat facing each other across the kitchen table and I told him about the accident I'd kept secret from him and Ma. I hadn't felt well that evening, I told him. I'd been feeling slightly dizzy and mildly nauseous – symptoms of the bug that had been going around the paper – so I cancelled the early-evening dinner I was supposed to have with a contact and headed home.

Lillian and I shared a flat on Randolph Avenue in Maida Vale – a top-floor flat in a tall, white-stuccoed terrace, not far from the canal. We reckoned it would have been used as servants' quarters back in the day when the house accommodated just one family. There was no lift.

As I climbed the stairs, after finally making it home, I could feel myself growing more and more exhausted. Just my luck, I thought to myself. James was coming down from Edinburgh for the weekend and I'd been looking forward to seeing him. But, from the way I was feeling, I knew I'd be in bed long before his train got in.

I remembered reaching the top of the staircase that stretched up through four floors.

I remembered hoping that Lillian might have managed to get home early for a change, because she might run down to the pharmacy and get me some ibuprofen for the headache that was now so bad my eyes were closing.

And then, nothing.

I opened my eyes and shut them again, dazzled by the bright-ness of the light above me. Everything hurt. Especially my head. I felt the floor under my head and my back. I opened my eyes again and saw a blurred shape in front of me: Lillian.

'Orla, thank God you're all right! I was so worried!'

I squinted at her, trying to focus my eyes, and saw she had tears running down her face. And she was gripping my hand so tightly that I winced.

'Wh-what's wrong? What happened?' I asked, looking beyond her and recognising where I was: the next landing down from our flat. My head seemed to be splitting in two from the pain, which was so bad I thought I was going to be sick.

'I don't know. I just came home now and found you lying here. I've called for an ambulance. It'll be here soon.'

'Did I fall?' I asked, confused. 'I don't remember falling. All I can remember is . . . I think I got to our door, but maybe I slipped on the top step.'

'That bloody step – it was bound to trip one of us up at some point. I'll get someone in to stick the carpet down properly,' she said. 'Oh, God; I'm so glad you're all right! I was so afraid . . .'

She stopped speaking and began to choke on her tears.

'James,' I said. 'He doesn't have a key . . . How will he get in?'

'It's okay. I've called him. He's still on the train. I'll call him again from the hospital.'

The hospital kept me in overnight. The only obvious damage I had sustained in the fall was a bump on the head, a sprained ankle and a few bruises. A head X-ray showed nothing untoward, but, because no one knew how long I'd been unconscious, I also had a brain scan. That, too, seemed to be clear, so the doctors weren't too concerned, though my inability to remember the actual fall did worry them a little, and they suggested that I talk to my GP about a possible second scan.

James spent what was meant to be a fun weekend looking after me. We'd planned to spend Saturday afternoon at Tate Modern, and then wander up to Galvin on Baker Street for dinner. I suggested he go to Tate Modern with Lillian, but he insisted on keeping me company. It was still early days in our long-distance romance, but his attentiveness made me think he might be a good bet.

The dreams began when I left the hospital and went back to the flat. They varied in intensity. Sometimes, I fell slowly. That was the least frightening version of the dream. Sometimes, the fall was fast and terrifying. But all the versions had one thing in common: the fall never ended. I didn't have them every night. They might come once a week or once every couple of weeks, but they kept coming. And then they stopped – until now.

Dad was disturbed by what I had told him. He said the dreams were almost certainly a natural reaction to what had happened, that I was probably reliving my fall subconsciously and that the dreams would probably stop eventually. But he was particularly worried by my inability to remember what had caused me to fall.

'Well, you know what it's like when you faint,' I said. 'You're doing one thing one minute and you're on the ground the next. You don't remember what happened in between, do you? There was a bit of carpet that was loose and we were always saying we'd get it sorted. I'm sure that was it.'

'What about the brain scan?' Dad asked.

'That was okay. Nothing dodgy showed up on it,' I said.

'I'm talking about the second one the doctors suggested.'

'Oh, that wasn't definitely going to happen. It was just something they said I should mention to my GP.'

'And did you?'

I shook my head. 'I've been fine, really, so I never went to the GP.'

'Maybe you should chase it up?'

'I suppose so.'

'And I hope you got the carpet stuck down properly?'

I smiled. 'James fixed it.'

'When are we going to meet this James of yours?' Dad asked.

I shrugged, but said nothing.

My relationship with James was one of the reasons I hadn't, as Dad put it, 'been myself'. He seemed to blow hot and cold, and I didn't know where I was with him. He said he was stressed at work, that teaching was much tougher than he had expected. I could believe that, but I couldn't understand why he had to bring that stress to our relationship. Sometimes I thought about suggesting we take a break from each other for a while. But I always baulked when it came down to saying the words, because I was afraid that, if we took a break from each other, it might be the end of him and me.

It hadn't been like that at the beginning. It was instant attraction for both of us when we met on the Eurostar from Paris. He had been on a cookery course in France and was on his way back to Edinburgh, via London, for the start of the new school year. He was very good looking, with dark, mischievous eyes, dimples that appeared in his cheeks when he smiled and a head of unruly black hair. He looked like a character from one of the Georgette Heyer novels I'd devoured in my teens after graduating from the Chalet School books.

When we pulled into Waterloo, we went our separate ways, but not without exchanging numbers. First, there were telephone calls. Then we began to meet. I didn't have much faith in long-distance relationships, but this was one I was prepared to nurture, and I did it by going to Edinburgh as often as I could, where he loved to try out his cooking skills on me. Lillian teased me about hiding him away from everyone.

'Are you sure you haven't made him up?' she asked.

'I assure you, I haven't made him up! But I'm trying to keep my cool – not read too much into things too soon. It may not last. It probably won't.'

'Well, since he's so gorgeous,' Lillian said, 'do you not think it would be a good idea to let everyone meet him, before he disappears?'

I remembered her words now, as I sat facing my father: *before he disappears*. But she was the one who had disappeared, not James.

And there was something else I hadn't told my father – something I was finding hard to admit, even to myself. My inability to remember what had caused my fall down the stairs had made me question my ability to remember anything properly. I had lost a lot of confidence at work. I was nervous of going to press conferences in case I misheard something or got something wrong. When I had to do an interview, I used two recorders in case one didn't work properly. I was so terrified of misquoting people that I replayed my recordings several times to be absolutely certain, and even then I fretted. And now Lillian was missing and I was in a constant state of anguish over whether I'd seen or heard something, but had failed to remember what – or who – it was.

Chapter Eight

He was working day and night. And Eily was pissed off. No, that wasn't the right term. She was incandescent a lot of the time with what seemed like barely suppressed anger. He couldn't keep up with her moods. She was angry, upset, resentful – all those things at different times and sometimes all at once. These moods would be followed by tearful repentance, and she would apologise for being so hard line about her demands when he was under such pressure. But then it would all start again, another cycle of recrimination followed by shorter cycles of repentance.

And his bewildered response was to work ever-longer hours. He didn't know how to address what was happening between him and Eily, short of giving up his job. But he couldn't do that. Finding out what had happened to Lillian Murray had transcended the obligations of mere police service. It had taken over his life.

He thought about little else. A young woman with everything

to live for had disappeared, vanished into thin air. It touched everything that had lain buried inside him for so long, and now those buried feelings were clawing their way out, exposing the dark part of him, the part of which he was most afraid. No one talked about *her* any more, that other young woman who had disappeared nearly two decades before. It was as if she had never existed. But he hadn't forgotten about her. He had had occasional glimpses of her in his mind's eye, glimpses that he always pushed away because to acknowledge them and let them expand would have been too much for him. But now, Lillian Murray's disappearance was bringing her back to him in high relief.

The buzzing of his telephone against the hard surface of his desk interrupted his thoughts. Just as well, he told himself. He was tired of thinking. The day had barely begun and he was already weary from the hopelessness of it all. He looked at the screen and saw that the caller was Orla Breslin. She had called him several times over the previous couple of weeks to ask him whether there was anything new, anything that would take them closer to finding out what had happened to Lillian. He had told her each time she called that there was nothing new, but that he and his colleagues were still doing their utmost to find her friend.

What he hadn't told her was that the search for Lillian was likely to be scaled back fairly soon and would probably be quietly abandoned in the not-too-distant future.

He could just about understand why: there was no evidence of Lillian having been abducted or murdered, or of the fire having been started deliberately, and there was every reason to believe that Patsy McLennan had simply been passing by on one of his wanderings and had gone inside to rescue the young woman he thought of as his friend. But Ned didn't like it. He didn't like it one bit.

'Orla. You're still here?' he said.

'Yes. I've taken unpaid leave from work. But I suppose I'll have to go back in the next week or two. Look, I need to talk to you about something. It probably doesn't mean anything, but . . . well, you said it was important to pass on anything, no matter how insignificant it might seem,' she said.

'Nothing's unimportant,' Ned said. 'I'm listening.'

'I don't know why I didn't mention this to you this before. Maybe it didn't seem important at the time. Lillian told me, months ago, just before she left London, that she and Aidan had a plan to turn Eaglewood into a boutique hotel. The idea was that Aidan's mother would basically hand the house over to them, but would still run the riding school. They hadn't discussed it with her at that point. But when we were on Skype . . . that night . . . Lillian said Aidan had talked to his mother earlier in the day about it. She said Mrs McManus had been a bit taken aback, but had come round to the idea. She told me to keep it to myself.'

'Did Lillian say anything else about this plan? For example, where the money was going to come from? Whether there was another partner?'

'No. That's it.'

'It's probably nothing, but thanks for telling me. I'll have a word with Aidan.'

'Can you keep my name out of it?'

'Of course. But why? I thought you were friendly with Aidan.'

'I thought so, too, but he hasn't been picking up when I've tried calling him. I can't think what I've done to make him upset with me.'

'Maybe he feels guilty that he wasn't at home and that you were the one to raise the alarm,' Ned said. 'I wouldn't worry about it. And, don't worry, I won't tell Aidan what you told me about the hotel plan. It's probably nothing important.'

It probably *was* nothing, he told himself when he ended the call, though a few thoughts ran through his mind. Could there have been an insurance angle? Could there have been a deliberate plan to burn down the cottage to get money for the hotel development? But that had to be bollocks, because a lot of money would have been spent doing up the cottage and extending it, and it was unlikely that whatever the insurance company might have paid out would cover both the restoration of the cottage *and* the conversion of Eaglewood into a boutique hotel. And, anyway, that didn't explain Lillian Murray's disappearance.

Still, there was no harm in talking to Aidan, so he got into his car and drove over to Eaglewood.

Although he was far from drunk, it was obvious that Aidan had been drinking – had probably been drinking steadily over several days. The smell of alcohol, mixed with that of cigarette smoke, seemed to ooze out of his pores. That wasn't going to help what was left of his rugby career. It was just as well he had been trying to set up a post-rugby future in the hotel business because, looking at the state of him now, Ned reckoned he was going to need one sooner rather than later.

'Aidan,' Ned said, when they were sitting down, 'I understand you're thinking of turning this place into a hotel.'

'Where did you get that from?' Aidan asked, a hint of belligerence in his voice.

Ned ignored the question. 'Is it true?'

'It *was*. Whether it will ever happen now, I don't know. It's not exactly at the top of my list of priorities at the moment.'

'No, of course not. I understand, though, that the plan would have involved your mother turning this house over to you and Lillian, and that your mother didn't wholeheartedly support the idea.'

'Is this relevant, what Lillian and I were hoping to do with the house?' Aidan asked. 'But you're wrong about my mother. At some point, she was going to sign the house over to me. We'd talked about it several times. She was glad I'd come up with a scheme to keep Eaglewood in the family. The alternative would have been to sell off the land, bit by bit, and then we'd have had housing estates right up to the gates. We might still end up with them. Have you any idea how much it costs to keep a place like this going?'

'I can only imagine. Turning it into a hotel wouldn't be cheap either, though. How were you going to fund that?' Ned asked. 'Have you got any other business partners?'

'My mother was going to provide the money. Again, all part of my inheritance. But everything has been turned on its head. My mother isn't in a position to provide anything very much at the moment.'

'How is your mother?' Ned asked.

Aidan grimaced and sighed. 'Medically, she's a lot better than she was. She's been moved from the stroke unit at the hospital to a nursing home, Kilfernagh. The doctors say she's improved a lot and that, after a couple of months of physio and other stuff, she'll probably be able to come back to Eaglewood. But I don't know. She's . . . different. Very shaken, very depressed. I'm not sure she'll ever be the same again.'

'How's her speech?'

'She says very little. I think she understands a lot, but she struggles to make words, and then, when she can't, she gets upset.'

'I'm sorry to hear that. We're hoping to talk to her at some point soon.'

Aidan gave another sigh and shook his head. 'I don't think she's anywhere near ready for that. She can just about cope with a visit from me,' he said.

As he left, Ned asked Aidan whether he had been in contact with Orla Breslin. 'You know she's in town?' he said.

'Yeah, I know she's here. She called me a few times, but . . . I can't face talking to her. You probably think I'm nuts, but it's just too . . . raw.'

'She's grieving too, Aidan,' Ned said.

He glanced back at the house as he walked to his car, which he had left outside the big iron gates. It was a bit bleak-looking now, a bit uncared for. But its location at the foot of the headland, with spectacular panoramic views across the sea and towards the mountains to the north, was enviable. He could see its potential as a small, exclusive hotel.

A group of journalists who had been standing on the road outside the gates besieged him.

'What did you and Aidan talk about?'

'Do you think Lillian might still be alive?'

'Is Aidan a suspect?'

'Sorry, folks; I have nothing for you,' he said, squeezing past them to his car. He looked in the rear-view mirror as he turned the engine on; several of them were on their mobiles, presumably telling their editors that Moynihan had been and gone, and had said nothing. The others had already forgotten about him and had resumed their previous positions, waiting for Aidan to emerge.

Fuck! he thought, as he drove away. He had forgotten to ask Aidan whether the cottage was insured and for how much. He would do that another time. Or he could phone him. Or get someone else to do it.

On the way back to the station, he saw the sign pointing to the Kilfernagh Nursing Home. Aidan had pretty much told him his mother was off-limits, but Ned was curious and this was like an invitation. He swung the car left into Kilfernagh Lane and, a few minutes later, he was driving into the grounds of the nursing home, an ivy-covered Victorian red brick house with modern extensions either side.

At the reception desk, he showed his ID and said he wanted to see Kathleen McManus. The receptionist said she'd have to ask her manager if he could be admitted. She picked up the phone and pressed a button. After listening for a few seconds, she replaced the receiver.

'She doesn't seem to be answering,' the receptionist said. 'Do you mind taking a seat over there, Inspector? I'll have to find her.'

'I just need to see how Mrs McManus is doing. I'm not planning to interview her or bother her. Couldn't you just point me in the direction of her room?'

'I'm really sorry, but it isn't allowed. We're not supposed to let anyone in to see her except her son and the doctors. I'll try to find Mrs Dillon, though. I'm sure she'll let you in, seeing as you're a guard.'

He waited, fully expecting this Mrs Dillon to march into the lobby and demand that he leave immediately. But, ten minutes later, there was still no sign of the manager.

'She must be on her lunch break,' the receptionist said.

He got up, thanked her for trying to find Mrs Dillon, and was walking towards the door when the receptionist called him back.

'Look, I'm sure it's all right. I'll get one of the care assistants to take you to Mrs McManus's room,' she said.

She made another phone call and, half a minute later, a young woman called Lenka was leading him into a lift and along a corridor.

'This is Mrs McManus's room,' she said. 'I will come in with you.'

He was about to say that this wasn't necessary, but then saw from Lenka's face that she had no intention of leaving him alone with a resident, even if he was a detective – maybe especially if he was a detective.

Kathleen McManus was dozing in an armchair, a woollen blanket across her legs. He hadn't seen her since his wedding, more than two decades earlier. But, even allowing for the passage of time, he was shocked by the change in her appearance. She'd once been a handsome woman, tall and haughty, aware of her standing as the mistress of one of the great houses in the area.

Now, she was greatly diminished, although the high cheekbones hinted at her former good looks.

He could see that she was well cared for. Her silver hair was brushed back into a neat bun and her clothes were spotless. He could smell lavender in the room.

'Don't disturb her. I'll wait for her to wake up,' Ned told Lenka, adding, 'You don't have to hang around.'

Lenka smiled. 'I will stay.'

So they waited together, and, just when he was beginning to wonder whether he was going to lose a whole afternoon before he got to talk to her, Kathleen McManus's eyes opened slowly, flickering several times, as if she wasn't quite sure whether she was awake or asleep, and then adjusting to his presence in her room.

'Who are you?'

The strength of her voice surprised him. He had expected something far weaker from someone who had suffered a debilitating stroke. And hadn't Aidan said she struggled to form words? But there was no hint of struggling here. She delivered the words in a demanding, imperious tone – the kind of tone, he suspected, that came naturally to her. The sagging skin seemed to tighten as she recovered whatever sleep had caused her to lose.

He leaned forward so that his eyes were level with hers. As he did so, she raised her chin. She was, the thought came to him, looking down her nose at him. He remembered that Eily hadn't shared her father's view of Kathleen McManus as a fine woman who was too good for her husband. *She's a snotty old witch*, Eily had said once. He hadn't seen it at his wedding. He barely remembered the McManuses being there. But he saw it now:

a sense of superiority that even the lightning blow of a stroke clearly hadn't mollified.

'My name is Ned Moynihan,' he said. 'Maybe you remember me? I'm married to Eily O'Donnell, Jack's daughter. You came to our wedding.'

The expression on her face changed in a flash. It made him think of one of those visual tricks in a horror film, where a face is revealed to be a mask that peels away. He saw the cold haughtiness vanish, to be replaced by something that he couldn't describe at first, as it spread across her face. But when he focused on her eyes again, he saw it more clearly. She was frightened. Her eyes were filled with some unspeakable terror, as if all the ghosts of her past, and even her future, were standing in front of her.

Her voice came out as a rasp now, as if she had overestimated the power she was able to give it. 'Go away! Go away!'

Ned looked at Lenka, who had jumped between him and Kathleen, as if to protect her charge.

'Don't worry; I'm going,' he said. 'I'm really sorry about this. I had no idea she was going to react this way.'

He made his escape, passing the reception desk.

'Was it okay?' the receptionist asked.

He gave her a rueful smile. 'Lenka will tell you all about it,' he said. 'Thanks for your help. If you have any problems with Mrs Dillon, put her on to me.'

His nerves jangled by his encounter with Kathleen McManus, he drove far too fast, just about managing to avoid causing an accident. Nothing about Lillian Murray's disappearance and Patsy McLennan's terrible, tragic death made any sense to him. And he was disturbed by the way Kathleen McManus had reacted to him. He hadn't told her he was a detective. He had mentioned only his wedding to Eily and Kathleen's presence as a guest. She had had a stroke. Maybe she would have screamed at anyone she didn't know or feel comfortable with. But he had a feeling she knew, once he had told her his name and that he was married to Eily, exactly who he was and what he did for a living.

But, if that was the case, why was she so terrified? He couldn't help wondering whether it was possible that she had been somehow involved in Lillian Murray's disappearance. Could she have been so possessive of her son that she had struck out against the woman he loved? She had been a strong woman, a domineering woman, used to being in charge. Maybe she had felt threatened by Lillian. And maybe she had abhorred the idea of her beloved home being turned into a hotel. But would she have had the physical strength to abduct and kill a young, healthy woman in her mid-twenties? No, that was ridiculous.

When he got back to his desk, there was a note from Fergus asking him to pop in.

Fuck! That was fast. Mrs Dillon must have been on the phone to the station to raise ructions within minutes of hearing about his visit to Kilfernagh. He made himself a coffee and went in to see Fergus, ready for the bollocking.

'There's been a complaint from Kilfernagh, I suppose,' he said, dropping into a chair and opening the conversation.

'Kilfernagh?'

Ned told him what had happened, admitted that he might have made an error of judgement, but suggested that they should still think about having a chat with Kathleen McManus – under medical supervision, if necessary. But Fergus didn't seem to be listening. He launched into a recap of how the Lillian Murray case had been developing, a recap that Ned quickly realised was going to turn into a justification for the scaling back that he hadn't thought would come quite so soon.

They had been working with hardly a break for several weeks, Fergus noted. The Met in London had come up with nothing of use, and none of Lillian's former colleagues knew of another colleague – or, indeed, anyone – who had been pestering Lillian.

'Aidan McManus, given the various time checks, would have needed supernatural powers to have killed his girlfriend and disposed of her body,' Fergus said.

Ned nodded in agreement.

Fergus continued: 'No one has seen sight or light of Lillian Murray, and the one person who might have been able to tell us something is dead. So I think we have to assume that Lillian did a runner.'

'Ah, come on, Fergus, I hope you're not telling me that you're closing down the investigation ... Jesus, you are! But that's ridiculous. It's not even a month. It's true the Met hasn't come up with anything useful. But what about that phone call a week before she went missing, even if we can't trace the number back to anyone? And the text Orla Breslin says she saw from someone with the initial R? What about him? Maybe he couldn't get over Lillian taking up with Aidan.'

Fergus sighed. 'And this character came all the way over from London and just happened to pick an evening when Aidan would be out to kill her?' he said, a note of frustration in his voice.

79

'Ned, we've had the Met check stuff out as far as they've been able to and they're drawing a blank. There's no body. If she fell or was pushed into the sea, she'd have washed up by now. And if someone has been holding her, you have to ask yourself why. There's been no ransom demand.'

'And Patsy McLennan? Are we assuming he just casually wandered into a blazing house?'

'We're not assuming anything. But, yes, maybe he did just wander into the house at the wrong time. Look, Ned, when we put everything together, we may not be getting an absolutely clear picture, but we're coming near enough to one. We can't go on pissing into the wind.'

'So that's it? Case closed? The press will have a field day.'

'No, we're not closing it. Of course we're not. But we're going to have to scale back a bit. And the press won't have a field day. Have you not read the papers lately or looked at the news? They've been digging into Lillian Murray's background and they've decided she may have been a bit unstable. Father died when she was just a kid and she was brought up by an alcoholic mother. They got hold of some neighbour who told them that Lillian and her mother were always fighting. They're all throwing into their stories the possibility that she decided she'd made a big mistake in coming back and just buggered off.'

'The same press that has been slinging enough mud at Aidan McManus to bury him? For fuck's sake, Fergus; this is the worst decision you've ever made, and some day it's going to come back and bite us all in the arse.'

Chapter Nine

It seemed as if everyone in Ardgreeney was at the Mass held for Lillian the day before I returned to London. The church was full to overflowing. It wasn't a proper requiem Mass because there was no body, but it might as well have been, because people looked as if they were attending a funeral. I didn't pay much attention to the liturgy or to the short sermon because my mind was stuck on the words of the Confiteor, which kept playing over and over in my head: *I have sinned in my thoughts and in my words, in what I have done and in what I have failed to do.* And I had failed Lillian. I had failed to keep watch when she was in danger. It didn't matter that neither of us had known of the danger. What mattered was that I had allowed my attention to wander. Had I been more attentive, had I caught a glimpse of the person who took her, I might have saved her.

Aidan sat with Lillian's mother, Nancy, at the front of the church, his arm around her shoulder throughout the Mass.

Afterwards, when everyone was standing outside, I looked for him, but he had disappeared. I wasn't surprised that he had made off as quickly as he could once he had seen the phalanx of TV cameras moving forward as the church emptied.

My parents took Nancy home to her house. She was broken, and I knew she would repair herself the only way she knew how: with alcohol. It was how she had always coped.

Her husband, Lillian's father, had died in a car accident when Lillian was twelve. That was when Nancy took to drink. Maybe it wasn't as simple as that. Maybe there were other triggers, other factors. But, if there were, they made little fundamental difference to Lillian, who had to watch her mother stagger between the house and the off-licence, who learned to recognise the signs that her mother had had her first drink of the day – the hint of a slur in her speech, the vacant look in her eyes, the sluggish movement of her mouth as she tried to form words. Lillian couldn't wait to leave home.

And while she was waiting to grow up, our house was her refuge. My parents' albums had nearly as many photographs of Lillian as they did of Fidelma and me. The urge to look through these albums came over me as I said goodbye to Nancy and walked back to our house.

I found the albums in a metal cabinet in the garage, which was where my parents decanted the overflow from the house. Over time, the garage had filled up so that there was no longer room for the car, which now lived on the little stretch of driveway to the side of the front garden.

I carried the albums into the kitchen and began to look through them. Sometimes, I laughed out loud at the ridiculous teenage poses we had struck, at our pouty faces trying to mimic the sultry looks of pop stars and models. And sometimes I just broke down in tears as I caught a glimpse of the vulnerability beneath Lillian's ebullient, confident façade. I hadn't seen it back then. But I saw it now and it broke my heart.

We had never really talked about the extent to which she'd been affected by the tragedy of her childhood. You don't lose your father at the age of twelve and not carry the scars, even if your mother isn't an alcoholic. Lillian and I had known each other all our lives. I knew her history, having grown up alongside it. And, eventually, I came to understand how sad and difficult this history had been. But, by the time I reached that point, there didn't seem to be a need to talk about it. I had got it all wrong, I thought now, as I saw beyond the veneer of the photographs.

I needed to find evidence of happier times, so I flicked back through an earlier album and found an ancient snap of the two of us on the strand. We must have been about eight or nine at the time. There was little to distinguish between us. We had identical masses of curly blonde hair. Our eyes were pinpricks, squinting into the sun. I remembered that day, all right. We had our swimsuits on, but we hadn't gone into the sea because of the jellyfish that had invaded the warm water. Some lay glistening on the strand, left there by the previous tide and soon to be covered by the incoming one. I remembered how we had edged up to stare at the dead jellyfish before running away, shrieking and laughing.

I became aware that the doorbell was ringing.

I opened the door to find Aidan standing there. I stared at him, lost for words.

'Can I come in?' he asked.

I didn't answer, at first. I didn't move, either. His unannounced arrival had taken me by surprise.

'I've tried to talk to you,' I said eventually. 'I've called you more times than I can count, but you haven't answered.'

He made an effort to look puzzled. 'What calls?'

I gave him a look that said, *Do you take me for an idiot?* and led him into the kitchen, where I picked up my mobile and pressed his number. His phone rang somewhere in his jacket.

'Those calls.'

He sighed. He seemed to be about to say something in response, and then he noticed the photograph albums. 'Do you mind?'

'Go ahead.'

He sat down and began to look through them. When he had finished, he stood up. 'I want you to come with me,' he said.

'Come where?' I asked.

'Where do you think?'

I got my coat and put it on, and we walked out of the house in silence and climbed into his Range Rover.

Neither of us spoke as he drove back into the town and on to the Seapoint Road. I knew where we were going. It couldn't have been anywhere else.

The blue tape was still there. We ducked under it and walked up the path and into the ruined house.

'Why are we here?' I asked.

'I'll tell you in a minute,' he said. 'Show me what you saw that night.'

I stretched my arm out to point at the now-empty space where the sofa had been. 'That's where Lillian was sitting,' I said.

'Show me how she was sitting, where the laptop was.'

I dug into the image I held in my mind of the way she had been on the sofa, leaning back into it, her legs curled up underneath her, and tried to imitate it as closely as possible, using my hands to make the shapes.

'And the laptop?'

'It was there,' I said, pointing to where the coffee table and laptop would have been.

'And yet you didn't see anything? Jesus, Orla; you *must* have seen something! Look around. Look behind you. You must have seen her walk out through the door. And the window – it's in full view of where the screen would have been. She disappeared in front of your eyes and you saw nothing? Are you blind?' He was shouting, now, distressed and angry.

But I was angry, too, and I lashed out. I had suffered as much as he had, maybe even more because I had seen too much and yet I hadn't seen enough to save Lillian.

'You think I don't ask myself those questions? You think I don't torture myself with them?' I shouted back. 'I saw the fire – I saw a man burn to death and I thought he was Lillian! That's what I saw. I saw more than you did. And where were you that night? Out getting pissed! That's where you were!'

His face seemed to crumble, and I realised I had been too cruel.

'I'm sorry, Aidan . . . Your mother . . . I'm so sorry,' I said.

'I'm sorry, too. It's not your fault. It's anything but your fault. I shouldn't have shouted at you. I just needed someone to blame so that I didn't have to blame myself. Because the truth is that, if I hadn't gone out that night, she'd still be here.'

I had to get out of the house, escape its blackened walls. I left him standing there and went outside again, desperate to empty my mind of his accusations. I walked to the bottom of the garden and looked out over the strand and across the granite-coloured sea. I thought I saw seals bobbing here and there, but everything was so grey that it was impossible to tell for sure. A couple of trawlers sat out on the blurred horizon, like paper boats perched on a crayoned line drawn across a page. In the distance, to the north, I saw black clouds suspended over the mountains.

It felt like the loneliest, most remote place in the world.

After a while, Aidan came and stood beside me.

'We were happy,' he said, not looking at me, but staring out across the water. 'We had plans. We were good together. I can't believe she just walked away and left.'

'No,' I said.

Lillian had always had a bit of a crush on Aidan. We all did, but he was older than we were and wouldn't have looked at us then. But all it took was a few years, and when he noticed Lillian at a party during one of her visits home, he wouldn't let her out of his sight. He was smitten, and she was, too.

She had been a bit slow in telling me that she was going to move back to Ireland to be with Aidan. They hadn't been together very long, only about three months, and hadn't even spent that much time together, because of his rugby commitments and training. But I'd had a feeling that something was going on. Her moods had been swinging all over the place for weeks. One minute she was upbeat and the next she was quiet and distracted, as if her mind was somewhere else entirely. It must have been a difficult decision, even if she was besotted with him.

When she eventually told me, I was shocked. I knew she

and Aidan had become serious about each other, but I hadn't expected her to throw her lot in with him so quickly.

'Are you absolutely sure about this?' I asked her. 'It's a massive step.'

'Of course I'm not absolutely sure,' she said. 'I've got doubts. Huge ones. But I know it's the right thing to do. It's the right thing for me. And, yeah, I know I'm going to have to deal with my mother more often than I've had to over here. But it's going to be different, now, because I'll have Aidan.'

'And you'll have his mother, as well,' I said. 'Where are you going to live? In the big house, with the pair of them?'

'No way! Are you out of your mind? I'd go nuts. God, she's such a cold fish. And I don't think I quite meet the criteria for marriage to her beloved son. Even Aidan – and he's devoted to her – wouldn't suggest we live with her. He's doing up a cottage for us. You know that place off the Seapoint Road, down a lane that comes to a dead end? It hasn't been lived in for years, but it's structurally sound and he's been building a massive extension.'

'But, Lillian, you're going to be living in Ardgreeney! It's not Dublin. It's a backwater. There aren't going to be many PR jobs there. At least, if you were going to Dublin – '

'To be honest, I'm not sure I'll be looking for a job,' she said, a cryptic smile spreading across her face.

'Jesus – you're not pregnant, are you?'

'I certainly am not! But . . . Well, keep this to yourself. We're thinking about turning Eaglewood into a boutique hotel, so I'm going to have plenty to keep me busy.'

'I can see that going down well with his mother. What are you going to do with her? Put her out to grass?'

Lillian laughed at that. 'Ha! I wish we could. She's such a superior old cow. But she'll be fine. She can continue to live in the house and run the riding bit. We'll need her for that. I can't tell one end of a horse from the other, and I have no intention of spending my days mucking out stables.'

'Does she know about this plan of yours and Aidan's?'

'Not exactly.'

'In other words, she doesn't know about it at all. Jesus. I almost feel sorry for her.'

And we both laughed.

But I didn't tell Aidan about that conversation as he drove me home. We didn't talk at all. I had no idea what he was thinking about. I was remembering the last time Lillian and I had been together. It was just a few short months ago, but it felt like years.

We had tried to make it as much like a normal Sunday as we could. Just as we did most Sundays, we went to Raoul's, on Clifton Road, for breakfast. But it wasn't a normal Sunday in any way. The winter had come late, but it had come with a vengeance. Everything had been covered in snow for what seemed like ages and the streets around the canal were like a postcard scene.

It would have been a perfect day, but for the fact that my best, my closest friend in the world was leaving. We laughed a lot that day, going back over the good times we'd had in London. But mostly we cried, walking arm in arm along the canal. I could see her clearly in my mind, remembering how she shivered in her new red coat, which was fashionably unstructured, but also unlined. She really should have been wearing something that would keep out the cold. Every bit of me, on the other hand, was wrapped up so that I looked like an Arctic explorer. All that was missing was the huskies and sled. We must have looked an incongruous pair.

We shuffled back to the flat and waited for the taxi to arrive to take her to Heathrow. She wouldn't let me go with her.

'I don't want the pair of us to be in floods of tears again,' she said.

'Call me tonight, then, just to let me know you've arrived okay. You never know, the flight might be cancelled because of the snow.'

She shook her head. 'No, if I call you tonight, I'll get into a state. The flight won't be cancelled. I'll call you in a couple of days, once I've started to accept that I don't live in London any more. I promise.'

I looked at Aidan now and I wished with all my heart that she had never met him. Because, if she hadn't taken up with him, she wouldn't have returned to Ardgreeney. And if she hadn't returned to Ardgreeney, she would still be alive. But I didn't say that to him. It would have been too cruel.

Nearly ten years later . . .

October 2016

Chapter Ten

Ned had no idea how long the envelope had been there. It might have been lurking innocuously for days among the bills and unsolicited junk mail that lay scattered on the mat by the front door. He hadn't bothered to pick up his post for the best part of a week. He looked at the envelope, with his name and address scrawled in big capital letters. He didn't need to open it to know what was inside, but he checked anyway.

Another to add to his collection. This one, just like all the others, asked him how he could live with himself, berated him for being a miserable failure.

YOU FUCKED UP. YOU DID NOTHING RIGHT. YOU DIDN'T LOOK IN THE RIGHT PLACE.

That last sentence struck him. The scrawl was slightly different, a bit hesitant, as if added as an afterthought. Or maybe it was meant to look different so that it would stand out. No name, no signature, but he was sure he knew who it was.

Orla Breslin. It had to be. He had heard on the grapevine a few months back that she had come back to live in Ardgreeney, and the letters started to arrive shortly after that.

But — if it was her — what did she mean by *You didn't look in the right place*? Did she know something, or was she just trying to stir him into some kind of action?

He stuffed the single sheet of paper back into its envelope, threw it on to the kitchen table and quickly made scrambled egg on toast and a pot of coffee. He tried to read yesterday's paper as he ate, but he couldn't concentrate. The final sentence of the letter bothered him. He didn't remember anything quite like that in the other letters. He got them out – he had a small stack of them by this point, and he kept them at home because no one at work was interested in them – and scanned quickly through them.

No, none of the others had a phrase quite like that. *You didn't look in the right place.* The right place for what? A body? The others were generally abusive – *you're stupid*; *your brains are in your arse* – but they didn't contain anything like this.

He reminded himself that his colleagues had attached little importance to any of the letters. Eily had told him to chuck them all in the bin and forget about them.

'Oh, for God's sake, Ned! Can't you just forget about what happened ten years ago?' she had said a while back, when he mentioned the arrival of the first couple of envelopes.

He had been surprised by the sharpness of her response. All he had said was that the letters had arrived out of the blue and that it seemed someone was keen to revive interest in the case. But she had reacted so angrily that he just shut up and didn't bring the subject of the letters into any of their subsequent conversations – if 'conversations' was the right word. Maybe the letters reminded her that their marriage had begun to break down around the time Lillian Murray disappeared.

When the first letter arrived, he had taken it straight to Fergus, expecting that, at the very least, it would provoke some discussion. But Fergus had been dismissive.

'There's nothing here, Ned,' he said, his eyebrows lifted. 'Some crank, looking to cause trouble.'

That had been Fergus's response each time a new letter arrived. Other colleagues were equally dismissive, telling him he was wasting his own time as well as theirs and that he would be better off putting his efforts into learning to play golf so that he had something to do when he eventually retired.

Golf! For fuck's sake.

Still, he was thinking about taking a sabbatical because he desperately needed a break. Just a year – the maximum time available. He had actually been thinking about going for early retirement, but Fergus, now a chief superintendent and probably heading even higher, had persuaded him not to take that final step. Not yet, anyway.

'Once you're out, you're out,' Fergus had told him bluntly. 'At least, if you go down the sabbatical route, you'll get a taste of what it's like to have nothing to do all day. You might like it, but I have a feeling that, in a year's time, you'll be more than ready to come back.'

'I wish I'd never taken early retirement,' Matty Walsh had told him a while back, when they were having a jar at Dolan's, the only pub in town you could still call a pub. All the others had taken to serving food, because that was what people expected these days, but Dolan's hadn't been spruced up in decades and it didn't even have crisps or peanuts, let alone food. It was the kind of drinking establishment where old men sat for hours with the same dark pint, in the kind of silence you could only dream about in other pubs.

'I thought I'd be out on the golf course every day. That was the grand plan. But herself had me mending this and fixing that, morning, noon and night. At least you don't have someone telling you the kitchen needs painting and the garden shed needs clearing out and the tiles around the bath need replacing – oh, and maybe you'd take the dog out for a walk, as well. Jaysus.'

Ned had to admit that the thought of full retirement was a scary one; that essay from the dark blue book of English prose from his schooldays, 'The Superannuated Man', kept springing up in his head. *I have lost all distinction of season. I do not know the day of the week, or of the month.* The thought of a year off was an attractive one, though. He wouldn't have to set the alarm clock. He wouldn't get phone calls at some ungodly hour, telling him to head off to Ballygonowhere. His relationship with the Ardgreeney traffic – a nightmare most hours of the day – would be transformed, because he wouldn't have to be anywhere by a certain time. His time would be his own.

Which might be a bit of a problem. He had never been very good at doing anything that wasn't related to work, and now, as if to demonstrate the point, he was starting two weeks of leave and hadn't planned a single thing. He probably should have booked a holiday in the Canaries, somewhere warm and sunny, but he hadn't really fancied getting on to a plane. He just needed the time off. But, now that he had it, what was he going to do with it?

It was shaping up to be a fine autumn day. That was the strange thing about Irish weather: you could be dreading the winter after a wet, dull and cold summer, and then autumn would throw up these magnificent days, warm and sunny, and you would have to make the most of them.

He could call Annie and ask if she fancied lunch at one of those bistro places with tables outside, but he didn't want her to feel obliged to meet up with him. All too often, he caught her looking at him with something that seemed to border on pity. And he hated that, even though there was nothing he loved more than sitting with her, hearing her talk enthusiastically about everything she was up to, watching her turn into the stunning young woman he was soon going to lose to some smart-arse who didn't deserve her. He had to admit, though, that the current smart-arse she was seeing wasn't quite as obnoxious as the usual kind of annoying, arty-farty, full-of-himself prick she seemed to attract.

No harm in giving her a buzz, though. Just to check in. She picked up on the first ring.

'Da. Howiya?'

'Not a bother. I don't suppose you'd fancy a bit of lunch later?'

'Oh, Da, I'm sorry. I can't. We have a photographer coming in to do the new brochure for the gallery. I'd love to, but I have to be here.'

'Ah. It's all right. Another day. But make sure you get some-thing to eat. Don't be skipping lunch.'

She laughed. 'Didn't be worrying about me, Da! When did I ever skip a meal? Look, why don't you give me a ring tomorrow or later in the week? Lunchtimes are going to be busy, but maybe we can have a jar one of the evenings?'

'I will,' he said. 'Mind yourself,' he added, before he rang off.

Mind yourself. Funny how the old phrases stuck. *Mind yourself* was what his mother used to tell him as he left the house for school. His stepmother, Irene, used to say it, too.

Hours to kill and he'd rather not spend most of them sitting in his house or in one of the pubs, which was looking like a serious prospect if he didn't come up with something to fill his time. He had had a project in mind for a while, though. It had struck him a few years back, when the *Irish Times* ran a series called 'A History of Ireland in 100 Objects', that he knew feck all about the history of his own country beyond the Geraldines, the Fenians and the Easter Rising. Oh, and not forgetting Oliver Cromwell.

He had been intending for ages to take a journey through Ireland's past with a visit to the National Museum in Dublin, but he always managed to find a reason to postpone it. No excuse, he told himself now. He was going to do it today. He made a rough plan in his head. An hour, maybe two, at the museum. Then he would have lunch somewhere he hadn't been to, maybe that French place on Dawson Street that Annie had told him about. After that, he might pop across to the National Library and then to the National Gallery. And then he would be flaked out and in need of a drink, and he would amble down to the

Long Hall and, if there was no one already parked on it, sit on the bar stool Phil Lynott had sat on in the 'Old Town' video.

He took the train to Dublin because parking anywhere in the city was always a pain. He was delighted with himself as he emerged from Pearse Station and sauntered along to Kildare Street, congratulating himself that he was doing something constructive, something *improving*, as his stepmother would have said. He smiled. Poor Irene. He had given her a hard time when she first turned up on the scene. But eventually her simple kindness had won him over. He reminded himself that he must go to see her, maybe take her out for a nice lunch and give her a break from his father, the miserable old bastard.

In the museum, he spent ages looking at the Bronze Age gold artefacts on display, hoards of ornaments pulled out of bogs and other unlikely places. He was fascinated by the lunulae, torcs and bracelets, which looked incredibly modern, yet had been made thousands of years ago. He could imagine how some of them might look on Eily, still a beauty at fifty. But he stopped himself. There was no point in going there.

He continued wandering around the ground floor and found himself in a different kind of space, where the lighting was softer and the atmosphere still, and the silence had an air of reverence about it. He remembered now hearing Annie talking about it a few years ago, when she was still at school and he was still living at home with her and Tom and Eily in the family house on Clonard Hill.

'I don't think it's right,' she'd said. 'They shouldn't be on display.'

'But sure, they're dead, aren't they?' Tom had challenged.

'That's my point! They're dead. We should be showing some respect, not lining them up for a bunch of little gurriers like you to gawk at.'

Ned thought of Annie's words now, her indignation, as he heard the whine of a child's voice: 'Eewww! That's disgusting!'

He looked at the child. She was about seven or eight and accompanied by her parents. He couldn't blame the kid for her outburst, but he did wonder what point her parents had seeen in bringing her here.

He walked into the pod the family had just left.

The body was incomplete, just the upper torso and arms – no neck, no head. The skin was leathery and so wrinkled that it put Ned in mind of a giant walnut. This was Old Croghan Man, he read, who had died – had probably been murdered – at least 2,180 years ago. And as he read on, looking back and forth from the museum guide to the body, he found that he was thinking along the same lines as Annie: this was once a living, breathing human being and shouldn't be on show.

But he couldn't help staring in grim fascination at what was left of the body, drawn closer by the man's surprisingly elegant hands. The fingers curved gently inwards towards the palms. The fingernails were perfectly preserved. The right arm turned out from the shoulder and bent upwards at the elbow. The left arm turned in at the elbow, towards where his stomach or abdomen might have been. It was the shape someone might make as he lay asleep on his back.

He wasn't prepared for the wave of sadness that swept over him. He was shocked by the strength of it. But as he steadied himself, reminding himself that it was a long time since Old

Croghan Man had walked around what was now County Offaly, he began to understand the strange pain he felt. Because it wasn't a response to the torso of the long-murdered king or would-be king he was looking at now, but to the image of his mother, his beautiful mother with her long fingers which had sewn the tiniest of stitches into the dresses she made for herself and had danced across the keys of the piano with such agility. This leathery, distorted torso was bringing her back to him and he felt all the composure that he had regained over the past few years crumble.

There was a voice somewhere inside him making sounds that he couldn't quite decipher. But then he saw that people were staring at him and he realised that the sound he was hearing was coming from inside himself, only now it was beyond him and he was hearing it around him, too – one long, low, continuous groan.

Chapter Eleven

I knew I would miss London, but I never thought I'd miss its sounds: the shrieking of late-night police and ambulance sirens that sometimes woke me up; the sound of the Tube, starting off as a distant rumble and then becoming thunderous as the train emerged from the tunnel; the relentless cacophony of traffic.

I had always been able to shut out the London noise when I wanted to. Here, at the bottom of Quay Street, it was impossible to shut out the relentless sound of the sea, the whooshing as it sent the waves rolling to the shore on the incoming tide, or, when the weather turned rough, the wild beat of it against the walls of the harbour.

Some of the time, it was a comfort of sorts. There was a rhythm to it. The tide came in and went out. Stormy waters gave way to calmer ones. Late at night, in London, I'd always liked to listen to the shipping forecast on Radio 4, waiting for the inevitable 'becoming good' that would follow the gale warnings for Dogger, Fisher, German Bight and all those other exotic, almost mythological names of that dead-of-night litany.

On stormy nights in Ardgreeney, though, I felt a darkness I had never felt in London. It was, of course, all to do with Lillian, who had walked out into a dark, stormy night and had never returned. And I was anxious whenever I was alone in the house at night, even though it was just a stone's throw from the café, where James often stayed late to catch up on the bookkeeping or to prepare for the following day.

When we first opened the café, which we named Seabird, a few of the locals from the immediate area around the strand and the harbour wandered in for a cup of tea or coffee, or maybe even a sandwich. But they didn't come back very often. Maybe they thought our prices were excessive, James's food a little too unusual. Maybe they felt they had done their duty and had given us some custom – the minimum amount needed to be neighbourly. Or maybe it was something else: a morbid superstition about someone brought up on an estate on the far side of town, who'd had the temerity to pitch up ten years after her friend's disappearance from a house in which one of their own had, inexplicably, been burned to death.

Fortunately, we didn't have to rely on those immediate neighbours to spread the word. Our café was the first new restaurant to open in the town in several years, and it didn't take long for the young and upwardly mobile set to discover it. We also had some customers travel from further afield, lured by a couple of newspaper reviews praising this new café that offered not only meals based on good, fresh, local ingredients, but also stunning views across the sea. *What more could you want*, one reviewer had asked in her piece, *than the sight of a seal surfacing behind a fishing boat and the sun sparkling on the waves as you savour the delicate taste of freshly caught hake and sip from a glass of flinty Sancerre?*

A big part of our income, during the summer months, came from tourists. But, apart from the odd group of walkers, the tourists had fallen off now. The local custom, on which we were now largely dependent, was proving to be not quite enough and our takings were dropping proportionately. Of course, we'd known that the first couple of years wouldn't be easy. This was why I had been building up my freelance editing business, which was supposed to tide us over until next summer. But would it? I hoped we hadn't made a terrible miscalculation.

James looked worried a lot of the time. He tried not to show it, but when you've lived with someone for years, you know when something isn't right. My dilemma was, what to do about it? Starting up the café had been a big thing for him. He had always loved cooking and had wanted to go to catering college, but his doctor parents wanted him to study medicine or veterinary science. He had become neither a doctor nor a vet, his interest not having been high enough and his A-levels not good enough, and had ended up teaching, which he eventually came to loathe.

Two things happened that brought about our decision to move to Ardgreeney: James entered a major TV cooking competition and reached the finals, and, shortly after that, the *Tribune* offered attractive redundancy packages, and I applied. I'd been working for several years on the editing desk, away from active reporting, and although I quite liked the editing, I was fed up on the desk.

We had a vague idea that we would sell our flat and move out of London to Devon or Cornwall, where we would run a small bed and breakfast and I would take on freelance editing work. It was Fidelma who encouraged us to move to Ardgreeney, phoning to tell us that what I'd always thought of as the nasty little caff at the bottom of Quay Street was up for sale, and why didn't we take it on?

'What do you think?' James asked.

'What do *you* think?' I countered. 'I'm *from* Ardgreeney. You're the one who'd be making the biggest move. Psychologically, anyway.'

'I think . . .' he said slowly. 'I think I'd like to investigate it.'

I was far from certain that I wanted to do this. For James, who was now a regular visitor with me to Ardgreeney, the move would be an adventure. For me, it would be tangled up with my feelings about Lillian. Almost a decade on, I was still grieving for her, and my grief was complicated by the fact that she had never been found. Deep down, I knew she must be dead. Yet, every now and again, something inside me would raise the question of whether she had deceived us all and had planned to disappear, and I would think the worst of her. After that time Aidan made me go with him to the wreck of Oriel Cottage, I never went back again, and I hadn't seen him for nearly ten years.

Now, fate seemed to be stepping in and dictating that I return to Ardgreeney. I could say no to fate, but I could also see that James was quietly excited about it. So, as the phrase goes, I went with the flow.

We contacted the auctioneer and flew over to look around the café. In my wildest imagination, I could never have seen the potential of that unprepossessing dirty-white building with the flat roof and big metal window frames painted an institutional dark green. To me, it looked like a large public lavatory – a building that was so bleak and bare, you would only go into it if you were happy to drink what you were sure would be the worst cup of tea ever made, or if you were desperate to use the loo.

But James saw its potential immediately, I could tell, because, as we walked around it, I saw that his eyes were very focused and his mouth was clamped shut. A sure sign that he was making calculations.

'Listen,' he said, taking me aside, 'I know it doesn't look like a Michelin-starred restaurant, but I don't think it will cost an awful lot of money to do it up. We can go for a minimalist industrial look, if there's such a thing. It comes with all the basic equipment, so we won't need to spend a fortune on new ovens and fridges. We can start simply, just do easy café stuff, like salads and sandwiches and cakes and breakfasts, and then, over time, we can be a bit more ambitious.'

As it happened, the man who was selling the café was also selling his house, which was almost next door, at the bottom of Quay Street. So we bought both, and, a couple of months later, we were sitting on the harbour wall, opening a bottle of champagne as the sun went down.

'I can hardly believe how easy everything has been,' James said, handing me a glass.

Almost too easy, I thought. But I didn't say that. It would have spoiled the evening.

And now, several months into our adventure, I reminded myself of that thought. It *had* been ridiculously easy. During those first months, the café was so busy that it left James and me with little time to think about anything else. But now that the tourist season was over, we were going to have more time for each other. A lot more time. It wasn't just the fall-off in earnings that I was worried about. Things were changing between James and me, and I didn't know why. Instead of becoming closer, we seemed to be growing apart.

Chapter Twelve

'Sorry I'm late, Da,' Annie said, throwing herself down in front of him in the wine bar.

'No point in changing the habit of a lifetime,' Ned said, pouring her a glass of wine from the bottle that he had half emptied in the time he had been waiting for her.

'I'll ignore that. Some of us have to work, you know.'

'*Sláinte.*'

'*Sláinte.* What are you grinning at?'

'Can't a father be pleased to see his daughter? Especially when it's only once in a blue moon.' He couldn't help marvelling at this divine creature that he had helped create, even if her hair was currently an emerald green and her ears sported not one, but several pairs of studs.

'You're staring at me.'

'I'm trying to remember what colour your hair is. Brown? Blonde? Or were you born with green hair?'

'Feck off.'

They bantered like this for a while and then Ned asked how her mother and brother were.

'Grand. Tom's studying like mad for his Leaving Cert, as far as I know. I'm hardly ever at home. Ma . . . Well, you know what she's like. "You look a bit thin; are you eating properly?" Stuff like that. She's always trying to feed me up. Actually, I think she's bothered about something, but she'll do her usual thing and keep it all bottled up, and then she'll sort out whatever it is and she'll be back to normal and we'll never know what it was. Or else she'll explode at some point.'

Ned smiled. Annie knew her mother so well. Still, he was concerned to hear that Eily was bothered about something.

'She isn't sick, or anything, is she?'

'God, no! I hope not. But I don't think so.'

'Is she all right for money?' he asked.

'Yeah, I think so. Well, Garret's not exactly hard up, is he?'

Ned clamped his lips together and widened his mouth into a grimace that he hoped Annie would see as an attempt at a smile. He and Eily had been apart three years now. They were still legally married; they just hadn't bothered to get unmarried. He supposed that was the next thing that was going to hit him – Eily telling him she and Garret had decided they wanted to tie the knot, and could she have a divorce, please? He had nothing against Garret, a high-earning accountant, who, it had to be said, was a decent man and – most importantly – was fond of and well liked by the kids. Eily had met him singing in the choir; he was a sixty-three-year-old widower, with four grown-up kids from a happy marriage and no emotional baggage.

Unlike Ned.

He turned his attention back to Annie, who had just graduated with a modern languages degree from University College Dublin and was now back in Ardgreeney, working in the local art gallery.

'How's the job?,' he asked. 'Are you planning to stay in it?'

'It's fine. Busy. But . . . Da, I have something to tell you.'

Her face was still luminous and lovely under that green hair, but now it had a serious look, as if she was going to tell him something big.

Oh, Christ; she's getting married, or, worse, she's pregnant, he thought.

'Milo and me . . . Well, we're thinking of going to Australia for a couple of years. Actually, we're going. We've got it all sorted. We've booked our flights to Sydney for after Christmas.'

The words froze in his brain. *Milo and me . . . Australia . . . flights booked . . . after Christmas.* Jesus. That was just around the corner.

His face must have looked a picture of horror, because her voice, loud and sharp now, cut into the echo chamber of his brain, where her words, banging around, reverberating painfully against every imagined nerve, were all he had been able to hear.

'Da, I'm only going for a couple of years. It isn't going to be forever,' she said.

'But, Australia . . . It's the other side of the world. It's so far away. And you're only twenty-two. What if something happens? You read all sorts of stuff – '

'It's an aeroplane ride away, Da. We're not going to be taking off on the Space Shuttle. And nothing's going to happen. We're well able to take care of ourselves.'

She leaned forward and gave him as much of a hug as she could manage from the other side of the table.

'You're not to worry. We'll be back before you know we're gone.'

They rarely had dinner together on these occasions when they met up in the evening. Annie was always running off somewhere, to meet Milo – Jesus, she must be serious about him – or some friend or other. But, this time, she was the one who suggested that they go somewhere to eat. She was taking pity on him, but he didn't mind. He was grateful for this extra hour or two with her that would start the countdown to her leaving – *for two bloody years*. And then he thought, Two years is what she said, but maybe she's just saying that and she's really planning to stay there for the duration.

So they went to a quiet little restaurant that cost an arm and a leg and wasn't usually frequented by girls with green hair and holes in their jeans. But Ned didn't care. He was grateful, so grateful, for this precious time with her.

Back home in his quiet little house on Chapel Lane, he poured himself a whiskey and turned on the jazz he loved, hoping the combination of booze and music would soothe him. But it didn't. And when he eventually went to bed, hoping sleep would empty his head and heart of the loneliness that had invaded him, he lay awake for hours.

He woke up late and stumbled into the kitchen for breakfast. As he sat with his coffee and toast, he gave himself a lecture: 'You're not going to mope around all day, Moynihan. You're going to do something constructive.'

But what? No more museums. Not for the time being, anyway. The experience of the museum, what had happened when he stood in front of the bog body, still resonated. He didn't want anything else disturbing his peace. Idly, he picked up the letters that had begun arriving a few months earlier and glanced over the latest one. He looked at his watch, slugged down what was left of the coffee and grabbed his coat.

It was time to pay Orla Breslin a visit. She and her husband or partner had taken on that dive of a café at the bottom of Quay Street and seemed to be making a go of it. That was what he had been told, anyway. He hadn't actually gone in there yet. He tended to keep a distance from people he had had to deal with as part of his job. But it had struck him at some point early on that the letters had begun to arrive shortly after her return.

The Lillian Murray case had never left his mind. She had disappeared into thin air and the absence of a body allowed for the possibility that she had chosen to leave, even if no one really believed that. Nothing had ever suggested to him that Lillian just walked out the door of her own accord. Not on a night like that. He remembered it all too well. Slates were flying off roofs all over the country and the relatively short journey from his house on Clonard Hill to Oriel Cottage was on roads made treacherous by all manner of objects that the high winds had flung across them. At one point, he had to manoeuvre his car around a tree that had come down and was blocking most of the road.

He remembered how diminished Aidan McManus had looked that night and for a long time afterwards – nothing like the solidly-built captain of the Irish rugby team he had once been, the local hero who had helped to put Ardgreeney on the map for an entire sporting generation. And Ned remembered how Aidan had broken down several times, sobbing his regret that he had not been there with Lillian that evening.

Ned had spoken to him several times over the course of the investigation, but there had never been any evidence that Aidan might have played a role in Lillian's disappearance, although some of the more scurrilous tabloids had thrown out unsubstantiated hints to that effect, which they should have been sued over. Lillian had moved back to Ireland to live with Aidan only a few months before her disappearance, and everyone who knew them said they were a lovely couple, a grand couple. Orla Breslin had also attested to the loving relationship. And, according to Orla, Lillian had told her during that Skype conversation that things were going well for the pair of them.

In any case, Aidan's alibi was pretty solid. He had been out drinking with his pals and had left the pub only after receiving a call from his mother, who needed him to help her with the horses after a branch had fallen through the roof of one of the stables during the storm. That's where the guards had finally got hold of him, at his mother's house, by which time he had rung the emergency services to say his mother had collapsed and he thought it might be a stroke. The phone records and timings had backed up Aidan's account.

By the time Ned had made it out to the burning cottage, Aidan was looking as if he was about to have a stroke himself. Poor bastard. Talk about a double whammy. Your mother has a stroke in front of you and then the guards turn up at the same time as the ambulance to tell you your house is burning down and your girlfriend can't be found anywhere.

Aidan had never been the kind of man Ned would want to spend time with. He was too much of a hail-fellow-well-met, rugger-bugger type. Except that he wasn't playing any more, his career having clattered to an abrupt halt after a series of poor performances and an injury that kept him off the field, not long before Lillian's disappearance. Ned couldn't help but feel a twinge of pity when he saw the occasional newspaper photo of Aidan looking dishevelled and bloated, often accompanied by a paragraph or two of gossip about his heavy drinking.

Oddly enough, despite living and working in Ardgreeney, he hadn't actually seen or talked to Aidan for years. He hadn't seen Orla Breslin, either, since the case had been quietly dropped. When he first heard she was back in Ardgreeney, he was a bit surprised that she hadn't got in touch with him to tell him she was moving back from London. But, then, he thought at the time, why would she? She might have assumed he was no longer at Ardgreeney station. Or she might not have wanted to see or talk to him ever again. Now, though, the letters – if they were from her – suggested something different. He just didn't know what.

It took him just a few minutes to walk along to Quay Street. He had intended to go straight to the café, but saw that the lights were on in the last house, the one he knew Orla and her chap had moved into. He rang the doorbell.

She opened it almost straight away, as if she had been expecting him. But the expression on her face told him otherwise. He was struck now by how similar she was in looks to Lillian. They could have been sisters. He hadn't seen it, all those years ago. Certainly not that first time she had turned up at the station, when she had looked terrible, gaunt and in shock, diminished by the unfolding tragedy. Nor had he noticed it in the weeks that followed. But now he saw the extraordinary likeness between her and Lillian, photographs of whom he had pored over during the investigation. They had the same blonde curls, the same eyes – huge and sapphire blue – the same porcelain skin. Except that Lillian's porcelain skin would never age.

'Orla,' he said, extending a hand. 'Can I come in?'

She stared at him without saying a word. She didn't take his hand, either. But she stepped back and held the door open, silently inviting him in.

Chapter Thirteen

With winter on its way, the café didn't need two of us there all the time. I'd taken the day off to catch up on some of my editing work and was struggling with an annoying bit of gobbledygook when I heard the doorbell. I jumped. I hadn't been expecting anyone.

I recognised him the moment I opened the door. He had been the kindest of all the detectives. I remembered how he had a way of looking at me when I spoke that made me think he was really absorbing what I was saying and taking it seriously. But even he had stopped listening to me, after a while. Now he was standing outside my door, waiting to be invited in.

I held the door open and he stepped inside. I took him into the kitchen and went to the sink to fill the kettle, keeping my back to him while I got over the shock of his turning up. And then, while the kettle heated up, I busied myself with getting the teapot and the mugs ready, taking the milk out of the fridge.

My thoughts were racing, trying to work out why he was here. Was I supposed to have contacted him as soon as I returned to Ardgreeney? It wasn't that he hadn't come into my mind during the months following our move from London. From occasional mentions of his name in the local paper, I knew he was still in town. But it had never occurred to me that he would want to make contact. Yet here he was, in my house.

We sat down at the big table in the kitchen and he asked me how I was settling in. I told him about the café that James and I had taken on, and said I hadn't really had much time to think about anything else.

'I heard about the café,' he said. 'Is it doing well?'

'It's early days, but yes, I think so.'

He chatted on, but didn't mention Lillian. I began to think that maybe it was just a sort of courtesy call. But then he leaned forward in the chair and gave me the kind of look that told me the conversation was about to become more serious.

'I'd like to show you something,' he said.

He produced a bundle of envelopes from a pocket inside his jacket. I saw that they were all addressed to him, but at a private address in Chapel Lane, rather than at the Garda station.

'What are they?' I asked.

He gave me a look that was quite stern. 'Did you send these letters?' he asked.

'No. Why do you think I sent them? What do they say?'

He opened one of the envelopes, took out a letter and showed it to me, but held it back when I reached out to take it from him.

'I'd rather you didn't touch it.'

I read through the words scrawled in block capitals and recoiled. Involuntarily, my hands went up to my face.

'Who sent this?'

That hard look again. It seemed to have a drill attached to it, boring into me.

'Didn't you send it?'

I shook my head vigorously.

'Look, Orla,' he said. 'If you sent these letters to me, all you have to do is say so and we can have a chat about why. You're not going to be in trouble.'

'But I didn't send that letter – or any of them! I really didn't!'

He opened up all the envelopes, one by one, and held out the letters so that I could read them without touching them. They were all similar in content: accusations of failure and incompetence. Abusive letters.

'The thing is, Orla, *someone* has been sending these to me. So, if it isn't you, do you have any idea who it might be?'

I thought of Lillian's mother. She was just about existing, ever more reliant on booze to get her from one end of the day to the other. I couldn't see her going to the trouble of writing anonymous letters. I thought of Aidan. But he was a wreck of a man. He hardly had the enthusiasm to do more than lift a pint of Guinness to his mouth. Could Aidan have sent those letters? No, it was unlikely. I couldn't think of anyone else.

I shook my head. 'I'm sorry.'

He started talking about the night it happened, reminding me of what I had said in my statement. But I didn't need reminding. I could see and hear it all again: Lillian's face, lit by the flames from the fire; her voice upbeat, and then the question mark coming into it; the frown that spread across her forehead as she said there was someone at the door. Lillian gone. And then the flames spreading out beyond the fireplace . . .

I knew I couldn't have saved Patsy McLennan. But, as I remembered, I felt the same stab of guilt I'd felt time and time again because I hadn't been able to give the guards anything that might have led them to Lillian.

'All I know,' I said, 'is that Lillian went to the door. I don't remember hearing a knock, but she said there was someone at the door and she got up. She seemed to be surprised. There must have been someone there, knocking at the door, because, if she'd imagined it, she'd have come straight back, wouldn't she?'

I pointed at the letters.

'These must mean that someone else saw something. Someone knows what happened to her. Surely you can open the investigation again?'

He shook his head. 'The case was never officially closed. But you'd need an awful lot more than these letters to get it going again, and resources devoted to it.'

'There *is* one thing,' I said, 'but maybe you'll think I'm imagining it, so long after . . .'

I thought I saw his head incline slightly. He said nothing, though – just waited for me to continue.

I hesitated. I could still see those images, hear the sounds, as if they were happening there and then. But I had come to doubt them, afraid that, in my desperation to unlock what might be stored somewhere in my mind, I was conjuring up scenarios that seemed real, but weren't. Since James and I had moved to Ardgreeney, though, I'd had intermittent hints of a memory so faint that I couldn't be sure of it. I couldn't even describe it as a memory. More a sense of sound and light. Maybe it was my imagination working overtime now that I was back. Why, after all, hadn't I felt this at any point during the previous ten years? But I wondered whether coming back, being here, had opened the door to a real memory that I hadn't been able to access while I was in London.

'I get this . . . idea – I can't say I remember it – that I might have heard a car outside that night. I can't swear on it, but I keep thinking I heard the sound of a car above the wind. I have a sense of lights, too. The reflection of car lights.'

'Cars go along the Seapoint Road all the time,' he pointed out. 'It's only a short distance from the cottage.'

'That's the thing, though. The sound that comes into my head isn't like the sound of a car going past. It's more the sound of a car engine revving up. So, if there was a car, it must have been stationary. But there were no houses near enough to the cottage for a car to have stopped. So . . . why would a car have stopped?'

'You didn't say anything about a car before,' the inspector said.

'No, and I'm not sure I did hear one. It's just this . . . sense I've had since we moved here. Maybe it means nothing. But maybe being here all the time now, so close to where it all happened . . . maybe that's unlocked something.'

He started to get up from the table. 'Let me know if anything else comes back to you,' he said.

I pointed at the letters. 'I know I haven't been much help, but surely you have to take these seriously?'

'I am taking them seriously,' he said, putting them back inside his jacket.

I got up to show him out.

'I was surprised when I heard you'd come back here to live,' he said, as we walked to the door.

'I took a redundancy package, and we wanted to move out of London, do our own thing. So here we are.'

'Are you enjoying being back?'

'So far. We had a great summer. The café's had good write-ups in the papers. You'll have to come and try us out.'

'I will,' he said, giving me his card. 'If you need to get hold of me in the next few days, call the mobile. I'm on leave at the moment.'

'If you're on leave, why are you here?' I asked.

'I'm taking leave from the leave,' he said.

It was corny, but it made me laugh, and I remembered again how kind he had been to me before.

Just as I was about to close the door behind him, he turned around and asked whether I'd seen much of Aidan since coming back to Ardgreeney.

'Not really,' I said, shaking my head. 'He's a bit of a disaster. He's never recovered from what happened and, as far as I know, he hasn't had anything you could call a relationship. You're not going to talk to him about those letters, are you? I doubt he'll be very pleased to see you.'

'It's a bit of a walk, and I didn't bring the car,' he said, smiling.

But, instead of turning left and going back up Quay Street, he turned right towards the sea. I had seen that he was wearing trainers. Eaglewood was a bit of a walk, all right, but it was a good, exhilarating one, if you walked along the strand. I often ran on the beach, but I rarely went all way to Eaglewood because it meant passing the wooden steps leading to the cottage. When I did run past those steps, I kept my eyes fixed on the far distance.

I tried to get back to my editing, but it was hard to focus. I thought about Aidan. A visit from the detective who had investigated Lillian's disappearance was the last thing he needed – especially when Inspector Moynihan had only questions and no answers.

Aidan's rugby career had ended prematurely and he had turned increasingly to drink. In addition, the shadow over him following Lillian's disappearance and the fire in which Patsy McLennan died hadn't completely lifted. He might have been one of Ardgreeney's famous sons, but he came from a family that was not well liked. His grandfather's unexplained wealth was often mentioned, and his father had been regarded as a hard man. As for his mother – there hadn't been much affection for her, either. *She always thought she was a cut above buttermilk*, was the kind of thing people said about her.

And Inspector Moynihan's visit had left me feeling anxious. Nearly ten years after Lillian disappeared, I was still going over and over that night in my head and driving myself mad. I had never stopped questioning my memories. Now, I felt as if I were under suspicion somehow. But for what? For not remembering things properly? I closed my eyes and tried to concentrate on my memories. *Was* it possible that I had seen the flare of car lights on my laptop screen and heard the sound of an engine starting up? And had I really heard a cry – a short, strangled cry that I didn't mention to the inspector – or was that something that I imagined later, something that my fragile memory had constructed rather than unlocked?

It hadn't taken long for the guards to find out about my fall down the stairs – the fall that I still couldn't remember properly. I could remember climbing the stairs. I could remember finding myself lying on the landing, a flight of stairs down from the flat. But I still couldn't remember the fall. I couldn't remember tripping on that dodgy piece of carpet. It was just a few minutes. I could remember everything else. But I knew what they were thinking and I could understand why. Inspector Moynihan had somehow managed to tell me without spelling it out – I wasn't reliable. Even though I had seen Patsy McLennan burn to death, even though I hadn't changed a thing in my endless retelling of what had happened that night, anything I told them had to be taken with a pinch of salt.

I'd learned not to talk too much about Lillian over the years because James thought my preoccupation with her disappearance was obsessive, unhealthy.

It wasn't your fault. There was nothing you could have done. You did everything you could. It's time to let it go.

He had long grown weary of saying the same things over and over. So I tended to keep my thoughts to myself. But this was different. The detective had come to our house with a bunch of letters written by someone who might know something.

We sat down to eat the supper I'd prepared – roast monkfish wrapped in Parma ham, bright green petits pois and delicious little new potatoes, dripping with melted butter. Cooking wasn't my strongest point, but I took pleasure in producing something good, and I wanted to improve.

'Perfect,' James said, sipping the glass of Meursault, crisp and chilled after several hours in the fridge.

He cut into the monkfish then, and I waited for him to say something about it.

'Fantastic! This is cooked to perfection,' he said, and I smiled. I knew I had done a good job on the fish, but I also knew that he was probably exaggerating its perfection just a little bit.

After a few minutes of talking about the food, we lapsed into one of those silences that were becoming more frequent. His face took on the worried expression that was becoming a permanent feature. I hesitated about bringing up the detective's visit. The evening was never a good time to talk about troublesome things. Maybe it was best left until the following day. But I didn't want to keep anything from him. And, in any case, there wouldn't be time to talk about it tomorrow, during the day.

So I cut into the silence with my account of Inspector Moynihan's visit. I hadn't expected James to be overjoyed about this out-of-the-blue development, but I hadn't anticipated the intensity of his response.

'Oh, for God's sake!' he said, putting down his knife and fork with a clatter. 'I can't believe that business is starting up again.'

'Why are you so angry about it? It doesn't affect you directly,' I said.

'No, but it affects you. It sounds like that detective all but accused you of sending those letters. Look, Orla, I remember how you were at the time. You were a mental and emotional wreck. You don't need this to start all over again. *We* don't need it.'

I leaned towards him and put my hand over his.

'James, I can cope with this. I know I wasn't to blame for anything, even if I do torment myself sometimes. I'm not going to have some kind of breakdown over it,' I said. 'Those letters mean that someone must know what happened to Lillian. Maybe now we'll all get to know the truth.'

'Doesn't it occur to you that those letters have probably been written by some nutter, out to cause trouble, because he has nothing better to do?' he asked.

'You're probably right. It's just . . .'

'It's just what?'

'It's just that I have a feeling about it.'

He groaned. 'I really don't want to listen to any more of this. I don't want to hear you going on about everything you saw that night. No – correction – everything you *think* you saw. Everything that's been building in your head.'

I stared at him, waiting for what was coming next, because I could tell that he had more to say.

'Because no one knows how much you saw at all. Not even you.'

I gasped and made to get up from the table, but James jumped up and put his hands on my shoulders, pressing me back into the chair.

'I'm sorry. I shouldn't have said that,' he said. 'I'm really sorry. I didn't mean it.'

I shook my shoulders, pushing his hands away.

'You did mean it,' I said. 'But, don't worry, I won't mention Lillian or the detective or anything to do with the whole bloody thing ever again, because it obviously upsets you so much.'

Neither of us spoke through the rest of the meal, and then I rose from the table and went upstairs, leaving James to clear up.

He still hadn't come to bed by the time I fell asleep, but some time during the night I felt him stir slightly and murmur something. I turned around and looked at him, his face soft in the moonlight that was streaming into the room, his curly black hair still pulled back into the little bun he wore during the day to keep it under control in the kitchen. He must have been too exhausted even to think of loosening it. I had known he wouldn't be happy about Inspector Moynihan's visit, but his reaction had been stronger than I could have imagined. Perhaps, I thought, his own worries about our finances had left him frayed at the edges.

I moved closer and put my mouth on his shoulder – a peace offering. But he didn't respond. He was out for the count. Or maybe he was just pretending to be asleep.

That was another thing. I couldn't remember when we'd last had sex. It must have been months ago, shortly after we moved here. Building up the café had been exhausting and we often fell into bed after long days and evenings, too tired to do anything but sleep. But we knew the ropes now. We almost had the café down to a fine art. Sure, we had concerns about money, but he knew there was a good chance that my editing work would keep us going until next summer.

After so many years together, I knew that sex wasn't the be-all and end-all in a relationship. But surely no sex at all was something to worry about? I had to admit that I didn't have much enthusiasm, either, because it was hard to be enthusiastic if you thought you were going to be rejected.

I tried to match James's slow, rhythmic breathing, hoping that, if I could concentrate only on my breath and the way it moved in and out, I would fall asleep again soon. But I lay awake for a long time, listening to the muffled sound of the sea, just a short distance away, until, finally, I dropped off to sleep.

Chapter Fourteen

The wind was from the south and it was strong. Ned had to push into it as he walked along the strand towards Eaglewood, in two minds about whether he should be seeking out Aidan McManus at all. Orla Breslin had made it clear to him that a visit from a detective was the last thing the man needed. And it wasn't as if Aidan was likely to be the writer of the anonymous letters. Logically, why would someone whose life had been torn apart by the disappearance of his girlfriend and the suspicion that had hung over him for so long want to invite renewed attention by doing such a thing – even if his goal might be to push the Gardai into resuming their investigations? Ned resolved his dilemma by deciding that Aidan had a right to know about the letters.

He came up off the beach on to the rough track that led to Eaglewood. He hesitated again as he reached the iron gates that stood open between two big stone piers, but persuaded himself that, having walked the best part of two miles, there was no harm in telling Aidan about the letters, even if Fergus wasn't ready yet to do anything about them.

He walked up the drive to the house. The weeds growing through the gravel, the long-overgrown lawns and the peeling paint on the windows seemed to symbolise the state of dishevelment Orla Breslin had attributed to Aidan. Ned looked for a doorbell, but found none, so he lifted the heavy cast-iron knocker, banged it several times and waited. Silence. He thought about wandering around to the stable yard, in case Aidan might be there, but decided against it. It would be too intrusive, a detective turning up out of the blue and roaming about.

He looked around him. Behind Eaglewood, there was only the headland, stark and windswept. He walked back down to the strand and faced the way he had come. It was faster going, this time, the wind behind him propelling him forwards. He didn't often walk on the strand these days, or even visit it. He hadn't made a conscious decision to avoid it, but he wondered now, his bittersweet memories coming as fast and furious as the wind, whether something in his subconscious had made him stay away.

He hadn't known Eily O'Donnell when they were growing up. A five-year age difference is a big one when you're young. And then, one day, when he was home from Dublin for a couple of days, he had walked into the little shop at the top of Quay Street to buy a packet of cigarettes. He had been smitten the moment he saw her behind the counter – so smitten that he paid for the fags and left the shop without picking them up. It was only when he sat down on the harbour wall, still thinking about her, and reached into his pocket that he realised he didn't have them. So he rushed back to the shop and, as he pushed the door open, he saw that she was smiling, holding up the cigarettes. He asked her out there and then, even though he knew he shouldn't, because he had Rose.

Eily was a primary school teacher in Dublin. She, too, was home for just a couple of days, and helping her mother in the shop. She agreed to meet him later that afternoon, by the harbour, once she'd finished her stint behind the counter. He hadn't been convinced she'd turn up, but she did, and, as he watched her walk towards him, he felt more elated than he could ever have imagined. They had walked up and down the strand – north to Bellaher Point, south to Eagle Head and then back to the harbour – talking nineteen to the dozen and then not talking at all as they realised that something was happening to both of them.

He was lost from then on. And, it seemed, so was she. Within weeks they were talking about a future together and within months they were walking down the aisle.

He remembered now his excitement at knowing Eily had arrived when the organ started up the 'Bridal Chorus' from *Lohengrin*, his delight as he turned around to see her walking towards him on her father's arm, her eyes shining behind the veil and a marvellous beam of a smile lighting up her face. And he remembered exactly where they had stood on this very strand for the photographs. He had been so certain that his marriage would last a lifetime. But the lifetime had turned out to be little more than two decades.

Not that a long marriage guaranteed happiness, he thought. He thought of his father, still living in the house on the Bellaher

Road with Irene, still sour from the fallout of everything that he thought had gone wrong with his life, as if his perceived failure had been no fault of his own. Ned visited from time to time, but it was Irene he felt bound to, not his father. How Irene put up with his father he just didn't understand.

Back home, Ned put on an Ella Fitzgerald CD and started to prepare his lunch, an omelette with ham and onion. It would make a change from omelette with cheese. The phone rang just as he was slicing the onion, and because he was lost in thought about everything – the visit to Orla Breslin, Annie's plans to leave – the loudness of it took him by surprise and he nicked his finger with the knife. 'Shite,' he muttered, sticking his finger into his mouth to stop the blood.

'Ned.'

'Eily.'

'You called.'

'I did. Are you all right? Annie gave me the impression you were a bit under the weather.'

She didn't answer immediately and, when she did speak, her voice sounded hesitant. 'I'm fine. But I want to talk to you about Tom.'

Talk at me, more like, he thought. Eily had stopped consulting him about the kids a long time ago – long before the split. He was just never there; simple as that. She had made all the decisions and he had just nodded approval when she told him what they were. He thanked his blessings that at least he and Annie were close. Tom was a different kettle of fish; he had been only fourteen when Ned moved out and it had hit him hard. He wouldn't talk to Ned for a long time. Every time Ned tried to coax him out to a football or rugby match, Tom, who was fanatical about sport, made an excuse. He had a cold or he had homework. *Homework?* What kid used homework as an excuse not to see his father?

Eventually, his son did start talking to him again, but in a distant kind of way. The kind of way you might speak to a teacher. Sometimes, Ned talked about Tom to Annie, who didn't seem to think it was strange that her brother should be so uncommunicative.

'It's not as if he's only like that with you. He doesn't exactly go out of his way to be nice to Ma, either. He's still at the stage where he's not quite tame,' she told Ned at one point. 'Give him a year or two and he'll be grand.'

'How does he get on with Garret?' Ned had asked, and immediately wished he hadn't. He wasn't sure he wanted to know.

'He gets on all right with him,' Annie said. And then she added quickly, 'I don't mean they're the best of friends, or anything. I just mean that Tom's civil to him.'

God, I must sound jealous of Garret, he thought then. Which wasn't far from the truth, because Garret had pretty much everything Ned wanted. He didn't like the idea of Garret occupying the role of stepfather to his son. He wondered whether Tom looked up to Garret, sought his advice. Garret, he knew, had taken Tom on some jollies with clients. Corporate boxes for big GAA games at Croke Park and rugby internationals at Lansdowne Road. He had also taken him sailing once. Ned couldn't compete with that.

About a year back, Tom had shown some interest in joining the guards. Eily had hit the roof and had got on the phone to Ned, demanding that he do everything in his power to discourage his son from following the same path. Ned had no real objections to Tom becoming a guard, if that was what he really wanted. After all, he himself had gone his own way and joined up against his father's wishes. And he had loved his job. The trouble was that he had loved his job so much it had helped to end his marriage. He could understand why Eily didn't want this for her son, and, if he was honest with himself, he wasn't entirely sure *he* wanted it for Tom, either. So, on the few occasions Tom had brought up the subject of a career in the force, Ned tried to encourage him to go to university first, get a degree, and then make the decision about whether to join up.

'It's what I wish I'd done,' Ned told him. Which was at least half true.

'But you'd still have become a guard?' Tom had asked.

'Maybe not.'

'You would. I know you would. And I know Ma's been on to you, telling you to put me off the guards.'

'She hasn't –'

'God, you're pathetic!'

Since that conversation, he hadn't seen much of Tom. Eily was trying to steer him towards university and, with some relief, had told Ned at the beginning of the school year, in September, that Tom had been checking out when he could start the online application process with the CAO. Ned had duly tried to show some interest in Tom's plans, asking what degree course he might take. But Tom had just shrugged and said, 'Dunno.'

With the odd exception, Ned's conversations with Eily tended to be on the spiky side. From the brittle tone he heard so often in her voice, you'd never guess they had been married. Or maybe you would – and that *he* had done something bad enough to make a friendly chat impossible. Except that he hadn't. Not intentionally, anyway.

'Ned?' Eily's voice broke into his thoughts.

'Sorry, I got a bit sidetracked. I cut my finger. You were saying you wanted to talk about Tom. Does he need anything?'

'I'm really worried about him.'

Her voice seemed less strident than usual, less certain of her absolute rectitude, and he was seized by a fear that she was going to tell him something dreadful, that Tom had some serious illness, that he was going to die. He heard his heart beating so fast that he thought his chest was going to explode.

'Tom . . .' she said hesitantly. He could hear her breathing getting louder and faster.

Christ, don't let it be something bad.

'I don't know what you're going to think about this,' she said. Another short silence before she continued.

'He's not studying. He has the Leaving Cert coming up and he's barely opening a book.'

Is that all? *Deo gratias.*

He felt his chest collapse as he released the breath he had been keeping in. But – wait a minute – hadn't Annie said, just yesterday, that Tom was studying like mad? That was exactly what she'd said: *studying like mad.* But maybe Annie's version of studying like mad was a lot more relaxed than her mother's.

'I wouldn't be getting too worried, at this stage,' he said, trying to sound reassuring. 'There's months to go before the exams.'

Another silence. He waited.

'It isn't just that,' she said.

So now he knew that she really *was* worried about something and that it was something so serious that she couldn't just tell him straight off.

He held his breath again, waiting for her to continue.

'I'm a bit worried . . . He's been going off at weekends and I have no idea where. He won't tell me a thing.'

'What do you mean, "going off"?'

'He walks out of the house, early on a Saturday morning, with a backpack. I ask him where he's going and he says, "Nowhere." I ask him who he's going to meet and he says, "No one." And when he comes back, in the evening, we repeat the performance. And the same thing happens every Sunday. I know you're going to say he's probably hanging out with his friends. But he's not, because I've checked. He always used to hang around with Conor Roche, but Conor's mother says she hasn't seen Tom for ages. I'm just worried he's got himself mixed up in something . . . bad.'

Ned was tempted to tell Eily she was being overly dramatic, but he knew that would wind her up. She was an overprotective mother, always had been. He remembered only too well all the anxious phone calls, when the kids were younger, to tell him Annie hadn't come home yet from ballet class, and she should have been home half an hour ago, or that she'd allowed Tom to ride his bike to school, and now she was afraid he might have had an accident. He remembered, too, his own sullen responses, as a teenager, to Irene and his father when they wanted to know where he was going and with whom.

'I really doubt he's involved in anything bad or dangerous. He's not that kind of kid.'

'What would you know?' she demanded. 'You know sod all about him. You never see him.'

That stung. That was below the belt. He would see Tom every single day, if he could, but it was Tom who didn't want to see him, not the other way around. But there was no point in saying this to Eily, because she knew it.

'The thing is, Eily,' he said, 'Tom's eighteen. I don't know what I can do except try to talk to him and see if he'll tell me what he's up to.'

'That won't do much good. If he won't talk to me, he's hardly likely to talk to you. And, even if he does talk to you, he'll probably lie through his teeth.'

'What do you want me to do, then?'

'Follow him. I want you to follow him.'

Christ.

He woke with a slight headache, a consequence of the several glasses of whiskey he had drunk the previous night, and spent a few moments in a state of confusion as he waited for his mind to take control of his body. It was Saturday, and he had to fulfil the promise he had made to Eily a few days earlier. He wasn't worried about Tom. He was a good kid, even if their relationship wasn't exactly close.

'I'm still in love with my wife,' he said silently. And then he heard himself repeat the words aloud several times, like a mantra. It was true, though, and it was hopeless. But he was still leaping to her command, dancing to her tune. And now she wanted him to sneak around after their son, to see what he was up to. Ned didn't want to do that, but he had promised Eily that he would.

So now, even though he regretted that promise, he hauled himself out of the bed. He almost pressed Tom's mobile on his speed dial. Maybe he could just sort it all out with a quick, friendly chat and not have to do what Eily wanted him to do. But he knew that calling Tom at the crack of dawn on a Saturday morning wasn't going to elicit a friendly response. The phone was probably switched off, anyway.

He set about making breakfast. As he spooned coffee into the jug, he wondered whether Tom might have told Annie what he was up to, where he went every weekend. *Damn.* If he had talked to Annie – or if Eily had talked to Annie – he might not be having to act like some cheap private eye.

Annie and Eily wound each other up. But he and Annie were as close as a father and daughter could be. She had always told him everything she thought he needed to know. She was the first born, and he remembered now how his heart had almost burst at the sight of the slithery little creature as she entered the world, screaming for all she was worth. She was still screaming in her own glorious green-haired, body-pierced way, and Eily had never quite known how to handle her.

By a quarter to eight, he was approaching the house halfway up Clonard Hill – the house he'd broken an arm and a leg to buy, when he still thought they were going to be together forever. The house where Eily lived now with Garret. It was too low down the hill to have a direct view of the sea, but he hadn't minded that, preferring the privacy of a fine old detached house that was separated from its neighbours by a stone wall and trees running all around it. He walked past it now, towards the next house along and the conveniently-located tree that would shield him while he waited for Tom to emerge and, he hoped, turn left, down into the town. He hadn't worked out what he was going to say if Tom turned right to continue up the hill, and saw him. He hated the thought of sneaking around after his own son, of behaving as if Tom was some kind of villain, and he was so nervous about it that he took out a cigarette from the pack he had picked up on the way.

The wind was rising and it was starting to rain. He just about managed to strike a match and hold it to the cigarette long enough to light it.

When he looked up, he saw Tom turning out of the gate and striding down the hill, wearing a backpack. He started to move after him. He found himself fascinated by his son, who had no idea he was being observed and who now looked so different from the boy who normally slouched around. He walked with such purpose, his head only slightly bent into the wind and the rain, and with no obvious care for the worsening weather. It wasn't the walk of a gangly boy; it was the walk of a young man – a young man Ned had no business following, even if the young man was his son.

'Fuck it. Fuck it. I'm not doing this,' he muttered to himself, slowing down a few yards beyond Eily's house. She would want to know whether he had kept his promise and trailed Tom to wherever he was going, and he would tell her the truth: there was no way he was going to sneak around after his own son; there had to be some other way of getting to the bottom of this.

He often wondered, these days, whether Eily had played away

when they were still together and before she met Garret. He hadn't asked her – hadn't wanted to. But, even if she'd had an affair, the unbinding of their marriage had been set in train by none other than himself and his unbridled devotion to his job. He couldn't blame her. She had needed a real husband, not a virtual one. And, while he might have been the one to leave, it was Eily who had effectively brought their life together to an end by withdrawing from him, hardly speaking to him.

And when he asked her whether she would like him to move out, she had simply shrugged and said, 'If that's what you want.'

Maybe he should have told her that, no, it wasn't what he wanted. Maybe that would have started a process of repair. But, like the fool he was, he had said nothing.

Losing her still hurt him like a knife in the gut. Even now. He should have been thinking about Tom and how to get him to open up about these weekends that he refused to explain to his mother, but all he could think of was Eily and how quickly she had taken up with Garret, how settled she was with Garret. The pang of emotion kicked him in the stomach with the force of a blow.

He hadn't cheated on her while they were together. Not that he hadn't been tempted. He had worked with attractive, clever women over the years, and there had been a few times when, after celebrating the solving of a case, he had left the pub with one of his female colleagues and had indulged in a drunken, clumsy fumble in a dark doorway. But he had never gone all the way. No, he had never cheated. Not really.

And yet, even as he silently railed at her present happiness, at the life she was leading without him, he was able to acknowledge somewhere inside him that she wasn't treacherous by nature and that maybe, after all, her unremitting anger towards him, which continued even now, was a kind of proof of what must once have been her love for him.

He thought again about turning back the clock. If only he could rewind their lives right back to the beginning of his marriage. No, further back. If he could, he would go all the way back to nineteen sixty-eight, to the day his mother walked out, without a word to anyone, and never came back.

Chapter Fifteen

The tension between James and me was getting worse. I was treading on eggshells around him, wanting to talk to him about the letters Inspector Moynihan had shown me, but afraid of upsetting him again. He seemed wary of me, too. Our conversations were becoming stiff. We couldn't even talk about the dripping tap in the kitchen in a relaxed way.

I kept thinking about the letters, wondering who had sent them and why. It could be someone who wanted justice for Lillian and was trying to stir things up so that the guards would start looking again. But what if it was someone who really did know what had happened to her? And, if that was the case, why was this person writing cryptic, anonymous letters, instead of giving straightforward information to the guards? What if the anonymous writer was Lillian's killer? I thought of that day, nearly ten years earlier, when I had stood inside the burned-out ruin of the cottage and suddenly felt danger, as if someone unseen had been watching me. What if he was watching me now?

I was becoming confused from the effort of trying to make sense of all these thoughts that swirled around in my head.

And I was tired, which didn't help my brain. Working in a café is physical. I didn't have James's talent or instinct for cooking. You could pick a bunch of random ingredients from the fridge or store cupboard and tell James to see what he could come up with, and you would be astonished when he served up the most incredible meal. He had learned to cook by watching his mother, who had encouraged his interest by letting him help her in the kitchen. My mother, on the other hand, had shooed me out of the kitchen, telling me I was a hindrance rather than a help.

James was the creative one when it came to food. He was the one who invented the salads and cooked the dishes that had got us those newspaper reviews. I cleaned tables and floors. I chopped vegetables, peeled potatoes, washed up. I made tea and coffee, boiled and poached and fried eggs and popped bread into the toaster. I wasn't complaining, though. We were in this together and James's culinary skills were far greater than mine. But I did daydream sometimes about a not-too-distant future when the café would be doing so well that James could take on staff and I could concentrate on my editing work.

Now, with the end of summer and the drop in tourist custom, I was working fewer hours in the café and building up my editing business. But I was still exhausted from the physical work in the café, because every surface – tables, floors, walls – had to be scrubbed clean, whether we had customers or not.

My eyes felt strained and my back and shoulders were stiff. I needed a break, and the café was quiet now. The likelihood of anyone dropping in for more than a cup of tea or coffee and a piece of cake this late in the day was small.

'Do you mind if I knock off?' I asked James. 'I could do with a run while there's still light in the sky.'

'No, go ahead. There isn't much left to do.'

I walked back to the house, changed into my running gear and set off for the strand. I ran north to Bellaher Point and back again, emptying my mind of everything. But as soon as I slowed down, all the disturbing thoughts that the detective's visit had stirred up started to flow back in, so I picked up speed again and ran south towards the headland. I hadn't thought about the darkening sky and by the time I realised how quickly the light was fading, I was close to the wooden steps leading to Oriel Cottage. I was suddenly fearful of being alone so close to where Lillian had gone missing.

I saw something big and dark in the distance, coming towards me, and my heart began to pound. But then the shape revealed itself to be Aidan, riding a huge brown horse. I hadn't seen him in a while.

About a week after James and I moved here, we invited Aidan to dinner. It wasn't a great evening. James hadn't been keen on it from the start, having decided in advance that Aidan was a boorish drunk, and he wasn't exactly welcoming. And Aidan had fulfilled James's expectations by turning up already half-cut and in an obstreperous mood.

'I don't ever want to see that jerk in our house again,' James said afterwards.

I hadn't been particularly happy with Aidan that evening,

either, but I was inclined to give him the benefit of the doubt. My return to Ardgreeney must have stirred up so many memories for him. Small wonder that he hadn't coped very well with the evening.

But the past few months seemed to have produced a change in him. He had looked bloated and unhealthy on the night of the dinner. Now, as he rode towards me on the beach, I could see even in the poor light that he had shed the extra weight he'd been carrying. He looked leaner, more muscular – almost handsome. His eyes were keen and bright. Maybe something had happened. Maybe he had met someone.

'You're looking terrific, Aidan,' I said.

'Thanks. I suppose I just realised that I wasn't doing myself any good with all the booze and the fags. In fact . . . Well, it was that night at your place, when I behaved so badly – that's when I knew things had to change. I've almost gone teetotal. I wouldn't go so far as to say I'm a new man, but I'm getting there.'

'I'm glad,' I said, not quite sure what else to add.

Aidan suggested then that I might like to go back with him to Eaglewood for a cup of tea.

'I'll drive you back home afterwards,' he said.

I looked at my watch. I knew I should really go home, but reckoned that another half-hour wouldn't make any great difference. And maybe Aidan turning up was opportune, because I could talk to him about the detective's visit. He would understand in a way that James wouldn't.

'That would be grand,' I said. 'I'm absolutely knackered.'

He jumped down and insisted I take his place in the saddle.

'But I don't know how to ride!'

'Time you learned. You'll be fine with Petra, here. It will be like sitting in an armchair. I'll give you a leg-up.'

We didn't talk much on the way to Eaglewood. I liked the sensation of being on horseback, and soon I was adapting the movement of my body to Petra's gait, which, with me rather than Aidan in the saddle, had become lazy and swaying.

I hadn't been to Eaglewood before. There had never been a reason and, as far as I knew, Aidan wasn't into entertaining. When we did run into each other, it tended to be in the pub and he had often been a bit the worse for wear.

The darkness now was thickening. I could see the lighthouse flashing in the distance, but nothing else.

'This is weird,' I told Aidan, who I could just about see in front of me. 'I feel really disoriented.'

'We're just coming off the strand now. There's a track that will take us up in front of the house.'

There were no lights on in the house. We took Petra round to the stables at the back. Her loose box was one of about a dozen, but half of the others were empty. The riding school had been Mrs McManus's business until she had the stroke. Aidan had kept it going, but, according to the local gossip, he was no businessman and was struggling to keep the place afloat. I remembered him telling me a while back that, although he couldn't remember a time when he hadn't been able to ride, he had had to hire someone to run the place for a year while he obtained the qualifications that would enable him to teach. In addition, a shadow still hung over him following Lillian's disappearance, even though he had never been a suspect. *No smoke without fire,* I'd heard a few times in whispered conversations in the pub.

The house itself was big and imposing, a mansion that I knew was Georgian because I had once looked it up, but it had an air of dereliction about it. I wondered what it would be like inside, preparing myself for moth-eaten curtains and other signs of neglect. But, threadbare rugs aside, everything seemed clean.

'Mrs Kelly still comes in,' Aidan said, as if reading my mind. 'She used to clean for my mother.'

'How is she?'

'She's grand. The best cleaner ever.'

'I meant your mother.'

'Sorry, I couldn't resist that,' he said, laughing. 'I wish I could say my mother keeps improving, but I can't. She's got her speech back – well, as much of it as she's ever going to. And she has some mobility now, too. But she doesn't walk more than a few yards because she's afraid she's going to fall, and she doesn't have much to say because she's depressed. She never got her confidence back after that stroke. If you'd known her before . . . well, you'd see the difference. She was always so proud, and now she can't do very much for herself. And she doesn't want to come here, even for an hour or two. Eaglewood represents everything she's lost.'

'I'm so sorry,' I said. 'It must be terrible for her, but it's hard on you, too, having to cope with that after . . . after everything else.'

'Orla . . .' he said, moving closer.

A mild feeling of panic hit me. He was going to kiss me. I took a step backwards and something moved against my leg.

I looked down to see a big tabby cat, which was now curling its body around my ankles. I picked it up, grateful for the diversion it provided.

'That's Oscar. He turned up a while back, absolutely starving, and he never left.' Aidan gently tickled the cat's chin. The purr grew louder. 'He's such a tart. Right,' he said. 'Tea or coffee? Or would you like something stronger?'

'Tea, please.'

He made a pot of tea and we went into the drawing room, where two sofas faced each other. I chose one nervously, wondering what I would do if he came and sat beside me. But he made straight for the other, followed by the cat, which jumped up beside him and pushed its head into his hand, eager to be cosseted.

I wondered whether Inspector Moynihan had paid him a visit in the end, and whether Aidan would mention it if he had. He might not, especially if the detective hadn't told him he had also been to see me. So I brought it up, because I was desperate to know.

'Did you talk to Inspector Moynihan?' I asked.

He frowned. 'Moynihan? You mean the detective who worked on Lillian's case?'

'Yes ... You mean ... he didn't come to see you? When he left me, I had the impression he was going to drop in on you.'

He looked shocked. His mouth fell open. 'Really? No, he didn't come here. Or maybe he did and I wasn't around. When was this? And why did he call in on you? Has something happened?'

'He turned up the other day. Someone has been sending him anonymous letters about the way he ran the investigation. He thought they were from me. But they weren't.'

'Jesus!' He lowered his face into his hands and, when he looked up again, I saw that the skin around his forehead and his eyes was red where his fingers had pressed into it.

'What's in the letters? Did he tell you?' he asked.

'He showed them to me. I can't remember how many, but there were quite a few.'

I told him as much as I could remember about the contents of the letters. He asked whether this meant the case was going to be reopened.

'He said it had never been officially closed, but I don't know. He didn't give me the impression that they were going to rev it up again. Maybe he didn't want to encourage me to be too hopeful.'

'Still,' he said, and I heard a lilt of hope in his voice, 'it sounds as if he might be trying to do something, doesn't it?'

'I honestly don't know whether he's going to be able to do anything at all. Maybe the letters were from some crank. But I want to believe that something is going to turn up that will tell us what happened.'

'So do I,' he said in a quiet, fierce voice. 'So do I.'

Suddenly, he was beside me on the sofa, his arms around me, his mouth seeking mine. I breathed in his smell – earthy and male and mixed with the scent of horse and leather – and for a moment I was tempted.

And then I heard a voice in my head.

No, this is wrong, the voice said.

I pulled away.

'Sorry, Aidan. I think I'd better go.'

I tried not to look at him, but it was impossible not to catch sight of the bewildered expression on his face as I hurried towards the door.

Chapter Sixteen

Every so often, Ned and Fergus met up outside the station for a chat over a pint. They had been doing it for years, because they'd been friends for years, but, as the gap in seniority between them widened, they preferred not to flaunt their friendship in front of colleagues. They had arranged to meet, as usual, in Dolan's, where they were unlikely to see anyone from the station. At half past six in the evening, the place was empty save for the barman.

'This isn't the only pub in town, you know,' Fergus, who had already made deep inroads into his pint, said.

'No, but it's the only one I can think of where you're reasonably certain of a quiet drink,' Ned said, settling himself on to a stool and nodding to the barman to pour him a pint of Guinness and bring Fergus another.

'What's the story, so?' Fergus asked.

'I had a word with Orla Breslin the other day. About the letters.'

'You did what?' Fergus groaned. 'Jesus, Ned; can you not leave well enough alone?'

'I got another one a few days ago.'

'You're building up a nice little collection,' Fergus said.

'I am. Yeah. But the latest one – it was a bit different.'

'How so?'

Ned told him about the sentence that didn't appear in any of the previous letters. *You didn't look in the right place.*

Fergus wasn't impressed.

'You're reading too much into it, Ned. It's only a sentence. Maybe whoever's writing these letters is just starting to use his imagination. You need a lot of imagination to keep writing crap. Anyway, I suppose you asked the Breslin woman if she wrote the letters, and she said she didn't? And then I suppose you went and frightened the shite out of Aidan?'

'I didn't go anywhere near him,' Ned said. 'Well, I went to the house and he wasn't there. Orla seemed surprised by the letters. I believed her.'

'That's fine. So, leave it at that,' Fergus said.

'I don't understand why you're refusing to take this stuff seriously, Fergus. Maybe Lillian Murray did run off and disappear into thin air, but, given the way the weather was that night, that's unlikely. Someone must have taken her, and we haven't a clue who that might have been. And now, just as Orla Breslin shows up in Ardgreeney, I start getting anonymous notes about us not doing our job properly.'

Fergus let out a big sigh and put his pint down on the counter. 'But you just said you didn't think it was her sending the letters.'

'And I don't. But those letters started coming just around the time she came back here to live. My point is that someone is sending the bloody things, and there has to be some connection between her arrival and the letters. So, who the fuck is sending them? Someone we failed to turn up as a possible witness or even a suspect? Someone who knows something. Maybe someone who knows everything,' Ned said.

Fergus reached to pick up his pint again, but then left it on the counter. He gave another sigh and rolled his eyes heavenwards. 'And what might this individual, whoever he or she is, know?' he asked.

'How Lillian Murray died or was killed? Where she's buried? Because she has to be somewhere. If you want a list of what he or she might know, I can write one as long as your arm.'

'Look, Ned, the chances of resuming investigations for that case are nil. Whatever happened to Lillian Murray is something we're never going to find out. And whoever has been sending you the letters is probably some nutcase trying to stir things up. I don't know why you're so obsessed. Okay, a young woman disappeared and we don't know whether she's dead or alive, but she's probably dead. It's a tragedy. But, at this point, we're not going to find her or what's left of her. And who's to say she didn't just set it all up because she changed her mind about living in the back of beyond with a rugby player whose career was already over? People disappear all the time. Sometimes they want to disappear. We can't find them all.'

No, Ned thought. We can't find them all. But we can try, and we should never stop trying. It's what we're here for.

After his second pint, Fergus looked at his watch and jumped. 'Have to go, Ned. Sorry.' He pulled on his coat, rolled his hand into a fist and gave Ned a light thump in the arm. 'Look, a word of advice. Stop getting beyond yourself, because if you start rummaging around and Aidan says you're harassing him and puts in an official complaint . . . well, you know the score.'

Ned stayed a while longer in the pub, thinking. There was nothing he could do without a nod from Fergus, and Fergus was dead set against anything that would disturb the status quo. But he had a feeling he might not have to wait too long before that nod came, because he reckoned that the letters were going to keep arriving, and, if the latest was anything to go by, they might become a bit more explicit.

But, while he sat there, Fergus's words kept coming back into his mind: *People disappear all the time. Sometimes they want to disappear. We can't find them all.*

The day his mother left was still vivid in Ned's brain.

He remembered that she began to laugh when he turned up in the kitchen for his breakfast and that, when he looked at her, confused by her laughter, she pointed to his jumper. He had managed to put it on inside out. He couldn't see what was so funny about it, but he laughed anyway, because she was laughing. And then she ruffled his hair and said he looked as if he had been dragged through a hedge backwards. She took out a comb, then held it under the tap and ran it through his hair to smooth it down. He remembered that she was wearing the new dress she'd made – deep blue with shiny mother-of-pearl buttons down the front. And he remembered wondering whether there was something wrong with her, because he couldn't think of any reason she might be wearing her new dress, unless she was going to the doctor.

'Are you sick, Mammy?' he asked her.

'Sick? Not at all. I'm as right as rain,' she said.

And she laughed again, he remembered. A tinkling laugh that went up and down and up and down, like the sound of the bells the church played when there was a wedding.

She didn't look sick. She looked bright and happy, and she joked with him as she gave him his breakfast. He remembered that, too. She had made the porridge just how he liked it – with milk, adding sugar as well as salt. His father couldn't stand sugar in his porridge, so she made two lots. For his father, she started off with a handful of pinhead oatmeal, softening it in a small amount of hot water for several minutes, before adding the oats and the salt and more water.

There was no sign of his father that morning. He had already left for the school where he was the head teacher. He could have given Ned a lift, but he insisted that his son walk so that the other children would see that Mr Moynihan showed no favouritism, and especially none towards his own son. That didn't bother Ned. He liked walking to the school by himself, even when it was raining.

On that last day, Ned waved goodbye to his mother, wriggling out of the hug she tried to give him before he left the house. He would regret that for the remaining years of his childhood, convinced that his refusal to hug her had been instrumental in driving her away and that, if he had thrown his arms around her, she would have been there waiting for him when he got home from school.

After the bell rang for the end of the school day, he dawdled his way home, crossing the fields, as he often did, because there was no hurry on him and because he liked the feeling of being in the middle of nowhere, like an explorer. When he arrived at the house, he thought it was strange that the front door was closed. Whenever he was even the tiniest bit later than he should have been, his mother was by the gate, watching for him. It was strange, too, that, when he turned the handle of the door and went inside, calling 'Mammy!' there was no answer.

His father came home to find him sitting on the doorstep.

'What are you doing out here? You'll catch your death of cold,' his father said.

'Mammy's gone,' he remembered saying, words that had repeated and echoed in his head since that moment he had entered the house.

'Gone where?' his father said.

'I don't know.'

Things became blurred after that. He thought he remembered his father's face changing, becoming darker, but he wasn't sure. He wasn't sure about a lot of things that he thought were memories, but that might be his own edited versions of what happened on that day. He was nearly sure he remembered his father telling him to go inside and not to leave the house, and then getting back into the car and driving away. The strange thing was that Ned had known – almost from the moment he had pushed the door open – that his mother wasn't coming back.

He went inside, as his father had ordered, but after a few minutes he put his coat on and went out again to sit on the doorstep. He lost track of time, although the darkening sky and the hunger in his belly told him it was evening and would soon be night. He tried not to cry, but sometimes he couldn't stop himself. And, after each bout of crying, he wiped away the tears and the snot on the sleeve of his jumper because he didn't want to leave the doorstep in case she came back.

He kept thinking about her face. It was always the last thing he saw at night when she kissed his forehead before putting the light out, and tonight she wouldn't be there to say his prayers with him.

He knew this for sure when his father came back without her, his shoulders hunched forward and an odd look on his face – sad and angry at the same time. Ned looked up at him, hoping he would say that his mother had just gone away for a few days.

'Is Mammy coming back?'

His father sighed. 'Not tonight, no.'

Deep inside, he knew. She was gone. His father never mentioned his mother again and Ned never asked. And, years later, when his father told him he was getting married to Irene, he knew that his mother had been written off by everyone. He held on to that last image he had of her, dressed in blue, her thick, dark brown hair falling to her shoulders. But over the years her features became blurred. He couldn't remember her eyes or her nose or her mouth exactly as they were, and so he changed the image he had of her so that the shiny mother-of-pearl buttons threw light up into her face, dazzling him.

As the years went by, he tormented himself with questions he couldn't answer and couldn't have asked his father. Why had she left? Had she been abducted and murdered, and, if so, why? Had some random stranger turned up at the house? Had she been taken and killed by someone she knew? Or had she simply walked out, wanting to leave her son and husband behind?

He learned, as he grew older, from chance remarks by neighbours, that his mother had suffered from her nerves. Yet he had no recollection of those periods when, he was eventually told, she was absent for weeks at a time, in the psychiatric hospital. All he had ever been able to remember was that her smile, when he came downstairs every morning, lit up the kitchen, and that her face was the last thing he saw before he fell asleep at night.

He fretted that she might have gone off somewhere and had another family, another son. But he couldn't cope with such thoughts when they came, with the awful possibility that she might love another child more than she loved him.

Irene was nice. She was kind. His father brought her to the house a couple of years after his mother's disappearance. She explained to him that she and his father were very good friends and he would be seeing a lot of her because she would visit often. He wasn't to think for a minute that she was taking his mammy's place, she told him, because she could never do that, but if he was ever worried or upset about anything, he could talk to her.

Once, he asked her whether his mother might still be there if he hadn't been late home because he had gone across the fields after school. Maybe, if he had gone straight home after school, he could have stopped her leaving, he said. But Irene gave him a sad smile and a big hug and said, 'Ah, no, pet; not at all. Sure, it's nothing to do with you.' And that had comforted him.

He hadn't been sure about Irene at first, but, somehow, after she started coming to the house several times a week, he found that he wasn't getting up out of bed during the night to check that the fireguard had been put in front of the fire, the cooker turned off and the doors locked. He was sleeping all through the night.

And there was a change in his father, too. He wasn't drinking so much, and he smiled and even laughed sometimes. But he didn't talk about Ned's mother, not once, and Ned never forgave him for that.

Chapter Seventeen

'I hear you were up in the big house.'

I was in Mrs O'Brien's shop, at the top of Quay Street, buying a newspaper. I was rummaging through my purse for the exact money. The euro coins still confused me. I thought I hadn't heard her properly.

'Sorry – what?' I asked, looking up.

'You were up in the big house,' she said.

Christ almighty. News travelled even faster than I thought.

'Oh. Yes, I bumped into Aidan when I was out running,' I said.

This is ridiculous, I thought. Why am I telling her why I went to Eaglewood? But, of course, I knew why. I wanted to ingratiate myself with her and everyone else who lived in that old part of Ardgreeney.

'You'll be having riding lessons next,' she said, with a flattening and widening of her lips that seemed more like a smirk than a smile. Did she mean what I thought she meant, or was

I reading too much into her expression? I decided on the latter and smiled back.

'Oh, I doubt it,' I said. And then, chastising myself for being so eager that she should like me, I added, 'But you never know.'

My visit to the shop had set my nerves on edge. I felt guilty about that one moment of temptation. When I reached the café, James was taking an order from two hikers. He looked at me briefly and continued to talk to the hikers.

'Can you do one of these?' he asked coldly, when he came into the kitchen and saw me glancing at the paper.

I looked at the order, which was pretty straightforward. Smoked salmon and cream-cheese bagel. Scrambled egg on toast.

'Sure. I'll do the egg.'

Scrambled egg isn't exactly difficult, but I was still a little bit unnerved by the combination of Mrs O'Brien's snide comments and what seemed to be James's resentment at my having breezed in with a newspaper, and I managed to overcook the eggs. James gave a deep sigh and then said he would take over.

I felt like throwing the pan at him, but I didn't. I took off my apron, put my coat back on and left.

I didn't want to go back to the house. I needed to calm down. So I walked aimlessly through the town and then beyond it, until I found myself near the old burial ground, about half a mile inland. It was on the top of a hill and could only be reached by walking up through a field of cattle. As hills went, it was a small one, but from the top you could see for miles in every direction. The graveyard was small, too – almost completely contained within the crumbling stone wall that ringed what was left of the church.

I had never been to this older cemetery, built around the ruins of an ancient church and no longer used for burials, except in cases where an existing grave could be opened to admit an additional coffin.

I wandered around, reading the names on the headstones where they hadn't been weathered away, and I recognised a few as belonging to some of the families who had lived in Ardgreeney for generations. Many of the headstones looked as though they'd been battered by decades, even centuries, of changing weather, and their inscriptions were illegible. But there were some more recent and one of them made me stop.

Patrick Joseph McLennan

b. 1931

d. 2006

A gentle creature, sorely missed.

I stifled a sob at the short, simple and unbearably sad inscription, clenching my fist and putting it to my mouth. I stood, looking at the grave for a while. At least Patsy had a grave, something that, so far, had been denied Lillian.

I stood there for a long time, oblivious to the darkening sky. By the time I began to think about leaving, the church ruins and the gravestones had begun to look different – they seemed threatening now, dark and malevolent. I didn't believe in God or an afterlife. Ghosts didn't exist; they were simply a manifestation of one's fears, or even one's longings. But there was an indescribable tension inside me that I recognised immediately.

I had experienced it once before, not long after Lillian had disappeared and I had returned to London.

I had worked a late shift and was on my way home, walking the last part of the journey from the Tube station. As I came close to Clifton Road, where I would turn left, a woman passed me. Something made me notice her. Something in the glimpse I caught of her profile as she overtook me made me think of Lillian. And then, instead of maintaining the pace at which she had overtaken me, she slowed down to walk at my pace, but just a couple of yards ahead.

From behind, she looked like Lillian. She wore the kind of clothes Lillian did. She walked like Lillian. She held herself exactly the way Lillian did. And, every so often, she would turn her head just enough to make me think she *was* Lillian.

But she couldn't be. Because Lillian wouldn't have walked past me. Because Lillian was dead.

Yet, I kept a close distance between us, unable to take my eyes off her.

The woman turned left into Clifton Road and my heart missed a beat.

I stayed behind her. She couldn't be Lillian. I knew that. She probably didn't even look like her. It was simply a case of my mind playing tricks. That's what I kept telling myself, even as I continued to be convinced that Lillian was somehow manifesting herself to me.

The woman crossed the road diagonally to the right and my heart beat faster. She's going to continue into Clifton Gardens, I thought, and even if she turns right into Randolph Avenue, it doesn't mean anything. But she turned into Randolph, keeping to the right-hand side of the street instead of crossing to the building where Lillian and I had lived. I began to feel silly for having imagined that Lillian's ghost was walking in front of me, leading me home.

But, even as I mentally laughed at myself for my ridiculous imaginings, the woman suddenly crossed to the other side of the road. She seemed to be slowing down now. She *was* slowing down, bending forward slightly, as if looking for something. A key, maybe? I stopped and waited to see what she would do when she came to my building, tension holding my body still. But then, with a slight turn of her head, she picked up speed again and walked on, and I let go of the breath I didn't know I had been holding in. It had been my overwrought imagination. But, all evening, and for hours into the night, I couldn't stop thinking about the feeling that had gripped me as I walked behind the woman-who-was-not-Lillian. I had felt fear. I had been afraid.

Chapter Eighteen

At one o'clock, when he knew the school would be on lunch break, Ned tried Tom's mobile. No answer, so he left a message saying he was going to wait for him outside the school at the end of the day. A few minutes later, Tom called him back.

'What's up?' he asked. His tone was sullen.

'I'll tell you when I see you, but it's nothing to be worried about.'

'You don't have to meet me at school. I'll come to yours.'

'Okay. If you like. Four o'clock, then?'

Should he call Eily and let her know that Tom was coming over? It would certainly put him in her good books. But, on the other hand, telling her would mean her putting a load of pressure on him to pass on whatever Tom might tell him – if he told him anything at all – and he didn't want to put himself in that position.

When Tom eventually announced his arrival, it was with the

lightest of touches on the bell, so that it barely made a sound. It was as if he was hoping that his father wouldn't hear and that he could slink away.

Ned opened the door. It had been lashing rain all day and Tom was soaked.

'Are you all right?' Ned asked. 'Do you want to dry your clothes on the radiators? I can give you a dressing gown.'

Tom grunted and shook his head.

'Tea?' Ned offered.

'Can I have a beer?'

Ned's first impulse was to refuse, but he reminded himself that his son was eighteen and could drink beer if he wanted to. He went to the fridge, took out a bottle and a glass and handed them to Tom, who ignored the glass and drank straight from the bottle. It was what all the kids did, Ned thought, but he remembered that, when he tried it for himself, he couldn't taste the beer properly.

He looked at Tom, tall and gangly, somewhere between a boy and a man and looking almost distressingly vulnerable in his wet clothes, and he wished he could find some way of connecting with him. They had little in common beyond shared genes, and, even then, it was hard to tell what he had passed on to his son. In looks, Tom was more like Eily, with his almond-shaped brown eyes and thick, dark brown hair, while Annie, though her eyes were green rather than blue and her hair a lighter brown – well, a light brown somewhere under the green – was more like him.

'Is everything all right at school?' Ned asked.

'Yeah. Why?'

'It's just that your mother is a bit concerned that you mightn't be putting enough study in. You have your exams coming up—'

'The Leaving is months away. It isn't even Christmas. Anyway, I *am* studying. She's just winding you up.'

'Why would she want to do that?' Ned asked.

'Because she wants to keep you running after her, that's why.'

If only, Ned thought. This wasn't going well.

'Tom,' he said, softly. 'Your mother is worried because you go off every weekend and won't tell her where. Okay, you're eighteen. You can vote. You can drink. You're an adult. But she's your mother and you can't blame her for thinking of you as her little boy, even if you're not that little boy any more.'

Tom bowed his head for a few seconds, and when he lifted it again the expression on his face was less antagonistic.

'If I tell you, will you leave me alone and stop her from pestering me?'

'If you convince me that you can handle whatever is going on, yes.'

'I don't have to handle anything. It's nothing. I . . . met this girl, that's all. I haven't told Mam because I don't want her bugging me.'

'So you see this girl every weekend?'

Tom nodded.

'Can I ask her name? And where she lives?'

'Her name is . . . Andrea. She lives in the town.'

'And are you . . . ?' Ned let the question tail off. It was a question he shouldn't even have started to ask.

Tom gave him a look that managed to encompass both anger

and contempt. 'Fuck off, Dad. Don't ask me any more questions, because I'm not going to answer them. Can I go now?'

'Of course, you can go. But, seeing as you're here, would you not like something to eat? I can make you something. Or we can go out.'

'I'm not hungry,' Tom said. 'I'm going home now. If that's all right with you?'

'Sure,' Ned said. 'It's fine.' He knew there was no point in trying to persuade his son to stay a while longer.

As Tom walked out the door, he turned back and said, 'And get Mam off my back. You promised.'

Ned nodded and watched his son until he disappeared. It hadn't been the easiest of encounters, but there had been worse. He could even think of it as a mildly successful one, not least because Tom had been relatively communicative. It was only when he went back inside that he realised he was actually feeling upbeat about Tom's short visit. And he knew exactly why. Tom had called him *Dad*. Ned couldn't remember when Tom had last addressed him as Dad. *Fuck off, Dad.* They were the best words he had heard in a very long time.

Ned smiled and opened another bottle of beer.

Eily was so sharp with him sometimes. When he told her he was thinking of taking a sabbatical, she had been scornful.

'What would you do all day?' she had asked him.

So he told her that, for the first month or so, he would do nothing at all, but was going to indulge in the kind of idleness he had dreamed of for years. What he didn't tell her was that his sabbatical – if he took it – was really going to be a trial retirement. He might not actually want to return to work. He might decide to do what had been at the back of his mind for a while: go to university as a mature student and get himself a degree, although he wasn't quite sure what he would study or what he would do with his eventual qualification.

Annie, surprisingly, had also been mildly disapproving when he mooted the sabbatical to her.

'I know you say that you need time to be lazy,' she told him. 'But I know what you're like. Unless you have something planned, all you'll do is end up staying later and later in bed and, before long, you'll be depressed.'

And the strange thing was, he realised now, as he sat in Dolan's by himself, she might well have a point. The other night, he had had a dream in which he went into the station and found a photograph of himself turned to face the wall. He woke up from the dream with the rage he felt while in it still burning.

Annie. Clever little madam and his pride and joy. How had she learned to understand him so well? And now she was going away to Australia for two whole fucking years and he couldn't bear the fucking bastarding thought of it, so he thought instead about how, when he was a boy, joining the guards was the be-all and end-all for him, and how all he wanted to do now was get out of the force.

With eight honours in his Leaving Certificate, he could have gone to university. He had enough points to do whatever subject he wanted. But it never even occurred to him to apply for a place. He had only one ambition, and that was to be a guard. He wasn't sure exactly when he came to know that this was what he wanted. Maybe it had come from some desperate, unconscious need to find out what had happened to his mother. Or maybe it had something to do with the fact that the father of his first girlfriend was a guard. Ned liked Barney Kelleher a lot. He was very different from Edward Moynihan; maybe not even half as clever, but he was a kinder man. A bigger man in every way.

The letter telling him he had been accepted for training arrived as he was leaving the house one Saturday morning to meet Rose Kelleher. He put it into his pocket and thought about it all day. In the evening, as he sat down for dinner, he put the envelope on the table. His father glanced at it, saw where it had come from and what it must mean, and then took a piece of bread and started buttering it.

'So that's the height of your ambition,' his father said, shaking his head. 'Directing traffic and patrolling the streets of some backwater.'

'I could do worse,' Ned said. Under his breath, he muttered, 'You haven't exactly had a glittering career yourself.'

'What was that?' his father asked, his voice as sharp as steel.

'Nothing.'

Irene had stepped in then, distracting his father's attention by asking whether it was true that one of his star pupils had won a scholarship to a top boarding school.

His father had once entertained political ambitions and, when Ned was a child, had run for a seat in the Dáil. But he didn't even come close to winning it and had taken the defeat badly.

Ned felt that he and his father had been spoiling for a fight for many years and, as the letter lay on the table between them, he knew there was something inside him that wanted to get it over and done with, either with words or fists. But the moment was gone. Irene, who hated conflict, had made sure of that.

His worst year at primary school had been his last year, when he entered sixth class and had to spend all day and every day being taught by his father, whom he had to address as Mr Moynihan. This prompted quiet fits of giggling from the other boys. He didn't mind the giggling – he too thought it was ridiculous to have to address his father in this way.

It wasn't that his father was especially hard on him. It was more the fact that he ignored him most of the time. So Ned stopped putting his hand up when his father threw out questions to the class, because there was no point – his father always pointed to one of the other boys for the answer. Maybe it was his way of ensuring that no one could ever think he favoured his son over the other pupils. Ned could see that now. At the time, though, it made him feel small and unimportant.

Secondary school was better. That was when he came into his own. He studied hard enough to avoid getting on the wrong side of the teachers, and, partly because he was reasonably good at sports, he was popular with the other boys. His father had assumed he would go to university or to teacher-training college. So had everyone else – except Rose Kelleher and her father, Barney.

Where was Rose now? he wondered. They'd carried on dating for years, all through his training in Templemore and his early postings. He had once thought he was in love with Rose. They were perfect for each other – that's what everyone said. At some point, they were going to get married and have kids. That was the unspoken understanding between them. But then he met Eily and everything changed.

Ned had realised pretty quickly that, with Rose, he had bought into a package that included Barney as the perfect father substitute. Now, having had his cosy little arrangement, his plans for a nice easy life, blown apart by the woman he recognised immediately as the one he had been waiting for, he knew he had to do the right thing. But he didn't do it. Not for a while, because it took him that long to get to grips with what had happened to him.

He still felt ashamed that he hadn't immediately told Rose about Eily. It had been pure cowardice on his part, because it hadn't been as if he was in any doubt. He had swung between the two of them for a few weeks, lying to both and hating himself for it. He had known for certain, though, that it was Eily he wanted, and so, after those first few weeks with her, he eventually broke it off with Rose and then hared back to Eily and asked her to marry him.

He hadn't really thought about Rose's feelings. He had thought only of his own certainty that he had to have Eily. Rose had been gracious. She hadn't even cried or asked him to reconsider, and he had seized on that as the nearest thing to absolution, or at least an indication that he wasn't actually ruining her life, that he was even doing her a favour in freeing her up to find someone more worthy of her. A few weeks later, she left her job in a solicitor's office and went to England, but, beyond that, he had no knowledge of what had happened to her.

He had tried to talk to Barney a couple of times – on the phone, of course, because he couldn't face standing in front of him. But Barney had been curt, telling him that whatever had happened was between himself and Rose, and that it was to her he should be talking. Ned wished now that he had been more of a man then and less of a coward. He wished he had behaved well.

But the excitement of Eily had pushed his guilt away. She was as different from Rose as it was possible to be. Rose wasn't what anyone would call a beautiful, or even pretty, woman. She was too solid for that. But she wasn't plain, either. She was attractive, with long, straight brown hair. Shiny hair. It was one of her best features. And she was intelligent and capable. She could do just about anything. Eily was a different creature altogether. She had an ethereal quality about her, as if she'd been formed from strands of mist and could slip through his fingers at any minute. Which was a ridiculous thought, really, in hindsight, because she had shown herself to be more than capable. She'd brought up two kids and run a household while he chased around after criminals. But, way back then, she was like an exotic, delicate bloom whose perfume filled every one of his senses, and he couldn't get enough of her. And it was still the same. Even now.

Chapter Nineteen

Something strange happened.

After working on a report for several hours without a break, I thought I might walk to Bellaher Point and back. I almost sped past the café; James probably wouldn't have noticed me pass by. But, on the spur of the moment, I thought I would casually drop in to the café to say hello. I hated the tension between us and found that I'd been almost continuously trying to think of ways to ease it. I knew that talking about it would make things worse. It would be better, I thought, to show him quietly that I cared. So I'd ordered a present for him: a book that I knew he wanted to read. I had also ironed his shirts that morning, something new for me. And now I would stop by to see him at work. I would be upbeat and good humoured. I wouldn't stay more than a few seconds.

He looked up from behind the counter as I pushed the door open, and I was pleased to see that he appeared welcoming. But then his expression seemed to change to a frown as he drew his eyebrows together. He had obviously been hoping for a customer and was disappointed to see that it was only me.

'Hello?'

I heard the question mark in his voice and my stomach tightened.

'I was on my way down to the strand for a walk. I just popped in to say hello.'

'Well, I'm a bit busy.'

I looked around the café. The busiest part of the day, lunchtime, was over and just a few people were dotted around the room, sipping tea or coffee, reading papers or books, or just staring out at the sea, which reflected the grey of the sky. 'Busy' wasn't the word I would have used.

But, as I moved closer to him, I saw that, while he had at first appeared to be still, his hands were fumbling with something – papers, I thought – that he hurriedly swept into the big pocket of his apron. He didn't try to explain.

'Sorry,' he said. 'I can't chat. I have a lot to do. I'll see you this evening.'

I turned away and left, bewildered and upset. I didn't go for my walk, but went back to the house, where I pulled down the box files in which we kept everything to do with the café and brought up the spreadsheets on the computer. I was certain now that he was hiding something that showed our financial situation to be a lot worse than he had let me believe. But what? Bills that we couldn't pay? A debt James had taken on without telling me?

I took every piece of paper out of the box files and printed out the spreadsheets. And then, over the next couple of hours, I reconciled every invoice, every relevant document, with every item listed in the spreadsheets. I was no accountant, but it all looked fine to me. I couldn't see anything untoward. Still, I was disturbed. I had mostly left the accounts to James, whose grasp of financial matters was significantly better than mine, despite my background as a financial journalist. Now, I was beginning to wonder whether I'd made a big mistake in doing so.

I felt helpless. It was one thing to have the anxiety over the anonymous letters that James refused to talk about, because it didn't affect our material future. But this was different. If James really was hiding a big debt from me, it put into question the whole point of our being together. And, not only that – if we lost the café . . .

Stop! You're getting beyond yourself, I thought. I was extrapolating too far – a bad habit that I had never been able to get rid of. I forced myself to close the computer and put the box files away, and then I turned on the television and watched a house makeover programme. I managed to relax a bit. But only a little bit, because the worry refused to go away.

When James came home, I found it difficult to stay quiet about what I had seen in the café. I was far too worried to think about his sensitivities.

'What's going on, James?' I asked, as he went straight to the fridge to get a bottle of beer.

He spun around. 'What do you mean?'

'I just . . . get the feeling that something is bothering you, and I wonder whether it's to do with money.'

'Money?'

'Oh, James, please don't treat me like an idiot. I know we're not going to have an easy time of it over the next few months. But I need to know how bad things are.'

'Things aren't bad. They're not perfect, but they're not bad,' he said. 'Look, if you're that worried, let me run you through the accounts.'

'There's no need. I've already looked through them.'

'There you are, then,' he said, turning away and opening the plastic container he had brought with him from the café. He laughed. 'My magnificent tofu and Brussels sprout creation didn't go down quite as well as I'd hoped, so I thought we could have it for supper.'

'James, you're not listening to me,' I said, trying to keep my voice level. 'When I dropped in today, you hid something from me. I want to know what it was. I want to know ... whether you've altered the accounts to make them look okay. I need to know whether we're in trouble.'

'We're *not in trouble*,' he said, with heavy emphasis. 'And,' he added, an expression of hurt on his face, 'I would never alter the accounts. You must have a very low opinion of me.'

I ignored that last comment. 'In that case, what were you stuffing into the pocket of your apron?'

He frowned, and then, as if something had only just occurred to him, said, 'Oh, *that*. It was nothing. Just a few notes I've been making for new recipes. I'm still thinking them through.'

I must have looked completely disbelieving, because his tone changed to something softer.

'Look, I'm sorry if I seem closed off. I don't mean to be. It's true that I'm a bit worried about our finances, but it's just the way I am. It's nothing to do with you and nothing to do with us. It's to do with the fact that I'm running a business for the first time and it's a bit scary. And those notes really were just notes. Honest.'

'Fine,' I said.

His explanation hadn't satisfied me, but there wasn't much else I could say. I had seen the cautious side of him before, the careful way he would think about something before doing it, whether it was an idea for a new dish or a reorganisation of the tables and chairs in the café. But I'd never seen him behave so secretively; he had never before swept something away so that I wouldn't see it. I felt hurt, but there was no point telling him that, because the chances were that he just wouldn't understand.

'I'm going to have a shower,' he said, disappearing upstairs.

I stared at his leather satchel, which he had left on a chair, tempted to look inside it. I'd never done anything like that before. But, then, I'd never had any reason to search through his things. I argued silently with myself. If I saw the recipe ideas he claimed to have been working on, I could relax. But if I didn't find any evidence of them, I would doubt him. And I was already aware that, in my thoughts, I had used the word 'claimed' – which meant that I already doubted him. Did I dare risk opening that bag and not finding his recipe jottings? No, I told myself. That was something I definitely wasn't ready to deal with.

It was just as well I had baulked at opening his satchel, because I heard his footsteps falling fast on the stairs. If I had opened the bag, I wouldn't have had time to move away.

I feigned surprise as he walked across the kitchen and filled a glass with water at the sink.

'That was a fast shower,' I said.

'Haven't had it yet. I just realised I've hardly drunk anything all day,' he said, drinking some of the water and then emptying the rest of it into the sink.

I pretended to be absorbed in the local newspaper. But, as he turned away from the sink to go back upstairs, I noticed that he swept the satchel up in a quick movement and took it with him. I was mystified. But, more than that, I was angry and upset.

It was then that my phone rang. Aidan.

I still felt uncomfortable about his attempt to kiss me, so when I saw his number flash up, all my imaginary red flags unfurled and whipped up to full mast. But I knew I couldn't just avoid him. We were bound together by Lillian, but I had James and he had nobody. He was sad and lonely. He could be excused for his errors of judgement. It was up to me to keep things at a manageable level.

'Aidan. How are things?' I asked as lightly as I could.

'Grand, thanks, Orla. I was wondering whether you'd like to have a lesson. I have a couple of hours free tomorrow.'

'Oh . . . I don't know . . . It's a lovely idea, but I'm up against a deadline to deliver a report I've been working on. And I'm terribly busy in the café. I can't really abandon James,' I said. 'And . . . well, we're on a tight budget at the moment.'

I thought my triple-pronged excuse – a deadline, the mention of James, money being tight – would be enough. But Aidan immediately said there would be no charge for my first lesson and that, if I did decide to continue, he would give me lessons at a heavily discounted rate.

'Why don't we just see how you get on?' he said. 'It sounds like you need a break from all your commitments.'

'Aidan, I don't think I can –'

'Actually . . .' he interjected, before I could finish, but then faltered. 'Actually, what I'm also trying to say is that I'm sorry about the other day. It won't happen again. I promise. I don't want you to feel you have to stay out of my way. I want us to be friends. And I really do think you'd enjoy learning to ride.'

My heart went out to him then.

'I really appreciate that, Aidan. And I'd love to learn to ride. Just let me talk to James first and get back to you.'

But, by the time James had come back downstairs after his shower and we were eating, I'd made up my mind. I was going to have at least that first lesson. And if I liked it, I was going to continue.

'I've just been talking to Aidan,' I said. 'I'm going over to Eaglewood tomorrow for a riding lesson.'

'What?'

'I'm going to learn to ride. Starting tomorrow.'

'But . . . won't that be expensive?'

'Not with the discount he's going to give me. And tomorrow's lesson is a taster, so it will be free.'

He frowned. 'But why would he give you discounted lessons?' he asked. 'I'm not sure I like the sound of this.'

'God, James – I know you can't stand Aidan, but you're so suspicious. Why are you looking for an ulterior motive?' I said.

I couldn't resist hurling the barb at him. I'd fretted over whether I should tell him about Aidan's move on me a few days earlier. But if there had ever been a chance that I might, there was none now.

*

I walked to Eaglewood and around to the stable yard, where Aidan was waiting. He didn't give me so much as a peck on the cheek or even come near me, which made me feel both relieved and, oddly, disappointed.

'I'm going to put you on Freddy. He's a big softie and he's as safe as houses,' Aidan said. 'Not that the others aren't, but you'll love him.'

He took me into the tack room and gave me a saddle and a bridle.

'First part of the lesson: tacking up,' he said.

Freddy, a big grey gelding, stood patiently while I fumbled about with the bridle. Eventually, I managed to get it on properly: the bit in his mouth, the headpiece behind his ears and the brow band in front of them.

'Poor horse,' I said. 'He's a saint to have suffered all the indignities I've just inflicted on him.'

Aidan laughed heartily. 'He is. Good job he couldn't see himself in a mirror, with the bridle on upside down. He'd have been mortified.'

The saddle was easier. Guided by Aidan, I eased it into the right position. Then I tightened the girth, but Aidan said it wasn't tight enough and told me to tighten it further.

'We don't want you sliding upside down.'

I loved the smell of the horse's body.

'It reminds me of jasmine,' I said, putting my nose against Freddy's shoulder and breathing in.

'I've never heard anyone say that before. Come on, let's go outside and get you up,' he said, handing me the hard hat that we'd agreed fitted me.

He didn't give me a leg-up. He didn't touch me at all, but showed me how to place my left foot in the stirrup while facing the horse's rear, and then swing up into the saddle. I was conscious of how ungraceful my attempt to mount had been, but at least now I was in the saddle and Aidan was leading me out of the yard, towards the paddock.

He taught me how to sit without looking like a sack of potatoes, how to hold the reins, how my feet and legs should be positioned. I learned how to make Freddy go forward, stop, and turn right and left, bringing my hands and legs and heels into play. I learned how to do a rising trot, moving forward and up, out of the saddle, in rhythm with the horse's gait, so that I didn't bounce around. It wasn't easy, but I eventually began to get the hang of it just as the lesson was ending.

'I think you've had enough for today,' Aidan said. 'I should warn you that your thighs will feel a bit stiff tomorrow, and even worse the day after that.'

'That was absolutely brilliant!' I said, brimful of enthusiasm, as we returned to the yard.

'Well, I think *you* were absolutely brilliant. You sit very well. You've taken to it like a duck to water. If only all my pupils were like you. So? What do you think? Have I convinced you that learning to ride is a good thing? And don't forget – I'm going to give you a good discount.'

'But, Aidan, why would you cut your rates for me?' I asked.

'Because I can. And because I want to,' he said. 'Today's lesson was free. Normally, I charge adults forty-five euro for a forty-five-minute private lesson. If you're really interested in coming regularly, I'll charge you twenty-five euro for an hour. So why not give it a go?'

I tried to think of excuses, but couldn't find any – not even one to do with money, because, that morning, one of the big corporations in Canary Wharf, in London, had offered me a very lucrative piece of work. And I'd had no idea that learning to ride would be such fun.

'It's really very nice of you,' I said. 'And, yes, I'd love to give it a go.'

'Fan*taaas*tic,' he said, lengthening the second syllable. 'And now,' he added, looking at his watch, 'I think it's time for something to drink.'

'I thought you'd given up the booze?'

'I have. Well, not completely – but I've cut down massively. I'm talking about tea. Or coffee. Or lemonade – though, I'm not sure I have any of that.'

I laughed. 'I think I'd better shoot off home,' I said. A cup of tea and a chat would have been a good way to end the afternoon, but I was wary, keen not to land myself in a difficult situation.

'Righty-ho. I'll give you a buzz in a few days, when I know what kind of schedule I've got. And, a piece of advice: have a good long soak tonight. It'll help with the aches.'

Chapter Twenty

'It's Eily. Call me, please.'

The message on his landline – she rarely phoned his mobile – was curt. The longer he left it before calling her back, the more likely he was to get it in the neck from her, so he dialled her number and waited for her to pick up.

'Garret Delaney.'

It was a confident voice; the voice of a man who had everything he wanted and needed. And, unfortunately, it was a likeable kind of voice, just as Garret was a likeable kind of chap.

'Hello, Garret.'

'Ah, Ned. How are you? Have you made your mind up yet about the sabbatical?'

'Still thinking about it, Garret.'

'You'll be wanting Eily, I suppose. Hold on and I'll get her for you. We'll have to have a drink, one of these days.'

'We will,' Ned said.

Garret had been suggesting for ages that they meet up for a drink, and Ned had been saying yes, they must. But they had still to do it, and Ned reckoned that Garret was probably as reluctant as he was, but felt he should make the effort to get on with Eily's former husband.

No, not *former* husband, he reminded himself. Husband. He was still married to Eily. Garret was just her partner. What a shite word that was: *partner*. As if they were in some kind of business joint venture. But, now he came to think about it, he would rather see them as a commercial enterprise than as a love match. He wasn't a bad-looking man, Garret, but he looked every one of his sixty-three years, plus a few extra ones on top. Did they . . . ? Ah, Jesus, he told himself. Stop it! Just stop it.

'Hello . . . hello . . . Ned? Are you there?'

'Yeah. Yeah, sorry; I was thinking about something else.'

'You're always thinking about something else. Anyway, since you haven't been in touch, I take it you haven't managed to find out what he's been up to.'

'I have, actually,' he said. 'I had a chat with him. I don't think there's anything to worry about. He's just found himself a girlfriend and he's a bit self-conscious about it all.'

'And who's this girlfriend?'

'Her name is Andrea something-or-other. I forget.' He didn't dare tell her that he hadn't even asked for a surname.

'Where does she live?'

'Somewhere in town. He wouldn't tell me anything beyond the fact that he has this girlfriend called Andrea. Honestly, Eily, I really do think we have to let him do his own thing, in his own way. He's eighteen.'

'You keep saying that.'

'Well, it's true. He's eighteen and you can't lock him up inside the house. You have to stop worrying. He's not going to do anything bad or stupid.'

'I hope you're right,' Eily said, sounding far from convinced. She ended the call without saying goodbye.

Ned poured himself a glass of whiskey, let out a sigh as he sat back on the sofa, and then turned the television on. He recognised the headland at Ardgreeney straight away, with Eaglewood in front of it and the sea behind it. But why was it filling his screen? Jesus, had something happened between his leaving the station and getting back to his house? Then the camera shifted to a man standing at the edge of the headland. Ned recognised him immediately: Professor Muiris Mac Aonghusa, a historian who popped up on television with amazing regularity. Between the TV appearances and the books he also seemed to have no trouble churning out, did the man ever actually turn up to teach his students at UCD? Ned wondered.

Mac Aonghusa was pointing down towards the rocks at the side of the headland and talking about the cave in which fugitive priests were supposed to have hidden during Cromwellian times. Ned knew all about the cave, though he had never been in it because, as far as he knew, it was inaccessible these days. The scene shifted suddenly, and now Mac Aonghusa was standing outside a castle in County Kildare. It was probably a very interesting programme, but a historical documentary wasn't what Ned wanted right now. He flipped through the channels and found one that was showing Hitchcock's *Dial M for Murder*.

Perfect. He picked up the phone, ordered a pizza and settled down to watch.

Later, as he put the remains of the pizza in the bin, the TV image of the headland and Eaglewood came into his mind. And then he thought about the cave, which, being at the side of the headland, was closer to Eaglewood than to Oriel Cottage. But there was that wooden staircase that went down from the cottage to the strand. Suppose whoever had taken Lillian Murray had wanted to keep her alive, for whatever reason? Suppose he had taken her to the cave? It wouldn't have been beyond the realms of possibility – there were all those nutters who had abducted women and kept them locked up for years, after all. It seemed so unlikely, though. Not only was that cave pretty inaccessible from either the beach or the headland, but, to his knowledge, it also filled up with water at high tide.

But what about access from the sea itself? Probably possible, but not on the night Lillian went missing. The storm was too violent, the sea wild. He remembered seeing the masts of the trawlers crowding the harbour. No boat could have negotiated those rocks to get anywhere near the cave. No, the idea that Lillian could have been put into that cave, whether alive or dead, was too far-fetched.

He tried to read in bed. Annie had given him a new thriller that 'everyone' was talking about.

'It's brilliant, Da,' she had said, adding, with a sly grin, 'You could learn a thing or two from it.'

That had made him laugh. So, tonight, not ready for sleep, he picked it up and tried to get into it, but his mind was still working out how anyone could get into that cave while a storm was raging, and it wasn't coming up with anything remotely feasible. Thoughts of his mother stole into his head, too. She had loved to walk along the shore, and he could imagine her now, crossing the fields to get on to the strand at Bellaher Point and striding all the way to Eagle Head and then back again. Had she walked on the headland? Had she stood above the rocks, looked down at them and lost her footing? How long might a body lie trapped in some crevice among the rocks? He shivered and sucked air in through his teeth.

He made himself concentrate on the thriller, sure, after just a few chapters, that he knew which of the characters would turn out to be the murderer. If only real life were as easy.

Chapter Twenty-One

When I arrived at the yard on Saturday, Aidan was talking to a girl who looked to be anywhere between sixteen and nineteen.

'Orla, meet Andrea,' he said. 'Andrea helps out here at weekends and sometimes after school, when the evenings are longer. She's going to become a riding teacher and have her own riding school, one day.'

Andrea beamed. Clearly, Aidan was someone she looked up to. And her parents couldn't be too bothered about any shadow still hanging over him, if they were happy for her to hang out at Eaglewood.

'Do you live around here?' I asked.

'Yeah. Abbeyfield,' she said, referring to one of the newer housing estates.

'A bit of trek, isn't it?'

'Nah. My dad usually drives us over.'

'Us?'

'Tom and me,' she said.

As if on cue, a young man of around the same age came out of the tack room and stood beside Andrea, who looked at him in an adoring way. He was tall and gangly, and he hung his head shyly, seemingly not quite sure where to look or what to say.

'Are you planning a career with horses, too, Tom?' I asked.

Tom shrugged. 'Dunno. I'll see how it goes,' he said.

Aidan gave me a surreptitious wink and I got the picture. I looked at them more closely. Andrea's red hair was pulled back severely into a ponytail, but her face had a soft prettiness to it. Tom had thick, dark brown hair. His skin was on the pale side and he was very skinny, but he was going to be a good-looking young man when he filled out a bit more.

'Okay, Orla,' Aidan said, tightening the girth on Petra's saddle. 'Let's get cracking.'

'Shall I get Freddy ready?' I asked, starting to move towards the tack room.

'Nope. You're on Petra today,' he said, adding, when he saw the look of shock on my face, 'Don't be nervous. She's the best teacher you could have.'

I had had a lesson every day for the past week and Aidan had told me I was a quick learner.

As we walked towards the paddock, I asked him about Andrea and Tom.

'Andrea's been coming for years,' he said. 'She had her first lessons from my mother. She's a bright kid, good at school – got honours in every subject in the Junior Cert and she'll probably do the same in the Leaving – but all she wants to do is work with horses.'

'And Tom?'

'He's very quiet, doesn't talk much. All I could get out of him was that his father's an accountant in some big Dublin firm. He started turning up with Andrea a couple of months back. I thought he was coming because of her, but actually he rides well and he's interested in the whole horse management thing. You don't have to ask him to do anything. He's always one step ahead. He anticipates what needs doing.'

'Maybe you'll end up hiring both of them?'

'I doubt it. Tom'll be off to uni in the autumn, he tells me. Anyway, let's get started. We're going to try some jumps today – just tiny little ones that you won't even notice.'

'But . . . so soon? I mean . . .'

I was apprehensive. More than that, I was scared. It was one thing to sit upright on a horse's back and trot or canter or gallop, and I'd already learned that it was harder to fall off than to stay on. But jumping was something else altogether. I'd watched those professional show jumpers on television. I had seen the way they leaned forward into their horses' necks as they took off and were still leaning forward as the horse came down on the other side. I wouldn't be able to do it. I was going to fall and I was terrified. I felt myself break out in a sweat.

'Are you all right?' Aidan asked, giving me an anxious look.

'I don't know if I want to do this,' I said. 'Something happened a long time ago. I had a fall . . .'

'From a horse?'

'No . . . it was down stairs. In London. Do you mind if we don't do jumps?'

'Of course I don't mind. I wouldn't dream of asking you to do anything you didn't want to. This is meant to be fun, not torture. How about we go out for a bit of a trek? Maybe a canter along the strand? I'll swap you on to Freddy and take Petra – she's a bit hard to manage when she's not confined to the paddock.'

It was the first time in years that I had felt so afraid of falling. Strangely, I wasn't afraid of being on horseback. I felt perfectly safe as we cantered along the shoreline towards Bellaher Point, the horses' hooves digging up the wet sand and flinging it into the air. It was just the thought of jumping that scared me, of losing that connection with the ground.

When we got back to Eaglewood, Andrea and Tom were nowhere to be seen.

'They usually leave around this time,' Aidan said. 'They come over almost at the crack of dawn and put in a lot of hours. I try to make sure they get to ride early on in the day.'

We put the horses into their boxes and I was about to leave when Aidan said, 'Let's go and have some tea and get warmed up. It's bloody freezing. Christ, if it's like this in November, what's it going to be like in January?'

This was the point at which I could have – should have – thanked him politely and gone straight home. But I didn't. It would have been rude, I convinced myself. So we went into the house and Aidan put the kettle on.

'Have you heard any more from the detective?' he asked.

'No. Has he been in touch with you?'

He shook his head. 'No. And I haven't contacted him, either. I suppose I'm afraid of everything opening up again. You know . . . all the grief I got before. I don't know if I want to face it again.'

'I can understand that. Anyway, he'll probably get in touch

with you at some point; although the fact that you haven't heard from him so far – and I haven't heard from him since – suggests that there isn't much going on.'

His mood was different now. He had been ebullient earlier. Now he was pensive. He seemed to have shrunk into himself.

'Lillian and I, we were going to get engaged that Christmas, you know. We didn't tell anyone. I had a ring for her, but she never saw it. It was my grandmother's.'

I shouldn't have been surprised, but I was. Had that been what Lillian was going to tell me that night?

'Can I show it to you?' Aidan asked.

I nodded.

He went out of the room and returned with an ancient-looking, dark-blue velvet box, which he opened and held out to me. It was an old-fashioned ring, with one big diamond set in a cluster of smaller stones. It shimmered and sparkled, but not in a brazen way. It was quietly beautiful and probably incredibly valuable.

'She would have loved this,' I said. 'It would have been perfect for her.'

'My grandfather, Phelim, went to London to buy it. Would you ... would you mind putting it on your finger? I just want to imagine what it would have looked like on her hand.'

I held out my hand and he slid the ring on to the third finger of my left hand. It fitted perfectly, but, even as I admired it, I felt it was all wrong. I shouldn't be doing this. I shouldn't be wearing the ring intended for Lillian, which she never got to see. And there was something else. The ring that Aidan had planned to give Lillian as a symbol of his love for her seemed to mock my relationship with James.

I started to remove the ring, but, just as I slid it to the top joint of my finger, Aidan put his hands on my shoulders and drew me towards him. I started to pull away, but then relented. I was still angry with James and he was being cool with me. And this was just a kiss. That was all. It didn't have to go anywhere.

But it did, because, although I knew it was wrong, I couldn't stop myself.

It was pitch dark outside when we finally pulled apart. Aidan went into the bathroom and I drifted in and out of sleep for a few minutes. When I eventually began to inhabit my body again, I rolled over to switch on the lamp on the table beside the bed. I was already succumbing to feelings of guilt at having betrayed both James and Lillian, and now I needed light to reflect on what I had done. I let out a small cry as I lay back on the pillows and found myself looking directly into Lillian's eyes.

James was already home from the café when I got back from Eaglewood. He tried to be chatty, but I could tell his interest was forced. When he asked me how I was getting on with the lessons, I told him I was enjoying them. I told him about Andrea and Tom being there, but I lied about how long they'd been around, telling James that the four of us had gone back to the house for tea and biscuits. I tried to keep the guilt I was feeling out of my face and voice, and nothing about James's expression as he listened suggested that he had seen through me. Or maybe he had and he didn't care. This made me feel even worse, so I tried to compensate by blaming him. If he had been less remote, I told myself, if he hadn't been shutting me out, if he hadn't hidden things from me, this would never have happened.

Later, in bed, I thought over and over again about what had happened that afternoon. In my mind's eye, I could still see myself drawing up the sheets around me to shield myself from Lillian's gaze. I could still see the huge framed black-and-white photograph of Lillian on the wall facing the bed. It was as if she was in the room. When Aidan woke up every morning, the first thing he must have seen was her face, a faintly Mona Lisa-ish smile traced across it, her eyes meeting his.

'Did you take it?' I asked him, when he emerged from the bathroom.

'Yeah. I'm a bit of a photographer when I have the time. What do you think?'

'It's good . . . She looks so beautiful, but . . .'

'But what?'

'It makes me feel guilty. It's as if she's watching me – watching us. Judging us.'

'It's a photograph, Orla. It's not Lillian. It's there to remind me of her. Not that I need reminding. You know that.'

'Seeing her in front of me like that . . . I was already feeling guilty and now I feel worse.'

Aidan was quiet for a few seconds.

'If you want to know the truth, I feel guilty, too,' he said eventually. 'But I can't help being attracted to you, Orla. It's not just because you look so much like her. It's also because . . . well, I can't explain it. I fancy you. I like you. I like you a lot.'

'We shouldn't have done this. I've cheated on James. And I feel like I've cheated on Lillian.'

'Don't feel guilty about either Lillian or James,' he said, moving to sit beside me on the bed. 'Lillian is gone. I've spent years mourning her and I'll never forget her. But now I have to get on with my life, and ... well, I'd like to think that you and I might—'

'No! This is all wrong. I can't do this to James. I shouldn't have done it,' I said, getting out of the bed and grabbing my clothes.

Aidan watched, making no effort to stop me.

'Look, I know that things between you and James aren't the best. That's been obvious to me for ages,' he said.

I shrugged, but said nothing. He wasn't telling me anything I didn't know. And then he said something that pierced me with a clarity of the sharpest, coldest kind.

'I don't know what you and James are hoping to find here, but it seems to me that you're not looking for the same thing.'

Chapter Twenty-Two

There was a new envelope waiting for Ned when he sifted through the bundle of post in the hall. He tore it open, wondering whether the letter inside would refer to Orla Breslin in some way. The four words he saw gave him a shock, although he wasn't quite sure what they meant.

I SMELL THE BLOOD

Were they a warning? They certainly seemed to be, but somewhere deep inside his brain they struck some kind of a chord – a memory, almost. He scratched his head, trying to make sense of them. There was something declamatory about them, something that made him imagine an actor reciting a poem. For a moment, he thought he had it. But, in less than a second, he realised that what he was thinking of was Joseph Mary Plunkett's 'I See His Blood Upon The Rose'.

It was a strange sentence. Why the definite article? *I smell blood* would have made more sense. There was no full stop and he wondered whether another letter would turn up with the end of the sentence. He was about to call Fergus to tell him about it when his phone rang. The landline at Bellaher flashed up on the screen.

'It's your father,' Irene said. 'He's not well. You'd better come.'

Ned didn't stop to think twice about it. He grabbed his keys and jumped into the car, and a few minutes later he was turning into the little lane, full of pot holes, that led to the house. He slowed down to manoeuvre the car through the gate, which was always left open these days because it was too old and heavy for Irene or his father to shift.

He got out of the car and walked up to the door. He felt as if everything was happening in slow motion. The clouds were low, oppressive. The sky was almost the same colour as the slate roof that had replaced the thatch before he was even born. The pebble-dashed walls of the house were meant to be white, but they had a dull grey tinge to them on this bleak November day. His chest felt tight, the way it always did when he came here.

Was this it? Was this the end? He couldn't get to grips with the jumble of thoughts and feelings that had pounded his head and his heart during the short drive. His father was dying and he was surprised – no, he was shocked – that he was feeling more emotional about it than he could ever have imagined.

Irene had the door open before he reached it. He bent down to give her a hug, but she was in too much of a hurry to get him inside and upstairs, and the embrace was clumsy. She walked up the stairs ahead of him, but stood back when they reached the top landing to let him go into the bedroom. The curtains were open, but the thick walls of the house meant that the light coming through the window was sparse and ungenerous. His father looked as if he might already be dead, but, when Ned sat down by the bed, the old man's eyes opened and flickered in recognition.

What should he say to him? He searched for words, but couldn't find any because he was thinking of all the words his father should have said to him, and didn't, when he was just a young boy, desperate for his mother. But Ned wasn't the one dying in the bed. He could afford to be generous. So, he took his father's hand, and that seemed to be a good thing to do, because he felt the hand grip his until, after a few seconds, it loosened. But he continued to hold his father's hand for what seemed like a long time, while he thought about the things he wanted to say, but didn't know how, until Irene came in and told him there was a pot of tea and a few scones, just out of the oven, waiting for him downstairs.

'Just give me another minute,' he said.

She gave him an odd look, an anxious look, and hesitated. But then she left, closing the door behind her, and Ned leaned in towards his father. He felt a pinprick of guilt because he would be taking advantage of an old man who was on his last legs. But this was probably his last chance to come out with the things he had never dared say to the old bastard before now.

'Dad, we have to talk about her,' he said.

His father said nothing, but Ned thought there was the smallest movement in the hand he held in his own. He had heard him all right.

'You never talked to me about her, Dad. I know you and I never got on, but surely you can talk to me now? You must have loved her once, but I never got a sense of that.'

Silence. He wasn't sure, but he thought he saw the tiniest flutter in his father's eyelids, so tiny that it was impossible to know whether it had really happened. He waited for a stronger signal, but it didn't come. Still, he was convinced that his father was listening to him, understood what was being said.

'I never got any sense you loved me, either,' Ned said. 'To be fair, I probably wasn't the easiest kid. So, this is our chance, Dad, to ...'

He was looking at his father's face, still outwardly impassive as he spoke. It didn't change now. But, without even the hint of a warning, and with surprising strength, the hand pulled away, and that was when Ned realised he might as well have saved his breath, because the old bastard had no intention, even with the grave only days away, of saying a word to him about his mother.

'Rot in fucking hell, for all I care,' Ned muttered to himself as he got up and left the room without a backward glance.

Irene was bustling about downstairs in the kitchen. He didn't look directly at her for fear he would give away the anger that was bubbling away inside him, but sat down at the table, where she had laid enough sandwiches and scones for six.

He took a scone and started to cut and butter it.

'Will you not have a sandwich?'

'I'm not hungry.'

'It's good you're here. He's not going to be around for too much longer.'

'No. It doesn't look like it.'

'You were a good boy, Ned. You're still a good boy. He should have shown you more affection. But . . .' She stopped speaking, as if searching for words that had been there, but had suddenly gone missing. 'It was just his way. He wasn't great at that kind of thing.'

'No, he wasn't,' Ned said, trying to keep the bitterness out of his voice as he remembered the times he had cried for his mother when he went to bed, and wondered why his father had been so incapable of comforting him. But, then, his father had always been the stern parent, the strict teacher, he reminded himself. There had been no play-acting in the school when he was around. *'The Strap' Moynihan* was what some of the boys used to call him. With this thought in his head, Ned frowned and looked at his stepmother.

'Was he good to you, Irene?' he asked.

'I haven't a thing to complain about,' she said. 'He was more than good to me.'

'He never . . . ?' Ned left the question unfinished, not quite sure how to phrase it, but she understood at once.

'He never lifted a hand to me.'

His question had changed the atmosphere between them. He could see that she was cross with him for asking it, though he wasn't sure whether she was cross on his father's behalf, or whether she was angry that he should even think that she might allow his father to strike her.

'I'd better head off. I don't want to be in your way,' he said. He was embarrassed by the lameness of his exit excuse.

Irene, though, gave no hint in her words or her voice that she wanted him to stay longer.

'You'll come back tomorrow?' she asked, as he opened the door of his car.

He nodded. Of course, he would return. What else could he do?

Back in his house, he called Eily to tell her that his father was on the way out.

'Do you want me to tell the kids?'

'Yeah. That would be great. Thanks. Annie might want to go and see him.'

'Okay. And, Ned . . .'

'Yeah?'

'I know he was a bit of a bastard to you, but I'm sorry, all the same.'

'I know. Thanks.'

The sight of his father, the miserable old fucker, on his deathbed had acted as a catalyst for an avalanche of memories of his mother, which pushed their way into his head and tumbled around it. They were just short little things, like something you'd record for a minute or so on a mobile phone – only these memories came from a time long before mobiles were invented.

She was irreverent. She taught him a song once, singing it over and over again, accompanying herself on the piano and getting him to join in.

One, two, three, o-lera
I saw De Valera
Sitting on his bumtilera
Eating chocolate ice cream

They were singing it together, Ned clapping his hands to the rhythm, when his father walked into the room.

'Daddy, come and sing!' Ned called out, still clapping his hands.

But his father didn't join in the singing.

'That's enough, Mary. Could you stop, please?' his father said.

His mother didn't stop, though. She kept going, repeating the ditty again and again.

How old would he have been at the time? He couldn't remember. But he remembered the angry look on his father's face and how it got angrier and angrier as his mother played and sang, louder and louder, banging the piano keys so hard that he put his hands over his ears.

'Go to your room, Ned,' his father ordered.

'No!' his mother yelled, grabbing hold of him and pulling him to her so tightly that his legs were jammed uncomfortably against the piano stool. And then she started playing again with just one hand, banging the keys harder and harder, and holding Ned to her with the other.

He had a vague memory of not being entirely sure of whether he should obey his father or cling to his mother and try to protect her. Did she need protecting? He pulled away from her and ran to his room, passing Father Jack and two other men in the hall. He didn't know who the two men were, but he thought he had seen them once or twice before. One old, one young. The piano went quiet.

Ned stayed in his room for ages, aware of the hum of voices from downstairs. He couldn't hear his mother's voice, though, and he thought that wasn't like her at all, to be so quiet, to give in so easily. She always had plenty to say and no one could stop her from saying it. She must have slipped out quietly, leaving the house to his father and Father Jack and the two other men, because, after a long time, he saw her coming back across the fields towards the house, striding the way she did when she went on one of her long walks, when she could disappear for hours. But then, probably because she saw the cars were still there, she went away again and didn't come back into the house until much later, when Father Jack and the men had gone and only his father and himself were there, waiting for her.

The men left before Father Jack. Ned saw them get into their car, a dark blue Anglia with flags and banners and a loudspeaker mounted on it, and drive out through the gate. Then he opened the door of his room quietly, tiptoed to the top of the stairs and listened.

Father Jack's voice came to him first.

'Merciful Jesus, man. You're going to have to keep her in line if we're to have any chance of getting you elected.'

And then he heard his father. He could imagine him standing there, scratching his head in exasperation and helplessness.

'Do you think I don't try? Jack, when she's like this . . .'

His father's voice trailed off and then Father Jack was talking again.

'Leave it with me. I'll see what I can do.'

That memory was like a piece from a jigsaw, but he didn't know where to put it. Then another started to assert itself: a memory of the whispers he had heard about his father – wasn't it a shame, wasn't it a great waste that he had lost so much.

Now, all those years later, he made the link. He had thought that those whispers were to do with his mother's disappearance.

But the timings he had attached to his scraps of memory were probably all over the place. No, he realised now, the whispers weren't about his mother disappearing and leaving his father wifeless and himself motherless, but about his father not fulfilling a political ambition to represent the county in the Dáil.

Now it all fitted into place and he wondered how he could have forgotten that his father had failed at the first hurdle and had been bitter ever since. He had blamed it on his wife, his beautiful, irreverent, unsettled wife, who was, as the neighbours used to say, 'highly strung'.

His mother's people were from just outside Ardgreeney, but they might as well have lived on the moon, as far as contact with them went. They were all distant, anyway. He had no aunts or uncles on his mother's side because she had been an only child, and she was also an orphan, brought up by her mother's sister, who had three children of her own. There had been some visits from the relatives, but his father had been unwelcoming. Small wonder that the relatives had stopped coming. He half wished now that he had kept up the contact, so that he could talk to them about his mother. Of course, there was nothing stopping him. He could get in touch with them, if he wanted, and he might do that. He wondered whether, once they saw the death notice in the paper, any of them would turn up for his father's funeral.

Father Jack was long dead. It would have been pointless talking to him, in any case. The priest was forceful, strong in his opinions. A bit more like Ned's mother, perhaps, than either he or she might want to admit. Ned could see that now. But, he wondered, what had Father Jack meant when he told Edward Moynihan that he would see what he could do?

It took several days for Edward Moynihan to die from the prostate cancer he had had for years. Ned went to the house every evening after work, but only to see Irene, and only for a few minutes. He didn't go upstairs and Irene, strangely, didn't ask him to. Her sister, Olive, had come across from Roscommon to be with her, so Ned didn't feel too bad about his flying visits.

It was Olive who called him, one morning, with the news that his father had died about half an hour before.

'The doctor's upstairs now. He says there's no need to move your father to the hospital. He's sending a nurse around to wash the body,' Olive said.

'I'll be over shortly,' he said.

But it was a couple of hours before he left the station and went to the house. Irene – or maybe it was the nurse, who was just leaving – had brought the waxy-skinned hands together and laced a set of rosary beads through the intertwined fingers. On the bedside table, there was a linen cloth and, on that, a crucifix and two candles, the flames of which were burning brightly. He should have felt sadness, and he did, but what he was feeling wasn't for his father. It was for every bloody thing that had ever happened in that godforsaken house.

When he went downstairs, he saw that Irene had started baking, while Olive had embarked on a cleaning frenzy.

'You don't need to be doing that,' Ned told them, but they insisted that bread and cakes needed to be baked for people coming to pay their respects, and that the house needed to be in order.

'Will I call Devlin's?' he asked, but they told him that they had already been in touch with the undertaker and that arrangements for the funeral were in hand.

Neighbours, most of them elderly, came and went throughout the day, climbing the stairs to sprinkle holy water over the body, say a few prayers and then drink tea, or maybe a glass of something stronger, and eat sandwiches and cake.

The removal to the church, later in the evening, was a quiet affair. Eily came with Annie and Tom. Ned recognised a few of the boys, now adults, he had been to school with. The priest said prayers over the coffin and spent a long time talking to Irene and Olive. Then Ned took them back to the house and stayed with them until they were ready to sleep.

The following morning, Eily and the kids walked with him behind the hearse to the graveyard. Annie, who had managed somehow to develop a relationship with her grandfather when she was younger, was upset and felt guilty that she hadn't visited him more often. Tom seemed to have distanced himself from the whole thing. He was there because Eily had dragged him along. But the four of them were together. Standing by the open grave, they looked like a complete family again, and Ned wanted to freeze time and then rewind it. It was wishful thinking, he knew, but he couldn't help it.

Chapter Twenty-Three

The envelope was lying on the mat, just inside the front door. I almost ignored it. James had already left, about half an hour earlier, and I was late. There was no address on it, and my first thought was that it was junk mail. But it wasn't the usual kind of envelope used for junk mail. It was just an ordinary white envelope, with no name on it, no address. And no stamp.

I picked it up hesitantly. I had a feeling that it contained something I wouldn't want to see, but I knew I had to open it. My fingers trembled as I pulled out and unfolded the sheet of paper inside. I gasped at the words.

I SAW YOU. I'M WATCHING YOU.

My first instinct was to drop it. My fingers let go of it as if they'd been burned. But after staring at it in horror for at least a minute, I picked it up again. I tried to stay calm, breathing deeply and as slowly as possible while I examined it. There was no signature. I couldn't remember exactly how the letters Inspector Moynihan had shown me were worded, but I knew that those letters and the one I was holding in my hand had been sent by the same person.

And I was afraid, because I realised that whoever had pushed the letter through the door must have known that I was alone in the house, must have waited for James to leave.

I SAW YOU.

I thought back to the night Lillian disappeared, when she and I were talking on Skype. Whoever had taken her, whoever had written the letter, had seen me on the screen, had watched me through the window.

I'M WATCHING YOU.

He had seen me then and he was watching me now. But why? I was shaking with fright. I opened the front door and looked up and down the street, but I didn't really expect the person who had delivered the letter to have hung around, and it was too early for most of the elderly people who lived around us to be up and about. I rushed around the house, checking that doors and windows were closed and locked. And then I grabbed my mobile and scrambled around in my bag for the card that Inspector Moynihan had given me. I called his landline at the Garda station, but the person who answered told me the inspector was at a funeral. I tapped out the number of his mobile. It went to voicemail without ringing.

'It's Orla Breslin. Please call me. It's urgent,' I said, my voice shaking.

I had to get out of the house. I stuffed the letter in my pocket, opened the door and ran the short distance to the café.

I held the letter out to James and saw his expression turn from initial curiosity, as he took it from me, to shock and then fear.

'Did you see anyone in the street?' he asked.

I shook my head. 'What can we do?' I asked him.

He didn't speak – just stood, rooted to the spot.

'James? Are you all right?'

He blinked and gave his head a shake, as if to wake himself up from a stupor.

'Yes . . . no . . . This is . . . worrying.'

Worrying? That was an understatement and a half. But I didn't say anything, because at least now he seemed to understand that he could no longer refuse to discuss the letters Inspector Moynihan had shown me.

'Maybe . . . it's a mistake. Maybe it's not meant for you,' James said.

'Who else can it be meant for? It's not meant for you, is it? And it's hardly meant for next door. Whoever wrote this waited for you to leave before putting it through the letter box.'

My phone rang at that moment and I heaved a sigh of relief as I saw that it was Inspector Moynihan.

'Orla, I got your message. What's up?'

'I've had a letter, like the ones you got. But this is worse – it's frightening.'

'Okay, I'm on my way over. Are you at your house?'

'No, I'm at the café with James.'

He arrived minutes later. Luckily, the café was empty. Immediately, Inspector Moynihan began asking questions. Had James noticed anyone in the street when he left he house? Was it possible that the envelope was already lying inside the front door when James was leaving, but had escaped his notice?

James said he hadn't seen anyone and he was certain the envelope hadn't been there when he left.

'It's entirely possible that what we have here is a crank who's getting a kick out of stirring things up,' the inspector said.

'But there's a big difference between this letter and the ones that you received,' I said. 'The letter I got seems . . . threatening. Someone is watching me. If a crank has written that, he's pretty sick.'

'It's certainly frightening, but there's no specific threat in there,' he said.

'So what happens now?' James asked.

'We'll keep an eye on the house – have a patrol car swing by a few times a day. And I'd like you to set up cameras at the front and back of the house. Can you do that? What's your security like?'

'Just the usual. We have locks on the doors. The windows . . . well, they're just old sash windows, but you can't open them unless the snib is pushed back,' James said.

'You can smash them, though,' I pointed out.

'I think you should go and stay with Fidelma,' James said. 'I'd feel much happier if you did.'

'It's not a bad idea, Orla,' Inspector Moynihan said.

'But what about James?'

'I'll be okay,' James said.

*

That afternoon, I packed a bag and went over to my sister's house, on the outskirts of Ardgreeney.

Although there were only three years between us, Fidelma had always seemed so much older than me, so much more organised and capable. Fidelma had had a plan and the plan had worked out. She was always perfectly turned out. Even as a child, she would spend ages choosing which clothes to wear, which left everyone exasperated. Her attention to detail paid off when she reached her mid-teens, because she had boys queuing to go out with her. Even in her school uniform, she looked attractive. She had a business degree, but her sights had always been set on a husband and children, rather than on a career. She met Harry, an investment banker, through work. He already earned a lot of money when she met him, and now, years later, he was earning an awful lot more.

Following their recent divorce, he was handing over a huge chunk of it to Fidelma, who also got to keep the beautiful house that some famous architect had designed.

Maybe it was just the desire to put that horrible letter out of my mind, but in a strange way I was almost looking forward to being part of Fidelma's world for a short while. No one meeting us together for the first time would have believed we were sisters. Always immaculately turned out, she was so different from me. We both had blonde hair, but while mine was curly, hers was straight and cut into a sharp bob that accentuated her angular features. And the difference in our personalities was just as big. She had incredible self-confidence; I was filled with self-doubt.

That she hadn't worked for years didn't dent her belief in herself at all. Her plan, which was still in its early stages, was to set up her own business. But she wasn't quite ready, she said at regular intervals, because, although the children were at boarding school, she nevertheless had to devote a considerable amount of attention to them.

We were sitting in Fidelma's massive kitchen now, drinking tea. She was beautifully dressed in a pink cashmere jumper, perfectly fitting jeans and little black ballet flats. I hadn't told her on the phone why I wanted to come and stay, so I told her now.

'Oh, Orla, that's horrible!' she said. 'But do you think you're in real danger? And what about James?'

'I don't think James is in any danger. I hope he isn't. But why would he be? As for me . . . to be honest, I just don't know. But I feel a lot better for having talked to Inspector Moynihan. He's going to have the guards keep an eye on the house.'

I'd never spent a lot of time with my sister before, but now that we were going to be together for a few days, I found myself opening up to Fidelma in a way that I wouldn't have thought possible just a day earlier. I told her about how strained my relationship with James had become, and I told her about Aidan. I expected her to be unsympathetic about my having cheated on James by sleeping with someone else, even if we'd been going through a bad patch and he had been freezing me out. But she didn't tell me off. Instead, she said, 'Good on you.'

Chapter Twenty-Four

Ned was glad Orla Breslin had opted to stay with her sister. The letter hadn't contained an explicit threat, but this new twist had made him fearful for her safety, especially in view of the letter he had received, with its mention of blood. But it puzzled him as to why the writer of these letters appeared now to be targeting someone who had been nowhere near Ardgreeney on the night of Lillian Murray's disappearance, and whose only role – albeit a crucial one – had been to raise the alarm. So why the letter to Orla? And why now?

He had taken the letter with him and would have it examined for fingerprints, but he knew that it would yield nothing, just as the collection he had amassed over several months had yielded nothing when he persuaded one of his pals in forensics to have a look. The same person had written all the letters, including the one delivered to Orla's house – of that he was certain; the scrawl looked identical to that on the letters he had received.

But there were two big differences. The letters sent to him had been addressed to him, and they'd been put through the postal system. The Dublin postmark meant nothing, because all mail from Ardgreeney was taken to Dublin for processing. Orla's letter, on the other hand, had been neither addressed nor put through the postal system, but had been delivered by hand.

He wasn't sure what that meant. He had assumed the writer of the anonymous letters to be from the Ardgreeney area, and the delivery by hand to Orla's house certainly suggested someone local. But who? An obvious possibility was Aidan McManus, but Ned didn't think it was likely – unless he was on some kind of a mission to get the guards to resume their investigation. But would he have sent such a disturbing letter to Orla? From what he was hearing from Matty Walsh, whose ear for gossip was second to none, Aidan and Orla were becoming quite friendly.

Reluctant to turn up at Eaglewood without warning, despite it being less than two miles along the road, Ned had called Aidan as he got into his car and had left a message saying he would like to have a chat with him – later that day, if possible. Aidan hadn't called back yet.

Fergus had listened this time. He hadn't said much, but he had nodded assent when Ned said he wanted to have the letter examined for fingerprints. He had also agreed that it would be a good idea to have a patrol car make an occasional swing past Orla's house, where James Weston would now be living alone while she was staying with her sister.

Ned had hardly had a minute to think about the funeral – or about Rose.

He had seen her out of the corner of his eye as he and Eily and the kids walked down through the church, behind the coffin. She was several rows from the back, at the far end of the pew. He wasn't sure it was really her, and he was nervous about staring. But he caught sight of her again in the graveyard, and that time he was certain.

He watched out for her in the pub, where everyone was gathering for drinks and sandwiches. He was afraid she would turn up and, at the same time, afraid she wouldn't. He started walking towards her as soon as he saw her come through the door.

'Rose,' he said, and then clammed up. What was he going to say? *Thanks for coming*? Or, *Let me get you a drink*? But that was the kind of shite claptrap he could say to anyone else. He couldn't just act as if they hadn't had a past, as if he hadn't ruined her life.

'I'm sorry,' she said, and for a moment he was confused.

Why is she telling me she's sorry? What has she got to be sorry about? I'm the bastard who should be sorry. And then he got it. Of course, she was saying she was sorry about his father having died.

He offered to get her a drink and she said she'd like a glass of white wine. As he waited for the barman to pour it, he kept turning around to smile at her, to reassure her that her drink was on the way. But he was looking at her, too, taking in every inch of her. The light brown hair with hardly a sign of grey in it that she still wore to her shoulders, the grey-green eyes, the dimples in her cheeks and the surprisingly full lips. He had forgotten about those lips, which softened an otherwise serious-looking face. She hadn't changed much. He would recognise her anywhere. She looked older, of course. But, then, so did he.

He handed her the glass of wine and they walked towards the back of the pub, where there were fewer people. He had already checked to see where Eily was, and was relieved to see that she seemed to be busy enough, talking to a small group of people.

'Are you still in London?' he asked. 'I heard you'd moved there ...'

'In principle, yes. But I came back a couple of months ago. My father needed to be looked after.'

'Oh. Is he ... ?'

'He's still alive, but going downhill. He has prostate cancer too. Very advanced.'

'God, that's shocking, Rose. I'm so sorry. He was such a strong, proud man,' Ned said.

'He still is. He's still very proud, and, in spite of everything, he's surprisingly strong. He was very fond of you, Ned.'

'And I of him.' He hung his head briefly, ashamed of having dropped contact with Barney Kelleher and wondering what he could do to repair the damage.

'Maybe you'll pop in to see him?'

'Do you not think I'd be the last person he'd want to see?'

She shook her head. 'All that was a long time ago. I think he would be glad to see you.'

'In that case, I will.'

He wanted to ask her how her life had been, but he didn't. He wanted to hear that she had had a wonderful life, the kind of life she wouldn't have had if he hadn't dumped her. But he was afraid to ask because he was afraid of the answer.

They talked for a while, avoiding the past and the years they had spent together. It was easier to talk about work. She had worked as a bookseller in London for years, and now ran her own small bookshop in Acton.

'I suppose you're terribly senior, now,' she said, turning the focus on to him.

'I'm not terribly anything any more. Rank-wise, I'm an inspector. It's fine. I've had a good career, but I'm looking at taking early retirement,' he said. And then, suddenly anxious about what he had agreed to do, asked, 'Are you sure it's okay for me to visit Barney?'

'I'm sure. We should exchange numbers so we can arrange a time.'

Ned tapped her number into his phone and pressed the call button.

'There,' he said, as he heard her mobile ring somewhere in her bag. 'Now you have my number. You can let me know whether Barney is willing to see me and, if he is, when it would be convenient for me to drop in.'

'I will,' Rose said. 'I'd better be going,' she added, looking at her watch. 'I don't like to leave him for too long.'

He watched her walk away from him towards the door, but lost her in the sea of bodies and faces.

'Who's that?' Eily asked, appearing beside him.

Why do you care? Why should I tell you? You've probably worked it out already.

'Someone I knew long ago.'

That was all he was going to tell her.

They stood side by side for a while. Seconds? Minutes? He wasn't sure. He was confused again – confused and ashamed.

Apart from his mother and Annie, the two most important women ever to grace his life had stood beside him in the same room, and he had messed up the lives of both of them.

Eily walked away and Annie took her place.

'Are you all right, Da?'

'Yeah. Strange day.'

'Who's the woman you were talking to?'

'Your mother.'

'Da! Feck off. You know who I mean.'

'An old girlfriend of mine. Her name is Rose Kelleher. I haven't seen her for years.'

'Since you dumped her for Ma?'

'How did you know about that?'

'I didn't. I just made an informed guess. Ma has that effect on men. Look at that oul' fella over there, making a beeline for her. Were you and Rose together for a long time?'

'A few years.'

'Were you going to get married?'

'I suppose so. We never actually discussed it, but I suppose it was . . . well, understood.'

'Do you regret not staying with her?'

'Jesus, Annie! What kind of question is that? I hope you don't expect me to give you an answer.'

'It's just a question, Da, and you *have* given me an answer, whether you realise it or not.'

'Then you'll know that sometimes I do wonder about it, yeah. Because, if I'd stayed with Rose, I probably wouldn't be living on my own now. But, on the other hand, if I hadn't taken up with your mother, I wouldn't have you. So, on the whole, I'd have to say I have no regrets. And don't repeat any of this to your mother.'

'Are you going to see her again?'

'I said I'd pay a visit to her father. He's on the way out. He was my mentor, I suppose. He was the one who encouraged me to join the guards. I haven't seen him for years, either. It was all a bit embarrassing. It's a bit embarrassing still.'

'Life's too short for that, Da. Go and see the man. It'll do you good and it might even do him a bit of good. And take Rose out for a drink or dinner. She looks nice.'

'She *is* very nice,' he said. 'Are you trying to get me fixed up?'

'I wouldn't dare. But you could do with a bit of female company to take the rough edges off you. You're a fine thing, Da. All my friends say that. Don't hang around forever, hoping Ma will give Garret the boot.'

He put his arm around her shoulder and bent down to kiss her green hair, which, he noticed now, had thin strands of blue running through it as well.

'What am I going to do without you?' he asked.

Chapter Twenty-Five

Fidelma was making plans for the future. She was thinking about getting into property, buying a couple of houses, refurbishing them and letting them out or selling them, and we were poring over the brochures she had picked up from the various auctioneers around Ardgreeney. I did wonder, though, whether she'd invented this new interest just to try to take my mind off that awful letter.

I was thinking about how kind she was being when my phone rang. Aidan. I hesitated. An image of the two of us in bed came into my mind, and then I thought of James and me. I didn't know what to do.

As if reading my mind, Fidelma said, 'Talk to him. He hasn't done anything wrong. You can't just cut him off because you feel guilty.'

She was right. I took a deep breath.

'Aidan, hello.'

'I was just wondering how you were . . . Thought I'd say hello,' he said.

'I'm fine.'

'Orla . . . about the other day . . .'

'I shouldn't have done it. It's not going to happen again.'

'I'm not saying it should. I really did just want to see how you were and to say . . . to say that I want us to stay friends. I don't want you to feel you have to stop coming for lessons or start avoiding me.'

'I'm not avoiding you. Actually, something a bit frightening has happened.'

I told him about finding the letter.

'Jesus Christ! That's horrible. When you told me about those letters that were sent to Ned Moynihan, I thought they were probably a good thing, on balance. But now . . . I don't like the sound of this. And the fact that whoever wrote that letter was outside your door . . . Look, I wasn't going to tell you this: I got a letter, too.'

'No! What did it say?'

'That's the thing. It was blank. Unless there's something written in invisible ink.'

'When did you get it? Yesterday morning?'

'No – this morning. Well, it could have been overnight, but I saw it today, when I got up. Just like yours, it wasn't sent through the post, but was put through the door.'

I shivered. 'Have you called Inspector Moynihan?'

'No. I wasn't sure whether there was any point. But I will now.'

'Listen, Aidan – you must ask him to arrange for the guards to keep an eye on your house. Just in case. They're already watching ours. He's taking all this very seriously.'

He went quiet for a few seconds, as if he was mulling over something he wanted to say.

I cut into the silence: 'Sorry, Aidan,' I said. 'I have to go. Let me know how it goes with Inspector Moynihan. And take care.'

I called James. I wasn't really worried that he might be in any danger. The letter had been meant for me – that was clear. But I wanted to check that he was all right. And I needed to assuage the guilt I was still feeling in waves whenever Aidan came into my mind. Talking to Aidan just now had prompted a tsunami of guilt. How could I have jumped into bed with him so easily? Yes, I had been feeling spurned, physically, by James. Yes, I had felt emotionally isolated from James. But it didn't say much for me that a few months of tension between us had been enough to send me into another man's bed.

I should have been able to understand that James might not welcome a renewed focus on Lillian's disappearance. I had been a mess a decade ago. I had heaped blame on myself. Reason told me that I had been only a witness to her vanishing, but I felt I should somehow have been able to save her. I felt power-less. I questioned everything I remembered about that night. I questioned everything about myself. I had failed my best, my truest friend.

James had rescued me. He listened to my self-questioning, self-hating monologues and then tried to talk sense into me. He held me close and comforted me, told me I had only ever done my best for Lillian. And, over time, I came to believe that. Except when I didn't. But he had coped with that, too.

And look how I had repaid him. I felt a twinge of nausea as I pressed his number on my mobile.

'Is everything all right?' I asked.

'I think so. No dodgy post. No one lurking in the garden, in the dark.'

'It's not funny, James,' I said. 'This is scary and I'm afraid – for both of us.'

'Sorry. I'm just trying to make light of it. It is scary and . . .'

'And what?'

'I wonder whether we shouldn't just throw in the towel and go back to London. Or somewhere else.'

'But we can't just leave. We'd have to sell the house and the café, and that could take months. And where would we go?'

'Anywhere but here. I'm serious, Orla. We were fine until we came here. We had no worries, apart from the fact that I hated teaching and wanted to get out of it. It's my fault we're here. I should have known that coming here to live would have . . . implications.'

'I don't know . . . Maybe you're right. Do you want to come over and we can talk about it?'

'Not tonight; I'm flaked out. But when I get back to the house, I'll start thinking properly about what we might be able to do. Are you okay at Fidelma's? What have you been up to?'

'We've been catching up. It's been quite nice, actually, considering everything.'

I wondered whether I should mention the letter Aidan had received. If I did, he would wonder why I had been talking to Aidan and I didn't want to give him any reason to suspect that there had been more between us than a series of riding lessons. I could tell him that I had heard about it from Inspector Moynihan, but that would be a lie that could fall apart if James and the inspector had a conversation.

So I said nothing. There was no point.

Chapter Twenty-Six

The words came from a rhyme in a fairy tale, one he remembered his mother telling him when he was a child. No wonder they'd sounded familiar. What he hadn't known until he had done an internet search was that Shakespeare had used a version of the phrase in *King Lear*, including the three words that hadn't appeared in the letter, but suggested the nearest thing to a name. But what did it amount to? It didn't seem to make a lot of sense, if the letter writer was pointing a finger of blame over Lillian Murray's disappearance. But, even if it was an unpleasant bit of mischief making, he felt he had to check it out.

With Fergus's blessing, Ned set one of the junior detectives to work.

'I'd be surprised if all the records went back that far, but I have a feeling we might get some joy from the credit-card companies,' he told him.

Aidan McManus had finally returned his call and Ned had

driven over to Eaglewood. Aidan, he was glad to see, seemed to be a lot healthier, both mentally and physically, than he had been in the years immediately following Lillian's disappearance. Indeed, he looked the picture of health, although, as soon as they got down to the business of why Ned was there, Aidan began to look worried.

'I got a letter the other day. Well, "letter" isn't the right word, because there was nothing written on it. Here, have a look,' he said. 'I have to admit, I'm concerned. Not so much about myself as about the horses. I can lock the house at night, but I can't prevent some headcase going to the yard. And I'm worried about Orla Breslin. She told me about the letter she got.'

'Do you have any thoughts as to who might be doing this?' Ned asked.

Aidan shook his head. 'I just don't know. I can't understand why it's happening now, after so long. Except . . .'

Ned raised his eyebrows, waiting for whatever was coming next.

'Years ago, when it happened . . . you know . . . I got a lot of hate mail. Hardly a week went by without some disgusting accusation coming through the letter box.' Aidan stopped speaking and shuddered. 'It still makes me sick to think about it.'

'Have you kept any of them?' Ned asked.

'Most of them. The first few, I burned or tore up. They were . . . vile. There were some I didn't even open, because I had a good idea what was inside; I threw them straight into the fire. And then I just put each one that came into a drawer.'

'I don't remember you telling us about them,' Ned said.

'What would have been the point? Would you have gone

looking for the people who sent them? Anyway, all I wanted was for Lillian to be found.'

'I'd like to see them,' Ned said.

Aidan left the room and came back with a big Manila envelope. Ned glanced inside at the envelopes that filled it.

'I'll have these looked at,' he said, getting up to leave. 'And, in the meantime, if you receive any more letters or spot anything untoward around the place, let me know.'

Aidan walked with him to his car. The sound of a horse whinnying came from somewhere behind the house.

'How's business these days?' Ned asked.

'Not too bad. Things were going downhill for a long time. Partly my own fault. I wasn't exactly in the best state to be running anything. But I've got my act together now. At least, I think I have. Take tomorrow – there was a point, a couple of years ago, when a Saturday wasn't much better than any other day. But I'm booked up all day tomorrow.'

'Glad to hear that,' Ned said.

Back at the station, he looked through the letters Aidan had received over a period of about a year, beginning after Lillian's disappearance. Aidan hadn't opened any of them, so Ned had to extract the sheets of paper from the envelopes with great care. They all accused Aidan of having murdered his girlfriend. So no surprises there.

Ned was no handwriting expert, and he would certainly call one in, but he was pretty sure that all the old letters had been written by a number of different people, none of whom had made any attempt to disguise their writing. It was impossible to tell whether one of these poison-pen letter-writers of a decade earlier was behind the more recent correspondence – the short messages, scrawled in capitals, that he and Orla Breslin had received.

He had been putting it off, but he knew he should fulfil his promise to Rose Kelleher to visit her father. It was Saturday, and he wasn't on duty, so he had no excuses. He brought up her number on his phone and pressed the green button. He was half hoping the call would go to voicemail, though that would leave him with the dilemma of having to decide whether to leave a message or not. But she answered immediately with, 'Hello, Ned.'

'Rose. I was wondering whether today might be a good day to drop in on Barney,' he said.

'Today would be fine,' she told him. 'What time?'

'I can be there by twelve. Would that be all right? It's not too early, is it?'

'No, twelve is a good time.'

'Does he . . . ?'

'I told him the other day you'd be coming down to see him. Don't worry; he's not going to bite your head off. We'll see you later. You know where we are.'

He had been dreading the meeting, but, now that he was on his way, he felt less agitated about it. It was simply something he had to do, not just for himself, not just for Rose, but for Barney, who had once been more of a father to him than his own had been.

His mind less constrained now, he thought of Irene. Maybe he should pop in on her after his visit to Barney.

As he slowed down outside Barney's house, behind Market

Square, his anxiety started to pick up again, and, by the time he was getting out of the car, his palms were feeling damp.

Rose opened the door and invited him in. He hadn't been there for years, but nothing seemed to have changed. The black and white floor tiles, laid in a diagonal pattern in the hall, were exactly as he remembered them. The side table was still there, with the same vase of artificial roses. The walls were painted the same dark green that Rose had always disliked because it made the hall so gloomy.

'He's in the back parlour, next to the kitchen. It's the warmest room in the house,' she said, leading him along the hallway and calling, 'Dad, Ned's here.'

She stopped outside the room. 'Go on in. I'll make a pot of tea and then I'll leave you two to talk.'

Barney Kelleher was a shadow of his former self; he looked as if he had been shrunk to half his original size and weight. He was sitting in a big recliner and had started to fiddle around with the mechanism so that he could stand up. He looked as though he was on the point of collapse and Ned was half panicking because he didn't know whether to help him up or tell him to stay as he was. But Rose, who must have been watching from the doorway at that point, came to his rescue.

'It's all right, Dad. You don't have to get up,' she said, putting her hand on her father's shoulder to prevent him from pushing himself up and out of the chair.

'As you can see, Ned, I'm not as fit as I used to be,' Barney said, holding out his hand as Rose left to make the tea. 'I'll have to start going to the gymnasium.'

'You could do worse, Barney,' Ned said, grabbing the

outstretched hand in both of his and then immediately wondering whether he had said the wrong thing, because he didn't know how the conversation was meant to go. Was he supposed to acknowledge Barney's looming death, or engage in some well-meaning banter about how he would be right as rain in no time?

Barney, though, was in full command of the situation.

'I'm not long for this world, I'd say, but I'm not going to complain.' He nodded in the direction of the kitchen. 'I have the best daughter in the world.'

'I know you do,' Ned said. 'Barney ... I ...' he faltered.

Barney held up his hand. 'There's no need to go over the past, Ned. It's gone. It's good enough that you're here now.'

'I still want to say I'm sorry.'

'You've just said it. No more. I haven't time for that sort of thing. Now, tell me about yourself. I hear you've been looking into that old case, the McManus girlfriend. Oh, don't look so surprised. I still have my ears to the ground and my nose to the wind.'

Ned chuckled. 'Not much gets past you, Barney.'

'Peculiar case, that,' Barney said. 'I suppose you were never convinced she just walked off? Neither was I, but I was well retired by then. I was just picking up bits and pieces, the way I still do. Anyway, tell me, what's your thinking now?'

Ned told him about the anonymous letters that had been coming for several months, but he didn't give any details and Barney didn't ask for any.

'So we have something new to work on. But I can't help thinking I'm still missing something. The trouble is, no matter how much I rack my brains, I just haven't a clue what that something is.'

They moved on to other topics: football and the chances of Louth ever again winning the All-Ireland or even making it to the quarter-finals; the impact of the drink-drive laws on the pubs; the high taxes and poor services. And then, as if her antennae were finely tuned to her father's metabolism, Rose appeared with a bowl of soup and told Ned that Barney had had enough excitement for one day, and needed his lunch and then a rest.

Ned got up and took Barney's hand. 'It's great to see you, Barney. I'll come back another time,' he said.

'I'll give you a piece of advice, Ned. Sometimes, you can't just pick up from where you left off. Sometimes, you have to go all the way back to the beginning and start again.'

'You're right, Barney. And I'll do exactly that,' Ned said.

He thought Rose was dismissing him, but as he prepared to say goodbye to her, he saw that she was pulling her coat on.

'I thought we could have a drink and a sandwich in O'Dwyer's,' she said.

In the pub, she talked about her bookshop in London, and how it was beginning to make a name for itself by hosting a range of events where authors answered questions from an audience about their books.

'You'll have to come over sometime, when we have a crime evening,' she said, laughing. 'You could be a guest expert!'

Was that an invitation? An invitation lightly given, but an invitation all the same?

'What about you, Ned? What's been happening in your life?'

'I don't suppose you know that Eily and I are separated?' Ned said. 'Well, actually, "separated" is a bit of an understatement. She lives with someone else now, so I suppose at some point we'll be getting a divorce.'

'No, I didn't know. I'm sorry. Was it hard, the split?'

'Yeah, it was,' he said.

He nearly added that it still was hard. That sometimes, when he thought of what he had lost, his body felt as if it was closing in on itself and twisting tighter and tighter so that he couldn't breathe. But he couldn't say that to Rose, not when he must have made her feel just like that when he told her he was leaving her for Eily.

'I split up with someone, too,' Rose said. 'Just before Christmas, a year ago. We'd been together for a long time. There was no one else involved. It just kind of fell apart. It was hard. But it's getting easier.' She stopped for a moment, as if she was thinking over what she had just told him, then laughed. 'Looking after Dad has been keeping my mind off it.'

He felt sorry for her, but he also felt relief that she had found someone else after him, that he didn't have to feel quite as guilty as he had for so long.

'Children?' he asked.

She shook her head.

'Do you ever see him?'

'Her. And, no, not any more. We started up the bookshop together, but when we split up I bought her out.'

'Oh. I'm sorry . . . I . . .' He stuttered to a halt. What an idiot. He had made an assumption and it had been wrong. How many other wrong assumptions had he made?

'Don't be sorry. I was the one who ended it,' she said. 'My round. Same again?'

'Thanks.'

He was relieved to have a minute or two to process what she'd just told him. How was he to apply it to what had happened between them, two and a half decades ago? And what did it mean for them now? He didn't know what to make of what Barney had said, either, about not being able to pick up where you left off and having to go back to the beginning. He had a feeling now that Barney's advice had as much to do with him and Rose as it did to do with the Lillian Murray case.

But what was Barney expecting from him? And what about Rose? What did she want from him? If she wanted anything at all.

Chapter Twenty-Seven

There was something familiar-looking about the lanky young lad ahead of us, wearing a school uniform and carrying a huge satchel. As we passed him, I realised who he was.

'Can you stop, Fidelma? That's one of the kids who spend their weekends in Aidan's yard. I just want to say hello.'

Fidelma brought the car to a halt and I got out and waited for him to approach. He seemed to be in a world of his own. When I said, 'Hi, Tom,' he almost jumped out of his skin.

'Oh, hello,' he said. He didn't seem able to work out whether he should keep walking or stop.

Shy.

'Do you live out this way?' I asked.

'Erm ... yeah.'

'Would you like a lift? That's my sister in the car.'

'It's all right, thanks. I just live up there. It's not far.'

'Are you sure?'

'Yeah. Honest. It's fine. I'll walk.'

'Well, if you're sure . . .'

I was getting back into the car when the rain that had been falling softly suddenly became a downpour.

'Come on – get in. You're not walking home in this,' I said.

Obediently, he got into the car and I introduced him to Fidelma, who immediately began to fire questions at him. Who were his parents? What did they do?

'We're not from around here,' he said. 'My dad works in Dublin. He's an accountant.'

'Oh, what's his name?' Fidelma asked. 'My husband is in finance. He might know him.'

I shot her a puzzled glance. Why was she mentioning Harry in such a friendly way? Usually, when she made any mention of him these days, she referred to *my shithead husband* or *my bugwit husband*.

'His name is,' Tom began, and I thought I detected a slight hesitation, as if giving any information about himself or his family was a step too far, 'Garret.'

'Garret what?' Fidelma persisted.

'De-Devine. Garret Devine.'

A couple of minutes later, he told us we were coming up to where he lived. We stopped in front of what looked like an old house, set back from the road and reached through a wide gateway between two stone piers.

'Thanks,' Tom mumbled, opening his door and stepping out on to the pavement. At that point, a car came out through the gate. The driver, a woman, wound down her window.

'Tom!'

'That must be his mother,' I said to Fidelma.

The woman got out of her car, said something to Tom and then came towards our car. Tom, I noticed, looked uncomfortable. She was very good looking – tall and slim, and with thick dark shoulder-length hair. Tom clearly took after her.

'Thanks for stopping to pick Tom up. It's very nice of you. When I saw the rain coming down like that, I thought I'd better go and meet him,' she said. 'Would you like to come in for a cup of tea? Please do.'

I looked at my watch. We were on our way to Slane to look at a house that Fidelma thought she might buy as a rental property, and we were running late for our meeting with the auctioneer. But I also had a strong vibe from Tom that the last thing he wanted was for us to sit down drinking tea with his mother.

'Thanks, but we're late for something already,' I said. 'Bye, Tom. See you!'

As Fidelma moved the car back on to the road, I thought I heard his mother say something, but, if she did and she was talking to us, it was too late, because we were already approaching the bend in the road.

'Odd kid,' Fidelma said. 'What do you know about him?'

'Nothing, really. Why?'

'Well, maybe he's just shy and a bit gauche, but getting anything out of him, even his father's name, was like pulling teeth. I just wonder whether he might be your letter-writer.'

'Ah, no, Fidelma. That's just too off the wall – it's bonkers! He's just a kid. And he wouldn't have been more than seven or eight when Lillian disappeared. Why would he resort to sending threatening letters?'

She shrugged. 'I know it sounds mad. But he hangs out at the stables and you got that letter shortly after you started having lessons. Maybe he's obsessed with Aidan, or something like that, and sees you as some kind of interloper. Maybe he's just some weirdo.'

'But he doesn't know where I live.'

'Oh, Orla – don't be stupid. Everyone knows where everyone lives around here, and, if they don't, they can easily find out. I'm just saying there's no harm in asking your detective man to check him out.'

She did have a point. It was true that the letter I'd received arrived within days of my meeting Tom at Eaglewood. Was it possible that he was somehow obsessed with Aidan? He had come over as a bit shy and awkward, but maybe there was more to it than that. Maybe he saw my arrival at Eaglewood as a threat to his standing with Aidan. But, I thought, even if that was the case, it didn't even begin to explain why he might have been sending anonymous letters to Inspector Moynihan over several months.

Fidelma was right, though. There was no harm in mentioning Tom to Inspector Moynihan. But I would wait until the next time he got in touch with me. I wasn't going to make a big thing of it.

Chapter Twenty-Eight

Barney had told him to go back to the beginning. And Barney had been right. Ned knew now he had made big mistakes early on, because he had made assumptions. He hadn't been free or wide enough in his thinking, all those years ago. He really had fucked up. He knew now that he had failed Lillian Murray from the very beginning, because he hadn't asked the right questions – he had left them out. So, when the young detective gave him the information he had asked for, he hadn't the heart to be jubilant.

'I haven't had any luck with the airline records, but the credit-card records have come up with something interesting,' the detective said. 'Here's an amount, charged to the card and subsequently credited back to it.'

It was enough information to send Ned to Northern Ireland, where he was standing now with Stuart Patterson, a detective from the Police Service of Northern Ireland, at the front desk of Turley Lodge Hotel, a small family-run hotel, north of Belfast, which had kept handwritten guest records going back decades. Normal protocol would have meant the PSNI carrying out any interviews, but Patterson knew Ned from a long time back and was happy for him to be present.

The young manager, whose name badge suggested that he was part of the owning family, told them that, even when guests insisted on paying their bills in cash, the hotel always lodged a charge against a credit card on check-in and refunded it to the card on departure.

'To cover all eventualities,' he said. 'Now then, have a seat in the lounge and we'll bring the books. There's tea and biscuits on the way.'

When the manager returned to the lounge, a broad smile was on his face.

'Here you are,' he said, opening up the oblong leather-bound register. 'As you can see, the guest spent just one night with us. Here's the name printed out in capital letters and here's the signature. And that little mark, there, shows that the bill was paid in cash. As you know, we always take a credit card as a guarantee when a guest checks in.'

'Can you hold on to this book? We may need it,' Ned said.

'I will, of course. We've held on to it for ten years already, so it won't be going anywhere. Would you like a photocopy, in the meantime?'

'Thanks. That would be great.'

The light was beginning to leave the sky when Ned got back to Ardgreeney. But, instead of going back to the station, he drove through the town and turned left into Quay Street, where he left his car. Black clouds were tumbling across the sky. He could almost smell the rain in the air and he felt it on the wind. The café was empty except for James Weston, who was busy clearing tables and wiping them down.

'Inspector,' he said, his mouth broadening into an attempt at a smile. 'What can I get you? We've finished the hot food, but I can do you some tea or coffee and a sandwich. If you're looking for Orla, she's still at her sister's.'

'It's you I want to talk to, James.'

'Oh. Okay. Sure,' James said, wiping his hands on the apron he was wearing and then taking it off and folding it.

'Why don't we have that tea you mentioned, and then we can sit down and talk,' Ned said.

He watched James go through the process of making the pot of tea and carrying it on a tray, along with cups and saucers and milk and sugar, to one of the tables. The expression of concentration on James's face told him nothing, but his hand seemed to be less than steady as he poured the tea.

'Have you found out who sent that letter?' James asked.

'No. But that's not quite what I want to talk to you about.'

'Oh. What, then?'

'The thing is, James, we never talked to you about Lillian. It never occurred to us that we should.'

James shifted uncomfortably. He started to pour some milk into his cup, but had to put the jug down because his hand was shaking.

'I don't know why you would have wanted to talk to me,' he said. 'I wasn't anywhere near here.'

'Weren't you?'

238

'No. I was living in Scotland then,' James said. 'I hardly knew Lillian.'

'Are you absolutely sure you weren't in Ardgreeney that night, James? Because my understanding is that you were a long way from Scotland. You were here in Ardgreeney the night Lillian disappeared, weren't you?'

Ned watched James's face go through another series of changes before he answered.

'This is mad! I *was* in Scotland. I'd never even been to Ardgreeney then.'

'So you're saying you weren't anywhere in this area that night? That you weren't even in Ireland?'

'I told you I wasn't. I was in Scotland. That's where I was living at the time.'

'Can anyone verify where you were?'

'I don't know . . . I don't think so . . . I think I was probably in my flat, marking papers. I used to be a teacher.'

'No flatmates?'

'No. I lived on my own.'

'How well did you know Lillian Murray?'

'Well enough, I suppose. But we hardly ever saw each other, except when Orla was around. I had no contact with her beyond that.'

'Did anything ever happen between you and Lillian?' Ned asked.

'What do you mean?'

'Were you romantically involved with her?'

'No, of course not! I was with Orla – Lillian was her friend!'

'Look, James,' Ned said. 'You haven't told me everything. I

know you weren't in Scotland the night Lillian disappeared. I know that because you spent that very same night at a little hotel just north of Belfast.' Ned pulled the photocopied page from his inside pocket and laid it on the table for James to see. 'Here, have a look at this: your name and signature in the guest book. Now, you may say a stay in a hotel near Belfast doesn't mean you were anywhere near Ardgreeney. But, if I were you, I'd start telling the truth. We've already got proof that you were in Ireland, not Scotland, and it's only a matter of time before we get hold of someone who can place you here.'

James blanched. He looked as if he had been frozen in time.

'Why don't you take a minute or so to think about what you're going to tell me and I'll make us another pot of tea?' Ned said. 'Don't be too imaginative. The truth is always best.'

He took his time making the tea. When he finally returned to the table, James seemed more calm.

'It's true. I came here that night, but I didn't harm her. I didn't even talk to her,' James said, his voice so low that Ned could just about hear him.

'So why did you come to Ardgreeney?'

'I just . . . I can't explain.'

'Why don't you start at the beginning, James?' he said gently.

'It was never meant to happen. I was with Orla, but . . .' His voice petered out. He hung his head in what Ned took to be shame.

'You were sleeping with Lillian while you were with Orla?'

James nodded. 'It was a kind of madness. It was wrong . . . I shouldn't have . . . Neither of us should have . . .'

'What about Orla? Did she know?'

James looked away and shook his head. 'Lillian and me . . . we didn't plan it. I didn't want to hurt Orla, and Lillian didn't want to, either. And then it all kind of resolved itself, because she took up with Aidan. It was a relief, really.'

'So why did you come to Ardgreeney that night?'

'This is going to sound crazy, but I was still mad about her. I look back now and wonder how I ever got into that mess, because I knew, at the time, that Orla and I had something that would last. I knew it couldn't last with Lillian; it was too . . . intense. But . . . I had this idea that I'd just get into my car and get on to the ferry and drive over. I know it was stupid, and I knew it at the time, but I had this need to talk to her and make her see that she should be with me and not him.'

'What did she say?'

'I told you – I didn't talk to her.'

'Are you telling me that you came all this way and then turned around and drove back again?'

'I didn't talk to her because I realised there was no point.'

'You'll have to elaborate on that, James.'

'It's a bit embarrassing,' James said, lowering his eyes. 'I saw them through the window. They were . . . you know . . .'

'You watched Aidan and Lillian, through the window, having sex?' Ned asked.

James nodded miserably. 'They were on the sofa. I drove around for a bit. I was still thinking I could talk to her, once Aidan had gone out, but I knew then that nothing I could say would convince her.'

'How did you know Aidan would be going out that night?'

'She mentioned it on the phone, about a week before.'

'You were still in telephone contact?'

'Sometimes. Sometimes I called her and sometimes she called me. I can't remember exactly when, but I'd phoned her one night and she couldn't talk, but she told me to call her the following Saturday, because Aidan would be out for the evening.'

'What did you talk about during those phone calls?'

'I can't really remember what we talked about. What I do remember is how elated and how miserable I used to feel, all at the same time. When I look back now, I realise that Lillian was just keeping me hanging on. I think she liked the fact that I was still crazy about her, that she could have someone like me in reserve, in case things didn't work out with Aidan.'

They had used prepay mobiles all through their affair, James said, except for that final conversation, when he had tried her number, but hadn't been able to get through on it and had used her Irish mobile number instead.

'The mobiles were her idea. She was afraid that if I called her on her normal phone Orla might see the number come up on the screen. She got worried once when Orla saw a text I sent her.'

'Did you put your name on that text?'

'No . . . I always just used an initial: *R*.'

'*R* for . . . ?'

James looked embarrassed. He muttered something.

'Sorry, I didn't hear that. *R* for what?'

'Romeo. That's what we used as a kind of code name. Well, her middle name was Juliet . . .'

What a mess, Ned thought. What an absolutely appalling way for James to have behaved. But the awful thing, he thought, remembering those first few weeks after he met Eily, was that it was all too easy to get into that kind of situation. He had spent weeks telling elaborate lies to Rose. He had been a shit.

'Okay, let's skip forward a bit and talk about how you got yourself to Ardgreeney that night,' he said.

'It wasn't something I'd planned. I just did it. I drove to Stranraer and took my car over to Larne on the ferry, and then I drove down to Ardgreeney. I can't remember how long it took or what time I got there. I can't remember much about the drive back north, either. I wasn't in a good state.'

Ned reminded James that an elderly man had died in the fire at Oriel Cottage that night. James insisted he hadn't seen anyone near the cottage and that he hadn't seen the fire either.

'Did you kill Lillian, James?'

'No,' James said, looking directly into Ned's eyes. 'I didn't.' He became calmer then. His shoulders sagged. His body seemed to flop. 'What are you going to do now? Are you going to arrest me?'

'No. But you're going to have to come into the station for an interview under caution. If I were you, I'd think about a solicitor,' Ned said, adding, 'Have you told any of this to Orla?'

James shook his head miserably. 'No.'

'You might want to tell her before she finds out, which she will.'

Ned rose to leave, but before he reached the door, James was speaking again.

'I . . . I received letters, too.'

He went into the kitchen and emerged with a small satchel, from which he produced several envelopes, all stamped and addressed to him at the café. The notes inside, written in an upper-case scrawl that Ned was now familiar with, were menacing.

YOU THINK NO ONE KNOWS, BUT I DO

I KNOW EVERYTHING

I SAW YOU THAT NIGHT

YOU'RE GOING TO GET YOUR JUST DESSERTS

Ned looked at the date stamps on the envelopes, all of which had Dublin postmarks..

'I see the first one arrived within a month or so of you and Orla moving here? Do you have any suspicions as to who might have sent them?'

'No.'

'Has Orla seen them?'

'No. I always get here before she does, so she hasn't even seen the envelopes. I didn't . . . I didn't want to worry her.'

'And yet she is worried. She's frantic over that letter. Did it not occur to you that you should tell her about the ones you'd received?'

James lowered his head. He looked utterly miserable. 'I knew the letter she got was really meant for me,' he said. 'I knew it was meant to frighten me. That's why I said nothing. I know now I should have. But . . .'

Ned sighed. 'Don't go anywhere. As I said, you'll have to come in to make a statement. And,' he added, picking up the letters, 'I'll take these.'

Driving back to the station, he wondered whether he should have arrested James Weston on the spot. But on what grounds could he have made an arrest? There was no evidence, at this stage. Sure, he had been in Ardgreeney that night. But the only person who seemed to have knowledge of that was whoever had written the anonymous letters. What role had this person played in Lillian's disappearance? Had it been that of an observer? Or had it been something more sinister?

Ned felt sorry for Orla Breslin. What had she done to deserve being cheated on by both her best friend and her boyfriend? He wondered what her reaction would be when James told her that he had been two-timing her with Lillian and that he was now being investigated for possible involvement in Lillian's disappearance. *If* James had the guts to tell her. More likely, Ned thought, James would delay telling her for as long as he could, in the hope that it would all go away. But it wasn't going to go away. If anything, it was only just beginning.

Chapter Twenty-Nine

'Orla!' Fidelma called. 'James is here.'

I ran downstairs, bumping into Fidelma.

'I've left him in the sitting room. He looks a bit anxious. I hope he's okay. I'll be in the kitchen, if you need me.'

He was sitting on one of the sofas, but he was leaning forward, his elbows on his knees. He looked up as I entered the room and I saw something in his eyes that I'd never seen before: a look that seemed to say the worst thing that could have happened had come to pass.

'James, what is it? What's wrong?' I asked, rushing to his side and putting my arm around him. 'Has something happened?'

'I have to tell you something. About that night.'

'What night?' I was confused. Which night was he talking about?

'I don't know how to tell you . . . Lillian and I . . .'

What was he saying? But, even with the question ringing

in my head, I knew. The way he'd said 'Lillian and I' told me more than I wanted to know. I got up from the sofa and leaned against the opposite wall, as far from him as I could get without leaving the room.

He talked and talked, and I listened, my stomach tight, as if gripped by a vice. He told me how he and Lillian had somehow become involved with each other. It had happened without either of them realising it.

I felt my legs weaken and my back slide down the wall until I was sitting on the floor. I closed my eyes, not sure whether I was going to faint.

'Orla . . . Are you all right?'

I opened my eyes to see that he was starting to drop to his knees in front of me, his arms outstretched. I pushed him away so strongly that he lost his balance and ended up on the floor.

'Don't you dare come near me! You tell me something like this and you ask me if I'm *all right*? No, I'm not all right. Do you really have to ask me that? So, tell me – how did it start? Did your heart miss a beat? Did you suddenly think, Oh, I'm falling in love with Lillian?'

I could hear how scornful and angry my voice sounded. But the scorn was a kind of defence because, inside, I felt as if I was slowly dying.

'It wasn't like that,' he said. 'It just happened . . . She was always there, with us, in the flat, doing things with us . . .'

'And I suppose those weekends when you didn't come down to London, and Lillian just happened to be away somewhere . . . ?'

'She came up to Edinburgh, but only a couple of times. And sometimes things . . . happened in London. I'm desperately sorry.

It wasn't meant to be serious. It was a temporary madness. We didn't want to hurt you. We thought it would . . . sort itself out.'

We thought. There it was again. That *we* that stabbed me like a knife each time he said it.

'How?' I stared at him. 'Things don't just sort themselves out. Was it Lillian who sorted it out? When she took up with Aidan?'

'I suppose so.'

I couldn't listen to any more.

'I don't want to continue this conversation,' I said. 'I don't want to hear any more of this. You'd better go. Just fuck off out of here.'

He didn't move, so I turned towards the door. He could stay there as long as he liked, but I wasn't going to listen to him.

'Orla . . . there's more. And you have to hear it. Inspector Moynihan knows . . .'

His mention of the detective stopped me in my tracks. I turned around and stared at him. And what he told me then made me think I was in a living nightmare. James had gone to Ardgreeney the night Lillian disappeared, but had left without talking to her. Inspector Moynihan had found out about his trip and was investigating whether he might have had anything to do with her disappearance.

'I didn't harm her, Orla. You've got to believe me; I didn't go near her.'

'Do you honestly expect me to believe anything you say? You've kept this from me for ten years. I've been living with someone who could be a murderer.'

'I'm not a murderer,' he said, so quietly that I almost did believe him.

I searched his face, trying to work him out, but gave up. 'I don't know who you are any more,' I said. And then, with a bitter laugh, I added, 'I don't think I ever knew you. And now I'd like you to go.'

I held the door open and watched him walk slowly through it. And then I collapsed on to the sofa. For a few minutes, I couldn't think or move. I saw it all again, all the scenes from that awful night, as if they were happening in front of me. Only this time there were additional scenes. Now I saw James outside with Lillian – a soundless scene in which their faces told a story of anger, desperation and fear. I saw Lillian lifeless, bundled into a car to be disposed of. And I saw the shape of a man falling through the flames, and my mind conjured up a horrific image of James pushing Patsy McLennan into the blazing house.

I wailed – a long, loud wail that brought Fidelma rushing into the room.

'Orla! Jesus, what is it? What happened?' Fidelma was beside me now, gripping my arms, trying to get through to me.

'James – it was James!'

'What do you mean? What do you mean, "It was James"?' Fidelma asked, her voice insistent, her fingers digging into my arms.

'He killed Lillian.'

'Don't be ridiculous, Orla! He couldn't have killed her. Why are you saying that?'

'Because he was in Ardgreeney the night she went missing. He told me he was here. Just now.'

'But why would he have killed her? Did he tell you he killed her?'

'He said he didn't see her. But he came here to see her because he wanted her. Fidelma, they had an affair! They were sleeping together behind my back!'

I told her everything he had told me. I was calmer now, although my insides still churned and I kept feeling I was going to throw up.

'Is he going to be arrested? Do the guards think he did away with her?'

'I don't know. He said Inspector Moynihan knew he was in Ardgreeney.'

'But what do *you* think?' Fidelma asked. 'Do you really think James could have killed Lillian? And that old man?'

It was a question that I couldn't, until now, have imagined being asked. Did I think James – the man I had lived with for the best part of ten years, the man I had expected to spend the rest of my life with – was capable of killing another human being? Did I believe that he had killed not only Lillian but also an old man he didn't know? To kill a person, surely you would have to be capable of unimaginable anger. I had seen James cross, moody, uncommunicative. But I had never seen him so angry that I'd been fearful.

I shook my head. 'I can't imagine him doing anything like that,' I said. 'But I never imagined that he and Lillian were having an affair. Although . . . you know, maybe the clues were there and I just didn't spot them.'

I thought back to what James had said. He told me that his affair with Lillian had 'just happened'. He didn't tell me *how* it had happened, who had made the first move. Had Lillian wanted James all along? Had she initiated their affair, made

James fall for her to prove to herself that she could have him, and then dumped him when Aidan came along? I couldn't imagine James having made the first move – not now I knew how weak willed he was. But why had he stayed with me? Was I no more than a consolation prize because he couldn't have Lillian?

I had so many questions. But there was one thing that was clear, and that was how little I had known either my best friend or the man I loved – the man I thought loved me.

'What a fucking tosser,' Fidelma said. And, in spite of the awfulness of it all, I had to laugh, because my sister had never been given to vulgarity or swearing.

But then I stopped laughing and all the shock, the gloom and the fear descended on me again.

'I don't know what to do now,' I said.

'Why don't you talk to that inspector of yours?' Fidelma suggested. 'I think it would be a good idea. He might be able to tell you more than James has told you.'

Did I want to know more than I already knew? Part of me wanted to shut down, draw the curtains. But I couldn't do that. I knew that whatever happened now wouldn't affect just James and me; it would affect everyone I was close to, including my parents, who had no idea of what was going on, and Fidelma.

I thought suddenly of Aidan. Should I tell him that James had been in Ardgreeney that night and was being investigated by the guards? I brought his number up on my phone, but I hesitated, unable to bring myself to make the call. With a jolt, I realised that I was hoping with all my heart that James had told me the truth – that he hadn't seen Lillian that night, that he hadn't killed her.

I called Inspector Moynihan, but when he answered all I could do was sob into the phone. Fidelma took the phone from me and I heard her tell him that we would call him later.

Chapter Thirty

All he could hear was an explosion of sobbing. James must have talked to her shortly after leaving the Garda station, where he had given a statement. Ned waited, and after a few seconds the sound of the sobbing grew distant and he heard a female voice addressing him by name.

'Inspector Moynihan, I'm Fidelma Thornbury, Orla's sister. Can we call you back in a little while? She's just been talking to James and she's very upset.'

'Would it help if I came and talked to her?' he asked.

'Oh, I'm sure it would. Thank you.'

He wrote down the address she gave him and told her he would be there within the hour.

Ned knew the house by sight, but hadn't known until now who lived behind the electronic gates and high walls. It was the kind of house he couldn't even dream of living in: a modern, architect-designed mansion built out of concrete, wood, metal and glass. Fidelma Thornbury and her husband must be worth a fortune. He was about to get out of his car to look for an entryphone when the security gates in front of the house began to open, so he turned in through the gates and, by the time he switched the engine off, a woman was walking towards him.

'Hello, Inspector. Thank you for coming,' she said, holding out her hand to him.

Fidelma looked nothing like her sister, Ned thought. And she seemed much more confident – as well she might be, if she had the wherewithal to be living in a house like this. She led him into a spacious hall that, in turn, led to a big reception room overlooking a landscaped garden at the rear.

'I'll just go and get Orla. I made her go and lie down for a while.'

He almost didn't recognise Orla when she came into the room. She looked dreadful, and he was reminded of his first meeting with her, a decade earlier. She looked as if her entire world had fallen apart.

'So, James has talked to you?'

She nodded. 'He told me he was in Ardgreeney the night Lillian went missing. He told me they'd had an affair. I never knew about that. And he told me he didn't hurt her,' she said in a monotone voice, her head downcast. And then she looked up at him, her eyes pleading. 'Did he hurt her?'

'I don't know, Orla.'

'How did you find out about James being in Ardgreeney? He was supposed to be at a university reunion that night. That was why I couldn't get hold of him –'

She broke off suddenly, as if realising some horrible truth.

Ned, too, had a sense of having learned something: James had told him he was in his flat, marking papers, but he had told Orla something completely different.

Should he tell Orla exactly how the anonymous letter had directed him to James? Probably not, but he decided there was no harm in her knowing.

'I received another letter. It said, *I smell the blood*.'

She stared at him, frowning, not understanding.

He finished the rhyme: '*I smell the blood of an Englishman*. It's from "Jack and the Beanstalk". It also makes an appearance in *King Lear*.'

'But . . . but that's not evidence!'

'No, of course it's not. But it's what made us think of James. And then we found evidence that he spent that night near Belfast, and the hotel confirmed it. When I talked to James, he admitted he had not only been in Belfast, but also in Ardgreeney.'

'But he didn't tell you he harmed Lillian.'

'No.'

'I need to know what you think . . . Do you think James killed Lillian? You must have met people who've committed murder. Do you think James is the type of person who could have done something like that?'

'I can't tell you that, Orla, because I honestly don't know,' he said gently. 'I'm sorry.'

Privately, Ned thought that the chances of finding any real evidence against James were low, maybe negligible. Would anyone in Ardgreeney remember having seen him on a night, ten years ago, when the appalling weather would have kept most people at home in their houses? Clearly, *someone* had seen him, but that person wasn't ready to reveal himself. Not yet, anyway. And maybe never. Still, who knew what other information was going to come to light, either from the anonymous scribe or from James himself.

'Did James tell you about the letters that were sent to him?'

'James got letters? But I didn't know ... He didn't tell me. What did they say?'

'They were similar to the letter you saw. That letter was probably meant for him.'

'And he never said a word,' she said, her eyes filling with tears. 'He let me think I was being threatened.'

As he drove away from Fidelma's house, Irene rang, telling him she was sorry to bother him, but she had to talk to him about something, and would he mind dropping over now?

He groaned inwardly. He could have done with just going back home. It had been a busy and exhausting day. They had taken a statement from James Weston that morning. Fergus had agreed with Ned that arresting James would be premature. It was more important to work on getting their evidence straight because, for now, anyway, the press had no idea that anything was going on. And, Fergus had said, there was a big question mark over the anonymous letter-writer's role and motivation.

Ned was at a loss as to how he was going to track down whoever had been writing the letters, and Fergus hadn't been able to offer any advice beyond the suggestion that they set up hidden surveillance cameras at the house in Quay Street, the café and Eaglewood, to monitor any comings and goings. Ned told him he had already suggested that to Orla, but that he would mention it to Aidan, too, and make sure something was sorted out the following day.

Tiredness swept over him. He was tempted to tell Irene he was busy on an important matter and that he would drop in sometime the following day, but he knew that his stepmother would have given whatever she wanted to discuss with him a lot of consideration, and he felt obliged to go to her, there and then. In any case, it wasn't taking him far out of his way.

'I've been doing a lot of thinking and I don't want to stay here on my own,' she told him when the tea was poured and they were sitting down. 'I'm going back to Roscommon. I'll live with my sister. She's been rattling around that big house on her own since John died. So I'm making this place over to you.'

He sighed and shook his head in protest. He didn't want the house; the memories were mostly bad ones. Once Irene had gone, he never wanted to see it again.

'Listen, Irene – the house is yours. You've earned it. Sell it and go to Roscommon. Use the money on yourself,' he said, adding, 'I don't need the house and I don't want it, either.'

But she insisted. She had already instructed the solicitor to draw up the necessary documents. 'I'm well provided for. No, Ned, the house is yours by right. I won't change my mind.'

'And I won't, either, so we're going to be talking about this again. When were you thinking of going to Roscommon?'

'Oh, I don't know. Soon enough, I suppose. There's no point in hanging on when I've made up my mind. I'm not going to be taking much. Sure, what would I need at this hour of my life apart from a few skirts and cardigans and a couple of pairs of shoes?'

'Do something for me, Irene,' he said. 'Give it some more thought. You're still . . . in mourning. Don't make this kind of decision yet.'

'You were always a good boy. I was always very fond of you.'

The way she phrased her words made them sound like a farewell, he thought. And, in a way, it was a farewell. He knew her well. He had no doubt that she would leave and that, once she had left, she was unlikely to come back. He knew, too, that the likelihood of him driving across the country to Roscommon on anything like a regular basis was small.

'I was wondering,' she said, breaking into his thoughts, 'whether you might take a look through your father's things. In case you might want to keep anything. And, if you don't mind, can you take the rest to the Vincent de Paul?'

'Sure,' he said, standing up. 'Do you want to come up with me?'

'No. I have things to do down here. And I'd rather not,' she said. 'Here, take these bags with you. You'll need them for the clothes.

Upstairs, he stood in front of the wardrobe, an ancient mahogany affair with a mirrored panel between two doors – the kind of wardrobe you only saw these days in the houses of the elderly. Irene's clothes hung on the left-hand side and his father's to the right. He lifted out his father's suits and trousers, shirts and jackets in one big armful, and threw them on to the bed.

The chest of drawers was similarly segregated: drawers for Irene and drawers for his father. He took a pile of folded woollen jumpers out of it and put them on the bed, his nose taking in the old-man smell of them. And he winced, because, for a moment, the musty smell made him think of his father not as the rigid disciplinarian, full of physical strength, even in his later years, but as the weakened old man who had held on to his hand when he had given it.

He opened another drawer. It was stuffed with old vests and trunks, sad and pathetic relics of a different time. He couldn't have bought new underwear for years. No Calvin Kleins here. The underwear could go straight into the bin, but the other clothes were in relatively good nick and he folded them into the two big black bin bags and put them on the landing. He would drop them off at the Vincent de Paul shop.

He noticed that the door of his old room was slightly ajar. He hadn't stood inside it for years, and he was tempted just to pull the door shut and walk away. But he pushed it open and went in, ready to face whatever demons it would throw at him. Nothing happened. There was nothing there beyond a bed, a bookcase, a small wardrobe and a chest of drawers. Nothing of him remained in this room. It was only when he exhaled that he realised he had been holding his breath.

He wandered over to the window, and that was when the past came swooping back over him like a big black crow. He remembered the dark night of nineteen sixty-eight, when he had stood there, looking out, straining his eyes for the lights of a car in the far distance that might have been one of the local taxis bringing his mother home. He remembered, too, the long days and nights after that, when he had somehow known that she wasn't coming back, yet had nurtured a desperate hope that he was wrong and that she would just turn up out of the blue one afternoon, that when he came home from school he would see her on the doorstep and she would run to meet him and scoop him into her arms.

He was fifty-five now, not the child he once was, but it was all still there – all the tears and snot of the seven-year-old boy he had been – and it threatened to erupt now. He hurried away, out of the room, and pulled the door closed behind him.

Downstairs, Irene looked away when she saw the black bags. 'Thanks, Ned. I couldn't have done it myself,' she said.

He bent down to hug her and, as he put his arms around her, he was shocked by how thin and small her bones seemed. It was as if she was starting to shrink away.

The route he drove back home took him past Rose's house. He wondered what she was doing. He wondered whether he came into her thoughts the way she was breaking into his when he least expected.

Part of it, he was certain, was that he wanted to feel absolved for having treated her so badly, and surely what she had told him about her relationship meant that he could felt less guilt about the way he had left her. Because, even if neither of them knew it at the time, she hadn't really been into him, or men, at all. That's what he kept telling himself. But he knew it wasn't as simple as that. He felt that there was something else going on below the surface, and he'd had a sense of something being rekindled between them as they'd sat together in the pub the other night. Unless, of course, he was imagining it.

Chapter Thirty-One

I wanted so badly to believe James.

I knew now that it hadn't been our finances that had made him so tense and unapproachable for all those months, but the letters that had started to arrive soon after we came to live in Ardgreeney.

I wanted to believe him when he insisted that he had done Lillian no harm, that he hadn't even seen her.

He and I had been together for years and they had been good years. He was kind and loving. He wasn't a violent man.

But every time I began to soften towards him, every time I tried to understand the terrible predicament he was in, the thought of him and Lillian together was like a physical assault. I didn't know which of them I hated more.

And then the hate would dissipate and I would try to find excuses for why they had both betrayed me. Maybe I hadn't been attentive enough towards either of them. Maybe I had been too laid-back about my relationship with James and my friendship with Lillian. And then I would be overwhelmed again by my love for him and the urge to comfort him, and the whole cycle would repeat itself: my longing for James giving way to hatred and then being followed by self-recrimination.

And always there was my anguish over Patsy McLennan, whose terrible death still haunted me.

I was a mess.

'What's going to happen, Fidelma?' I asked my sister. 'If he's charged with murder . . .'

I couldn't finish the sentence. It was too horrible to think about.

'Do people know that the guards have been talking to James?' Fidelma asked.

'I don't know. I don't think so.'

'What about Aidan? Does he know?'

'I haven't talked to him, but maybe Inspector Moynihan has.'

'I've been doing a lot of thinking about all this,' Fidelma said. 'Let's just go through it. James has admitted to being in Ardgreeney the night Lillian went missing, but he didn't actually lie to the guards about that in the first place, because they never talked to him when it happened. He hasn't been charged with anything – not at this stage, anyway – and I suspect he isn't likely to be charged unless something more substantial turns up. He was in Ardgreeney. He says he came here to try to talk to Lillian, but, in the end, he didn't, and he went away. He says he never even saw Patsy McLennan. Did anyone see him go to Lillian's place?'

'Do you think the guards will start going around asking people about James, and whether they saw him? Oh, God.' I put my hands to my mouth in horror as a thought hit me. 'Do you think they might put a notice in the paper, asking for information?'

Fidelma bit her lower lip. 'It's possible, I suppose. But, come on, let's not get ahead of ourselves. My point is that, so far, the guards haven't come up with enough evidence even to arrest him. I'm not saying they won't find any, but I'd lay bets on that inspector of yours being careful enough to look beyond James. For example, if I were him, I'd be wanting to know who's been writing those letters, because there's something very sinister going on there. Take the letter you saw – maybe you were meant to think it was for you?'

'You mean . . . that whoever put it through the door must have waited for James to leave so that I'd be the one to find it and open it.'

'Exactly. Suppose this person *wanted* you to be the one to find the letter. James had been getting letters, too, but he kept that from you. Maybe this person wanted to make sure you knew.'

'But why?'

'To increase the pressure on James by making you frightened, maybe? I don't know, it's just an idea, but it kind of makes sense to me.'

'So . . . what are you saying?' I asked.

'I'm saying you don't have to make your mind up about anything. Not yet.'

I knew I'd have to talk to James, even if the thought of it turned my stomach. We agreed that I'd meet him at the house on Quay Street. I got there a few minutes early, ringing the doorbell to let him know I'd arrived. But I heard no movement from inside. He hadn't arrived back from the café yet. As I let myself in, I took a deep breath, as if anticipating some awful discovery. But everything was the same inside, apart from the place being unusually tidy. James had always been zealous about keeping the café in order, but at home he tended to be careless, often leaving mugs on the floor beside the sofa, newspapers strewn across the kitchen table, clothes on the backs of chairs.

I heard James's key turn in the door. When he came into the kitchen and saw me, his face momentarily lit up. But, just as quickly, the light went out of it, and he seemed so forlorn that my heart ached for him. He looked like a wounded animal. Could he really have killed Lillian? And Patsy, an elderly man who had done him no harm? But, even as I asked myself those questions, I reminded myself that he had had an affair with Lillian and I hadn't been even remotely suspicious. He had lied about his trip to Ardgreeney the night she disappeared. What else was he capable of? I shuddered.

'Hello,' he said.

'Hello,' I said, after a short pause.

We stood silently for what seemed like a long time, and then James asked me whether I'd like tea or coffee.

'I don't mind. Whichever you prefer,' I said.

I watched him fumble through the tea-making process, my feelings veering between pity and anger. It was the anger that I was feeling most when we finally sat down at the table.

I knew there was no point in asking him again whether he had killed Lillian. But there was another question that had been burning inside me, which I had to ask him.

'How did it start, you and Lillian?' The words tasted bitter in my mouth. 'And don't tell me it just *happened*. I want to know *how* it happened.'

'I'd just got off the train and you called to say you'd be at least a couple of hours late because some big story had landed and it was all hands on deck, but that Lillian would be home and she'd let me in. We opened a bottle of wine. And then we opened another bottle. We were pissed.'

I remembered that evening now. I'd worked a late shift and had got home to find James on the sofa, watching television. He was far from sober and he told me Lillian had drunk a lot more than he had and had already gone to bed. I had laughed, pleased that the two of them were getting on well. I was glad that James hadn't had to spend the evening alone, waiting for me to return from work.

'Who made the first move? Was it you?'

He shook his head. 'But that's no excuse.'

'No,' I said. 'It's no excuse.'

Inside, I was screaming at Lillian, hating her for being so selfish. I'd loved her like a sister and I thought she had loved me, too. No, I was sure she'd loved me. But maybe her moral boundaries had been set more widely apart than mine. Maybe she hadn't believed I was serious about him. Maybe she just couldn't help herself. She probably hadn't even thought she was doing anything wrong.

I was trying to find reasons to exonerate her. After all, she had dropped James for Aidan. Perhaps she would have dropped him, anyway, to avoid hurting me. But the cold, hard fact was that the friend I had loved all my life and was still mourning, ten years after her disappearance, had seduced James, and that was something I would never understand.

I looked at James. He was watching me anxiously, waiting, perhaps, for an explosion of anger and hoping that, once it was out, we could begin a process of repair. There was no explosion. What I felt now wasn't anger; I didn't have a name to put on it.

'Why did you want to come to live here?' I asked. 'I don't understand that.'

'It's hard to explain. When Fidelma told us about the café being up for sale, it just seemed as if things were falling into place for both of us. It seemed as if . . .' He hesitated.

'As if what?' I pushed.

'As if we were meant to be here. As if it was all part of something that would finally make sense.'

'And does it make sense? It certainly doesn't to me. Thanks for nothing, James. Thanks for ruining my life.'

He started to say something, but I raised my hand to stop him. I'd had enough. I couldn't bear to look at him or listen to him.

I got up, took my coat and walked out, closing the door quietly behind me.

Chapter Thirty-Two

His mother's cousin, Agnes, lived in a bungalow within sight of the farmhouse she had passed on to her son and his family. Ned's mother had been an only child, orphaned at the age of two and brought up by her aunt, who had three children of her own: two boys and a girl. The boys were no longer alive, but Agnes was a sprightly ninety-year-old, in full possession of her faculties.

'I suppose you want to talk about Mary?' she had asked him when he called her.

He had been slightly taken aback by her directness, the way she had ignored the niceties people normally observed when someone telephoned out of the blue. But, as she told him when he was finally sitting in front of her, drinking the strongest tea he had ever tasted, she didn't have time to shilly-shally around, making small talk.

'What do you want to know, so? Have you questions for me or will I just tell you about her?'

'Maybe you could just tell me about her,' Ned said. 'What she was like.'

'Do you not remember much about her?'

'I only have a few memories. I don't actually know very much about her.'

'Did your father not talk to you about her?'

He shook his head. 'No.'

'Well,' Agnes said, 'I must have been about ten when your mother came to live with us, and I had to mind her a lot of the time. She was like a little doll, but, even then, you could tell she had a great brain on her. She had questions about everything. She'd drive you mad sometimes, but in a good way.'

He smiled. He thought he knew what she meant.

'And she was mad about music. Always practising the piano. I can still see her little fingers flying around it.' She held up her own hands, splaying her fingers wide. 'Mine were like sausages. No wonder I was useless.'

All of a sudden, her relaxed mood changed and her face tightened in on itself.

'I don't want to speak ill of the dead,' she said, 'but it's a crying shame that she ever met that father of yours. He was no good. No good.'

Ned was shocked by the vehemence in her voice. 'What did he do to her?'

'Oh, he didn't do anything *to* her, as such. He didn't hit her or starve her. But he had it in for her. She told me.'

'But why? What had she done to him?'

Agnes looked at him, as if trying to size him up. 'What do you know about how they met and got married?' she asked.

He told her what he knew. His father and mother had met at a dance and got married just a few months later. His mother had told him they had to wait a couple of years for him to be born.

'And that's all she told you?'

'Is there more?' he asked, and even as his question floated on the air, he knew that it was a stupid one.

'It was what we called a shotgun wedding,' Agnes said. 'Oh, they seemed happy enough, and they had a story all ready about the child being born a couple of months early . . .'

Shotgun wedding? Child? Ned felt palpitations in his chest. His breathing became shallow.

Agnes must have seen his distress because she rose and went to the kitchen, returning with a small glass of brandy.

'Have a sip of that,' she said. 'Tea's all very well, but there's nothing like this stuff when you've had a bit of a shock.'

He took a few sips of the brandy and sat back in the armchair.

'I'm fine. It's all right. Go on,' he said. 'And the child? What happened to it? Have I got a sibling somewhere?'

Agnes shook her head and resumed her story.

'She lost the child a few months in, sad to say. Devastated, she was. And that's when your father showed his true colours. He told her she'd ruined his life by tricking him into marriage, and now there was no need for him to have married her, after all.'

'She told you all that?'

'She did. We were like sisters,' she said. 'And she told me more besides. She took the loss of that child hard, you see. She had a spell in hospital with her nerves, before you were born. And she went in a few times after that, too, God love her. Was it any wonder she took to the drink? I don't blame her for it one bit. I'd have drunk Ireland dry if I'd been in her place. He had no kindness in him, that father of yours, and I hope you won't mind my saying it. Not one ounce of kindness.'

'No . . . he wasn't a kind man,' Ned said. 'Not to my mother and not to me, anyway.'

He was thinking of Irene, now. She had loved his father, had grieved for him and was still grieving. His father had been kind to her; he must have been. Maybe he should tell this to Agnes. But what would be the point? Agnes wouldn't change her mind about his father. She might hate him even more.

'When she went missing . . . what did you think?' Ned asked. 'Did you think she'd just run off because she couldn't stand it – couldn't stand him – any more?'

'I don't know what I thought at the time. Your father came over, demanding to know whether she was at our house. She wasn't, of course. And then he went off. It wasn't the first time he'd come looking for her – he expected her to be there, waiting for him, with his food on the table – so we weren't too worried. And then, well, we never saw her again.'

'Did you think she might have . . . done away with herself?'

'I didn't want to think it at the time. But what other explanation is there? I'll tell you one thing: she'd never have just gone off, leaving you behind.'

They both fell silent. He didn't know what Agnes was thinking. His own mind was still filled with questions, but what Agnes had just told him – that his mother would never have gone away and abandoned him – gave him a strange kind of comfort.

'Can I keep in touch with you? Come in and see you every now and again?' Ned asked, as he was leaving.

'You can come whenever you like. I'll be here for a few years yet,' she said.

She stood at the door and watched him get into his car. As he wound down the window, before driving away, he heard her voice, strong and clear, above the wind:

'You're the spit of your mother.'

Agnes's revelations burned like wild fires inside him. They crackled and blazed, making all his nerve endings scream in pain. But he understood now. Edward Moynihan, as if he had forgotten his own part in the story of mutual attraction that had led to an unplanned pregnancy, had seen his marriage as something that need never have happened. Ned imagined him filled not with grief for the child never born, but with resentment and distaste for the woman who had tricked him. What Ned didn't quite understand was why his father had resented him, too; but, he thought, maybe his very existence was a constant affront to a man who felt imprisoned by his marriage.

And what of his mother? Had she felt so trapped, so ground down by her marriage that she had consciously chosen to end her life, even if it would mean her son growing up without a mother? Maybe she had thought Edward Moynihan would be kinder to him if she weren't around.

These were painful questions, but he had to ask them. And he had to keep asking them while his feelings were so raw. He called Rose.

'How's Barney?' he asked.

'He hasn't got any worse since you were last here.'

'Would it be all right if I dropped in for a chat with him? And you, too, of course.'

'Sure. We'll both be delighted to see you. I'll put the kettle on.'

The sound of Rose's voice had raised his spirits. They could be friends – they *were* friends, he thought. Okay, there had been a years-long gap in the friendship, but surely some of what had drawn them together in the first place, when they were young, was still there? Maybe they should never have been anything but friends. Maybe they had mistaken friendship for romance. And if it hadn't been Eily who had blasted him out of that cosy, not intensely romantic relationship, it would probably have been someone else.

Barney looked happy to see him, and he realised that he was happy to see Barney. Somehow, they'd got over the years of estrangement and were easy with each other.

They talked about the new developments in the Lillian Murray case.

'Do you think James Weston is your man, then?' Barney asked.

'I don't know. I don't have any feel for this at all. I think I might be losing my touch.'

'I hear you've been talking about a sabbatical. Might that be a trial retirement, by any chance?'

'Jesus, Barney, no flies on you. They should have made you Garda Commissioner, and for life.'

Barney laughed heartily, and Ned marvelled that a man in the final months, maybe even weeks of his life could laugh like that. But the Lillian Murray case wasn't the only thing he wanted to talk to Barney about.

'I wanted to ask you something, Barney. I was wondering whether you remembered anything about ... the time my mother went missing.'

'Well, now, I wasn't expecting you to ask that,' Barney said. 'It was a long time ago. I'm not sure I remember much. What do you want to know?'

'How long the guards looked for her. What they thought. Whatever you can remember.'

Barney scratched his head. 'I never met your mother, but – and you'll forgive me for saying this – people said she was a bit on the highly-strung side. And she was in that place – near Crossakiel – with her nerves, a couple of times. So, from day one, the thinking was that she took a fit of the janglers and just went off somewhere and would show up–' He stopped abruptly, as if something had just struck him. 'In fact, that uncle of your father's, the priest, said he thought he'd seen her in Ardgreeney. He wasn't sure, but it made everyone think that at least no harm had come to her.'

Ned had never heard this before – Father Jack's sighting of his mother.

'When did he say this?'

'After your father reported her missing. A couple of lads went round to the house to talk to him, and the priest – Father Jack, wasn't that his name? – was there. That's what he'd said – that he thought he'd seen her going into a shop, earlier in the afternoon, when he was driving through the town.'

'But – are you sure? No one ever told me that. It just doesn't make sense. If he knew everyone was looking for her, why didn't he stop and check whether it was her he saw?'

'He saw her – or thought he did – before he knew she'd gone missing. Maybe he was mistaken. Sadly, we'll never know.'

'When did everyone stop looking for her, Barney? When did the guards give up?'

'I can't rightly remember, Ned, but I have to confess, I was never happy with the way the whole thing was conducted. Everyone was far too ready to go along with the idea that she'd had a bit of breakdown and that she'd turn up somewhere a day a two later.'

'So they didn't do very much at all,' Ned said, bitterly.

'No. But, Ned, you have to remember they were different times. We didn't have computers. We didn't have mobile phones and the like. I'm not making excuses, but you've seen it yourself, the way things have changed and improved.'

'Why didn't you tell me all this when I was going out with Rose, years ago?' Ned asked.

Barney sighed. 'I should have told you. I know that. But, at the time . . . I didn't think any good could come of it. I'm sorry.'

'It's all right, Barney,' Ned said. It wasn't all right, but what was the point now in saying anything else? 'Look, I think I'll ask Rose if she'll come to the pub for a drink. If you don't mind?'

'Go on,' Barney said, waving him away.

Rose insisted on getting the drinks in the pub. He watched her as she waited for the pints, joining in the patter among the several elderly men sitting at the bar. How much easier life might have been with Rose, he thought. No shouting matches, no recriminations. She was the daughter of a guard. She would have understood that his dedication to the job didn't mean relegation to second place for her and the kids. There might not have been great passion, but, then, look where his love-at-first-sight great passion had got him.

'Did you have a good chat with Dad?' Rose asked, when she was sitting down beside him, the two pints in front of them.

'He told me something I didn't know.'

She raised her eyebrows.

'About the time my mother . . . went missing.'

'Do you want to talk about it?'

He shook his head. 'I don't think so. I have to get my head around it first. Thanks, though.'

She didn't seem to be offended by his reluctance to confide in her. He liked that in her, had always liked that in her. He remembered that, when they were courting, all those years ago, she was always easy to be with. They had enjoyed each other's company. They had laughed a lot. He had never had to tread on eggshells around her.

She hadn't been the jealous type, either. Whenever Eily had seen him talking to other women, especially if they were attractive, she had always interrupted the conversation and then grilled him later as to whether he fancied them. Not Rose. Although, when he was falling in love with Eily, Rose must have noticed that things were changing between them. Maybe she had guessed that he was seeing someone else, but had assumed she could simply wait it out, because it was probably a fling that wouldn't last.

How hurt she must have been. He cringed, remembering how he had told her about Eily. *I've met someone.* That's how he had said it, blurting it out. Oh, the crassness of it. And how dignified she had been. She hadn't cried or pleaded. She hadn't called him a shit. She had been gracious in heartbreak, and she was gracious now, accepting him, sitting here with him.

'You're looking very thoughtful,' she said, smiling.

'I'm thinking about the old days, when you and I were together. I didn't behave well.'

'No. But, as Dad told you, it's water under the bridge. A lot has happened since then. We're not the same people.'

'Aren't we?'

'No.'

'But we can be friends?'

'We'll always be friends, Ned.'

She looked directly at him as she said this. There was a smile in her eyes and on her lips. But he thought he saw something else, too, something that made him want to lean forward. He didn't, of course, because what they once had was over and he didn't dare. He smiled back and lifted his pint in a salute, because he didn't know what else to do.

Chapter Thirty-Three

I had no plan when I closed the door behind me. I seemed to be moving on autopilot and I found myself on the strand, walking towards Eagle Head. But, while my body was moving of its own accord, without any clear direction from me, my mind was overwhelmed by conflicting feelings of hurt and hate, helplessness and anger. And hopelessness. I couldn't stay in Ardgreeney, but where could I go?

I left the strand and climbed up on to the headland, where the wind cut through me like a knife, but it was cleansing, just as the salt on my tongue cleared away the bitter taste in my mouth. I was still standing there when I heard my name carried on the wind. I turned around to see Aidan striding towards me.

He was smiling. But the smile changed quickly to a frown as he came closer.

'What's happened?' he asked. 'You look as though you've been through something terrible.'

'I have,' I said. And I began to cry salty tears that even the strong wind couldn't blow away.

Aidan put his arms around me and hugged me tightly. 'Come on, let's get you to Eaglewood and we'll talk about it.'

We sat at the table in the kitchen. I had drunk most of a glass of brandy before I could tell him anything, and when I did start speaking, I sounded distant, as if mine was a disembodied voice coming from the radio, telling a story.

'James and Lillian had an affair,' I said, adding, when I saw the expression on his face flicker between incredulity and shock, 'but it was before she met you.'

'But . . . that can't be true! How do you know that?'

'James told me. And it's true. But . . . that's not the only thing. Aidan, I can't bear to tell you this – and maybe you know something already from Inspector Moynihan – '

'What do you mean, "know something from Inspector Moynihan"?'

'Or maybe he doesn't want anyone to know yet. James was in Ardgreeney the night Lillian disappeared. He wanted to persuade her to . . . Oh, I don't know what he wanted to persuade her to do. Go back to him. Leave you.'

Aidan's face was frozen in an expression of disbelief. His reaction seemed to mirror my own, when James told me his story.

'He says he didn't talk to her, after all, and that he drove back up to the north and got the ferry back to Scotland. But . . . Aidan, the guards are looking at him.'

'You mean . . .' he said, in a voice that seemed to struggle to come out. 'You mean that the guards think James killed Lillian?'

'I don't know if they really think that, but they're investigating him. He swears he never harmed her.'

'Jesus, Orla; I thought the worst time of my life was over, that nothing as bad as that could ever happen again . . . I'm sorry; I have to go outside.'

He stumbled out of the room and I heard the front door slam.

I waited a long time for him to come back and, when he didn't, I went outside to look for him. He wasn't by the front door, where I had thought he would be. I walked around the back, to the stables, and that was where I made out his shape in the darkness, head bowed, sitting on a mounting block in the middle of the yard. He turned around as I approached.

'I shouldn't have left you alone just now. I was only thinking about myself, but you're suffering, too,' he said.

He shifted slightly on the mounting block and I perched beside him.

'What do you think, Orla? Did he kill her? You know him better than anyone.'

I opened my mouth to speak and, as my breath escaped, it made wispy ghosts in the cold air, ethereal shapes that vanished into the darkness. They seemed to represent everything I had thought was real and true – like James; like Lillian.

'I don't know him at all,' I said. 'Anyway, I've . . . I've left him. I can't be with him, knowing that, at best, he lied to me and, at worst . . .'

I didn't finish. Aidan took my hand and led me inside. I went with him willingly. I no longer had any feelings of guilt about betraying James and Lillian, because they had betrayed me a long time ago.

Later, as Aidan cooked supper, a text landed from Fidelma.

> How did it go with James? Are you OK?
> It wasn't fun. Am at Aidan's. Will prbly stay night. x
> Is that wise? Call me.
> Can't talk now. Don't be cross. See you tomorrow. x

I didn't wait for her response, but turned my phone off.

We talked a lot and we drank a lot, and when I woke the following morning the daylight coming through the window and the cold empty space beside me in the bed told me that Aidan had probably been up for several hours. I stared into Lillian's eyes and, for a moment, that sense of having done something wrong came into my head. But, just as quickly, another feeling replaced it, and I mouthed the words, 'Fucking bitch!'

There was a text from James on my phone. It asked me whether I was all right and would I please call him, just to let him know that I was okay.

I snorted. *Okay*? How could I be *okay*? I was falling apart at the seams. I deleted the text without replying.

There was nothing from Fidelma.

I pulled on my clothes and wandered down to the yard, where I knew Aidan would be. Andrea and Tom were with him. Of course. It was Sunday. I looked at Tom, who seemed to be listening intently to Aidan. Was it really possible that this kid could be behind the letters? He had certainly had the opportunity. But the motive? I was reluctant to talk to Inspector

Moynihan about Tom, but there was no harm in talking to Aidan about him. More likely than not, Aidan would laugh his head off.

'Orla! Good morning. Have you had breakfast yet?' Aidan called out as he saw me approach. Then, turning to Tom and Andrea, he said, 'You remember Orla, don't you?'

They both mumbled hello, but I could tell they were embarrassed. Aidan's question about whether I'd had breakfast had told them more than they needed to know.

'I'll come and show you how that coffee maker works. It's a bit temperamental. Andrea and Tom, can you start tacking up for the ten o'clock ride?'

In the kitchen, he pulled me to him and kissed me, and then made me sit down while he made toast and coffee.

'The coffee maker works perfectly,' he said. 'I just wanted to come in with you. And I wanted to ask you to stay. For a day. For a few days. For as long as you like. Because I think we need each other right now. Do you not feel that?'

I did feel it. My sister was wonderful, but she didn't – *couldn't* – understand exactly how I felt. The only person I could really share this terrible burden with was Aidan. But I knew I should go back to Fidelma. She and I had become closer than I could ever have imagined. I didn't want to lose that closeness and I was afraid she might think I'd been using her.

'I'd like to, but I really need to talk to Fidelma about a few things. And I need to do some work.'

'Shame. But I understand,' he said, kissing me on the forehead and then beginning to pour the coffee.

'Listen, Aidan,' I said. 'I know this might sound a bit odd, and

I have to say that I think Fidelma is off the wall, but . . . do you think Tom might be the person writing those letters?'

A look of incredulity spread across his face.

'Tom? Why would Tom send anonymous letters?'

'It's something Fidelma came up with. We saw him on the road the other day and gave him a lift because it was lashing rain. She wonders whether he sees me as some kind of interloper. I honestly don't think so – I mean, look at him – he's just a kid and you said yourself that he's planning to go off to university. But I thought I'd mention it to you.'

He looked thoughtful for a few moments.

'I'll keep an eye on Tom, but he's not the type to do that kind of stuff. And, even if he had sent letters to you and me, why would he have sent letters to Ned Moynihan? He wouldn't even have been ten years of age when . . . when all that happened.'

He drank his coffee quickly and got up from the table.

'I wish I didn't have to work today,' he said. 'Look, why don't you come over tomorrow morning? The stables will be closed and we can go out for a ride. It would do you good.'

'Okay,' I agreed.

I stayed in the house for another couple of hours. Being at Eaglewood, away from James and from Fidelma, and even from Aidan himself, felt like being on holiday from the world and, strangely, from the emotional turmoil I'd been suffering. I lay back on one of the big sofas in the drawing room, doing nothing. I heard cars come and go and, sometimes, the sound of hooves clip-clopping as Aidan led a ride out. Sometimes, I dozed off. Eventually though, it was time to go.

*

No sooner had I walked through Fidelma's front door than she was in front of me, looking annoyed but anxious.

'Did you sleep with him?' she asked.

I didn't answer.

'Oh, God – how's that going to look?'

'I'm beyond caring, at this point,' I told her. 'Oh, Fidelma; I'm sorry! I don't mean that. But it's just that he's been on the receiving end of all this stuff as well. I can talk to him.'

It struck me then that Aidan and I hadn't actually done much talking – not once had I told him what I knew. But then, I thought, we didn't need to talk about it, because it all came down to each of us simply understanding what the other was going through.

I told her about my meeting with James the previous day, how his and Lillian's treachery had begun in the flat she and I had shared. How Lillian had made the first move.

'But I can't just blame *her*. He went along with it. I'm sorry to keep going on about it, but you just can't imagine what that feels like – your partner and your best friend doing all that behind your back,' I said.

'I can, actually,' Fidelma said. 'Several times over. Harry slept with every friend I ever had.'

'I'm sorry. I never guessed . . . I never asked.'

'And I never told you. What I'm trying to say is that I understand more than you think I do. Okay?'

'Okay.'

As Fidelma bustled around in the kitchen, I thought about Aidan and how easy we had been in each other's company. He had seemed so content, even happy, to have me at Eaglewood. But I knew that was an illusion. How could he be happy? How could either of us ever be happy again?

Chapter Thirty-Four

Ned was busy, but he called Irene, as he did every couple of days, to see how she was coping. She told him she was coping fine, that she was still intent on giving him the house and moving to Roscommon, but that she would do as he had asked and leave it for a little while before legally passing the house over to him. She was keeping herself occupied and neighbours were dropping in regularly for chats.

'I'll drop over myself in the next day or two,' he said, preparing to end the call.

'I don't suppose you could come now,' she said. 'There's something I want to talk to you about, and I don't want to talk about it on the phone.'

It wasn't ideal timing, but he knew her well enough to know that whatever she wanted to discuss with him was important – to her, at least. He would humour her.

He wondered what this latest request was all about. He had

dealt with his father's clothes and they'd put the issue of the house on hold. Maybe she just wanted to talk about her life with his father and how much she missed him. Maybe it was as simple as that, even if he couldn't understand why she had ever managed to love a man like Edward Moynihan.

He had never seen his father touch Irene affectionately, hold her hand or let an arm fall around her shoulder. Still, there must have been a strong bond between them. He supposed she must have unlocked something in his father, something that became apparent only when they were alone.

And his mother? Had she had to keep searching for the key to his father's heart, only to find that it didn't exist for her? Ned didn't remember a lot about the way his parents were with each other, only the way they were with him, and he thought of his mother as warm and loving, and his father as cold – as cold and hard as the rocks at the side of the headland. Agnes had said that Edward Moynihan saw his marriage as a trap and punished his wife by being distant and domineering. But had he had a change of heart when she was no longer there? Had he realised the depth of his loss and responded by retreating deeper into himself and turning to drink? And then, when Irene came along, had he understood that she was offering him a chance he couldn't turn down?

Ned had grown to love Irene, although she couldn't replace his mother. He had fought against her initially, but she had slowly gathered him to her and mended him. She'd been a teacher, which was how his father came to meet her at one of those annual conventions that moved around the country.

Irene had been on the scene for years before Ned's mother

could be declared dead and his father was free to marry her, and he wondered now whether she was going to confess to him that she had slept in his father's bed for all those years they were supposed to be just courting. The lie they had maintained was that Irene slept in a spare room when she came to visit for a few days, and that had seemed to satisfy everyone. She did, indeed, have a room of her own when she came to stay, but Ned had known that she rarely slept in it.

Now he was parking the car outside the house and Irene had the front door open before he had even turned off the engine.

'Come in, Ned,' she said.

There was something different about her, something he couldn't quite put his finger on. She was leading him to the sitting room – the parlour, as she called it – instead of the kitchen, which had always been the hub of the house. All of a sudden, she seemed older than her seventy-eight years, and shakier, too – which, he supposed, wasn't all that surprising, given that she'd had to look after his father, watch him die, bury him and then, when all the fuss was over, let it all sink in and get used to being on her own.

He wondered whether she kept seeing, in her mind, snapshots of happy times, just as his own memories of that last morning with his mother still ran like a reel of film in his head, repeating over and over.

The sitting room had a smell to it, not unpleasant, but suggestive of an industrial-scale bout of cleaning and polishing, followed by months of disuse with door and windows closed. He couldn't remember when he had last been in this room. Looking around it now, he felt a great sadness as he took in the ancient patterned carpet, the beige sofa and matching armchairs, the picture of the Sacred Heart above the fireplace, the upright piano that his mother had played and the long-broken radiogram that still occupied almost an entire wall.

'Sit down and I'll make the tea,' Irene said.

She was treating him as if he were an important visitor rather than someone who had grown up in this house and had always veered naturally towards the kitchen. But he humoured her, because it was clear that she was anxious about whatever it was she wanted to talk about. Oh, God; I hope she's not going to tell me she's dying, he thought.

While he waited for her to return with the tea and, no doubt, the scones or cake she had probably put into the oven within minutes of calling him, he walked over to the piano, lifted the lid and sat down on the stool. He remembered the way his mother used to hold her hands above the keyboard for a few seconds before inclining her head forward and to one side, as if giving the signal to her hands to fall on to the keys and draw the music out of them.

He closed the piano and turned his attention to the radiogram, with its turntable and stack of old vinyl long-playing records.

Most of them were his father's, and most of them were compilations of light classical music, bought from *Reader's Digest*. Mozart's *Eine kleine Nachtmusik*. Strauss waltzes. He moved on to his mother's LPs: Ella Fitzgerald, Frank Sinatra, Louis Armstrong. And then he looked at his own small collection, a mishmash of pop and heavy metal and jazz that charted his passage from child to adult.

He got a bit of a jolt when he saw the Peggy Lee album, and his eyes immediately fixed on one song: 'Is That All There Is?' He had rushed out and bought it after hearing it on the radio, because it had struck something in him, addressed the emptiness and sense of loss that he couldn't shake. He used to play that song endlessly when he was in his teens, asking himself what the whole fucking point of everything was.

The clattering of cups and saucers brought him back to the present and he rushed to help Irene with the heavy tray. There was a lot of fussing as she cut the sponge cake, which was still warm from the oven, insisting that one slice wouldn't be enough for a big man like him and that he must have at least two. It was an excellent cake, well up to her high standards of baking. But he noticed that she didn't touch the slice she had cut for herself and that her hand was shaking so much as she lifted her cup that she was in danger of spilling its contents. He reached out a hand, took the cup and saucer from her and put them down on the coffee table.

'What's wrong, Irene?' he asked. 'You're starting to worry me.'

She looked at him, her eyes dark and wet and her face troubled, and took several deep breaths.

'I wasn't going to tell you this, but I haven't been able to sleep, worrying about it ... He told me not to say anything, and you're supposed to respect the wishes of the dying, but ...'

'It's all right, Irene. Really. You don't have to tell me anything if it upsets you.'

'No, I have to ... I know it's the right thing to do. And if I don't tell you, you'll never know.'

*

289

He managed to get himself home somehow. The minute he closed the front door behind him, he went straight to the bottle of whiskey. All he wanted to do was blot out everything that was in his head. But the whiskey couldn't soften the images that had assembled in his mind as Irene told him what his father had told her while he was dying but still conscious.

His mother, in her blue dress.

His father, stern in the old-fashioned tweed jacket he wore at school, even on the warmest summer days.

An argument.

A blow.

A fall.

The cracking of her head as it hit the tiles of the fireplace in the very room where he had sat drinking tea and eating cake with Irene as she told him about it.

A mad fucking ABC of what Irene said had been 'an accident'.

His father had come home from school at lunchtime to pick up something he had forgotten. His mother was drunk, dancing to her records in the sitting room. *Stotious* was the word Irene said his father had used. It wasn't the first time, she said. His mother was an alcoholic and God knew what else. She had mental problems; she had been in the hospital a few times with them. His father was at the end of his tether. He shouted at her. She shouted back. He raised his hand and hit her – not a heavy blow, but she fell back on to the hard tiles. She didn't move. She was still. She was dead. His father panicked. He thought about calling the guards, but was afraid they wouldn't believe it was an accident. So he put her in the boot of the car and went back to the school.

Ned remembered being unable to speak as he listened to Irene, incapable of interrupting the ghastly, unthinkable story she was telling him in full frantic flow. She had spoken so fast that she was unstoppable.

He knew now that, when he arrived home from school that day to the empty house, his mother was already dead, and that, when his father drove off, ostensibly to try to find her, he was taking her body away.

'Where did he take her?'

He was shouting now, and Irene shrank back, her face masked by fear.

'Sorry – I'm sorry,' he told her. 'Please, I won't shout. Just tell me . . . where?'

'I don't know,' she sobbed. 'I don't know, because he didn't tell me. He said . . . it was best that way.'

'And you believed him? That it was an accident?'

'I did, Ned! I did! I still believe him. He wouldn't have lied. Not to me.'

All those hours his father had been gone; Ned remembered that it had been light when he left and dark when he had come back. Where had he gone? Had he driven around for hours, trying to find a spot where she wouldn't be found? Unexpectedly and bizarrely, something came into Ned's mind: an old piece of lore he had learned in geography class about no part of Ireland being more than sixty-five miles from the sea. And then he heard a blackly comic voice in his head saying that the addition of all the roundabouts in the country had probably increased the sixty-five miles to a hundred.

Ned couldn't listen to Irene for another second. He told her he would come back the following day, that he was sorry to leave her in the state she was in, but he had to get away. He had driven like a maniac, his mind a torment and, behind his eyes, a pain so sharp that he felt sick and dizzy.

The images wouldn't go away. They kept flashing up in front of him all the way back to his house, and they were still flashing up in front of him now, as he sat sprawled across the sofa, a glass of whiskey in his hand and the bottle close by. There were other images, too, that he couldn't handle. His mother, drunk. His mother in the mental hospital. He had no recollection of ever having seen her drunk. He couldn't remember her ever having been away.

He couldn't believe this stuff. It was impossible. And yet something nagged at him, something he felt he should be able to grasp, but couldn't quite. Something that acknowledged the truth of what Irene had told him.

All his life, since that awful day in nineteen sixty-eight, his mother's disappearance had haunted him. Now, he was possessed of a terrible knowledge and he didn't know what to do with it. So he picked up the bottle and poured what was left of it into the glass.

He remembered that a lot of whiskey had been drunk that night his mother disappeared. He remembered that the first person to turn up at the house was his uncle, Father Jack.

Father Jack had liked his whiskey. Ned had watched as he drank glass after glass. And Ned saw that his father, who wasn't a big drinker, seemed to be matching the priest glass for glass.

They took no notice of him as they talked. He might as well

have been invisible. But, after a while, Father Jack turned to look at him.

'Go on, now, to your room; there's a good lad,' he said. 'Your father and I have a few things to talk about.'

So he had gone to his room and stood by the window, looking out and hoping he would see his mother turn in through the gate. But it was pitch dark and he couldn't see a thing. It was cold, too. Perishing. That was what he had heard Father Jack say to his father when he'd hurried into the house from his big black Ford Zodiac, rubbing his hands hard together and stomping straight to the electric heater. 'Christ almighty, man, this thing must be eating up the money.'

He couldn't remember how long he had waited upstairs. His mind had been everywhere and nowhere. Every so often, he would become aware of the distant buzz of conversation that came from downstairs, but the house was too big for him to make out what they were saying. Maybe they'd been saying the rosary. His uncle had great devotion to the Virgin Mary, his mother had often said with a big smile on her face. He thought she might have been making fun of Father Jack to his father when she said things like that.

When he'd heard the sound of another car engine, he thought it might be his mother coming home in a taxi. Maybe she had just gone to Dublin for the day and had forgotten to tell anyone. His heart was a little lighter as the car drew nearer. But when it came in through the gate, he saw the sign *GARDA* on it. Two guards got out of it and he heard them knock on the door, heard the door open and Father Jack's voice greeting them. He would have liked to have gone down and looked at the car, a

Vauxhall Victor. He wondered whether they might let him sit in it and play with the siren. But then his thoughts went back to his mother and he knew now for sure that, if the guards were here, something very bad had happened to her.

He'd wondered whether the guards might want to talk to him, so he went over and over, again and again, everything that had happened that day. Saying goodbye to her in the morning and going to school; coming home in the afternoon and finding the door closed and the house empty; his father coming home from school and then going away again. But they didn't call him downstairs and eventually he heard them drive away, without flashing the blue light or turning the siren on.

Father Jack and his father came upstairs.

'Now, Ned, how would you like to come back with me?' Father Jack asked him.

He looked at his father, waiting for a signal from him. But there was none. So he shook his head.

'He'd be far better off coming with me. He'd have Mrs McElroy to look after him for a few days,' Father Jack said.

'I know, but ... I'm not going to make him. It's going to be hard enough for him,' his father said.

The three of them had gone downstairs then, and his father heated up a pot of soup that his mother had made the day before, and they had it with bread and cheese. It was the first thing Ned had eaten since breakfast.

Father Jack came a lot, after that. He took Ned for spins in the Zodiac and sometimes they stopped and had ice cream, even though it was winter. The guards came a couple of times and sat in the kitchen, drinking tea with his father and, when

Father Jack was around, whiskey as well. Another man came, too, a younger man, and Ned recognised him as one of the men who were in the house the time his mother had played the song about De Valera.

Father Jack was long dead now. How much had he known? Had Edward Moynihan fed him the lie that his highly-strung wife had simply walked out, or had he told him what really happened? Had Father Jack helped him? Had Father Jack lied to the guards about having seen Mary Moynihan in a shop on the day she went missing? There would be no justice for his mother now, Ned thought bitterly. But even worse than that was the knowledge that her body had been disposed of somewhere it wouldn't be found, and that his father had denied him the comfort of a grave by which he could mourn.

Chapter Thirty-Five

I went back to Eaglewood on Monday morning and we tacked up and rode out on to the headland. The ride started out well, but the ground was uneven and muddy. Every time Freddy stumbled or slipped, I gasped, sure he was going to fall.

'Relax,' Aidan said. 'Freddy is out here every day of his life. He knows it well and he's not going to fall or do anything mad. He's far too lazy for that.'

As we trekked towards the highest point on the headland, I allowed myself to settle down as Freddy picked his way up through the boggy ground and the gorse. At the top, we dismounted and walked towards the furthest point on the headland, where the drop to the rocks below was sheer.

I went as close to the edge as I could without feeling dizzy. I could imagine only too well what it would be like to lose my footing and fall towards those vicious rocks. I shuddered.

'Are you all right?' Aidan asked.

'I'm fine.'

I wasn't fine and I knew he wasn't, either. I was getting to know that his way of dealing with grief and loss was to put up an I'm-all-right front.

'Did you come up here with Lillian?' I asked.

'A few times. But we walked up. She didn't like riding.'

'Do you hate her now?'

'No. I've been thinking about it. Her thing with James was before she and I got together. He was the one who couldn't let it go.'

'You don't think it continued?'

'No,' he said, his voice firm. But then he asked, 'Do you?' and I thought I heard a note of doubt.

I was tempted to tell him that, if she could betray me, she could betray him. But I shook my head instead.

We mounted again and began the descent towards Eaglewood. The incline wasn't steep, but Freddy seemed to stumble more frequently on the uneven, muddy ground than he had on the way up.

'You're doing fine,' Aidan said in encouragement. 'Freddy has been up here more times than I can count. He knows every inch of it. Trust him.'

I tried to relax. I looked at Aidan. He was comfortable on Petra, allowing her to decide where to put her feet. I managed a smile, but I was still tense. All too easily, I could imagine Freddy making a mistake – a mistake that would send the two of us tumbling down the hillside.

When it happened, it was so fast that I didn't have time to think about being frightened. Freddy stumbled heavily and I lost my own balance. He found his footing, but it was too late for me. I was falling, falling in slow motion. And then I felt the ground slap me.

My head is spinning. I see Lillian's face in front of me. I feel her hands against my shoulders, putting pressure on them.

Why is she pushing me away from the door?

I'm ill and exhausted. All I want to do is collapse into my bed. My headache is so bad and I'm feeling so dizzy that it's taken me several tries before I've managed to get the key into the lock.

But now Lillian is in front of me. She won't let me into the flat. 'No,' she's saying, 'you can't come in! You've got to go to the pub. Please! I'll see you there in a while.'

She's wearing a bathrobe and her face is flushed. Ah. Now I get it. But why is she being so coy about having some man in her room?

'Don't be silly, Lil,' I say.

And, even though my headache is getting worse by the second, I can't help smiling at her unusual display of modesty.

I try to push past her into the flat, but she keeps up the pressure on my shoulders. And now I'm trying to keep my balance, but I can't, and as I tumble down the stairs to the next landing, the last thing I see is her look of horror and the familiar face that appears behind her.

'Orla! Orla!'

For a second, I wondered who was shouting my name. I squinted into the low winter sun and made out Aidan's face. The worst thing had happened – I had had a fall. But I was still in one piece.

'Are you all right?'

'I think so,' I said.

But, in the space of an instant, I knew I wasn't all right, because now I remembered. I remembered in horrific detail why I had fallen down the stairs in Maida Vale. Lillian had pushed me. And James had watched her.

I looked up at Aidan.

'I think I'm going to be sick,' I said.

Chapter Thirty-Six

The pain in his head was excruciating. Ned was on the sofa, fully dressed, half lying, half sitting. He looked at the clock, which told him that he must have slept for hours after returning from Bellaher and drinking himself almost unconscious. He hauled himself into an upright position and the movement made him feel a rush of nausea. The nausea was almost a relief because he had to think about it for a few seconds, had to decide whether to race to the bathroom to throw up or wait and hope it would pass. He waited and it passed, and then everything came flying back at him. He groaned and sank back into the sofa and cried like a baby – long, loud wails that nobody could hear.

He tried to banish the images, but they refused to go away. They were multiplying, taking on a life of their own. He saw his father now, lifting his mother's body and putting her in the boot of the car, leaving her there by herself all afternoon. He saw him drive her body away, pretending he was going to search for her and telling Ned not to leave the house. He had thought his father wanted him to stay there in case his mother came back. Now, he knew that his father hadn't wanted him to talk to anyone or raise the alarm before he had got rid of his wife's body. In his mind's eye, he saw his father as he was then, looking tragic and stoical at the same time. Hypocrite.

But the strongest image of all now was of his mother on that final morning. She was in her blue dress with the shiny mother-of-pearl buttons, waiting for him in the kitchen. She laughed at his inside-out jumper, and he laughed, too. It was all the same as before, except this time, when she wrapped her arms around him as he left for school, he didn't wriggle out of her embrace.

For one terrifying moment, his mind was blank. The room was dark. He didn't know where he was. Worse, he didn't know who he was. And then, in a second, it all came flooding back and he groaned. Something – someone – stirred beside him. Another blank moment. But, as he felt her back against his side and her feet against his legs, he started to remember.

He had stumbled and staggered to her door the night before, had hesitated about disturbing her. But he had to see her. When he rang the doorbell, she answered at once. She led him inside, putting her finger to her lips as they passed the front room.

'Dad sleeps in there, now. It's easier for him if he doesn't have to go up and down the stairs,' she whispered.

In the kitchen, she made him sit down and poured him a brandy. He told her everything and she listened, her face a constantly changing picture of disbelief and revulsion.

'Oh, Ned,' she said, when he had finished his appalling story. 'What would you like me to do? Maybe we should talk to Dad?'

'No, don't. Don't tell anyone. I'll do it some day, but not now. I have to think of Irene,' he said. 'I shouldn't have put this burden on you. I'm sorry. I needed to talk . . .'

He made to leave then, apologising for having turned up so late and without warning, and for having forced her to listen to his terrible story. But she stopped him.

'I'm not letting you go home in the state you're in,' she said.

He didn't argue. He was too weak.

They went up the stairs quietly and she showed him into a room and told him she'd be back in a minute with sheets and pillowcases and towels.

'Can't I sleep in your bed, with you?' he pleaded. 'I don't want to be on my own.'

'Okay,' she said, but he heard the uncertainty in her voice.

He hadn't meant anything to happen, but he didn't stop himself when it did. He hadn't initiated anything. He hadn't so much as reached out for her hand. It was Rose who had pulled him to her in the dark, as he lay awake, haunted by the images that wouldn't go away.

And now, here they were, side by side in her bed at some unearthly hour of the morning, and Barney was downstairs with no idea of what had gone on during the night.

He watched her for a while as she slept, thinking about what it all meant and whether it meant anything at all. Had he gone back to the beginning, or was he picking up from where he left off, all those years ago? But all this thinking was too much for his knackered brain, and when she started to stir and turned to him, he abandoned any attempt at understanding.

There was no point in sneaking quietly out of the house, Rose told him. Barney had ears on elastic and would have heard him arrive the night before.

'Just come downstairs when you're ready and we'll have breakfast,' she said. 'I'll tell him I made up one of the spare rooms for you.'

'If his ears are that good, he won't believe a word of that.'

She pulled on a robe and went off to the bathroom, which Ned remembered now was just a couple of doors away. He looked at his watch: not quite seven. There was a whole day ahead of him and he wasn't sure how his mind was going to take him through it.

Rose came back to the room, smelling of shampoo and soap.

'Your turn,' she said. And when she saw that he wasn't moving in the bed, she tugged on the covers.

He still didn't move.

'Are you all right?' she asked.

'I'm just thinking about you and me,' he said. 'Rose, what does it mean? Are we . . . ? Are you . . . ?'

'I don't know, Ned,' she said. 'I don't feel I can make any kind of plan – even with you.'

'Especially not with me,' he said.

'I didn't say that. Let's just see how it goes, okay?'

'That sounds like a good plan,' he said.

Inside, he felt a flood of relief. But it was mixed with confusion. The thought that he and Rose might get together again had been in his head, but he hadn't expected the suddenness of what happened last night. The sex had been incredible, mind-blowing, but maybe that was because he had needed something to blow his mind so that the terrible memory of the day before would be pushed for a while into some dark recess of his brain. He didn't want to promise anything, and her apparent ambivalence about the significance of what had happened between them consoled him. Maybe, if they were to see more of each other, it would become clearer to both of them.

He wanted to think about Rose and about this new confusing state, even if it troubled him. Because thinking about anything was a refuge from the terrible, horrific truth that he would have to live with for the rest of his days: his father had killed his mother and had lied about it for all those years. Ned had to believe it was an accident. Because if he didn't, he would lose his mind.

Chapter Thirty-Seven

Aidan wanted to take me to the hospital, but I refused. I ached everywhere, but I knew that it was just muscle strain incurred as I fell. My head was a bit tender, too, and Aidan was worried.

'You were out for a couple of seconds,' he said. 'I really think we should get you checked over.'

'I'm fine. Honestly. I just have a few aches. I'm going to have a bath and clean myself. And then – I hope you don't mind – I'm going to go back to Fidelma's.'

'I'll drive you over.'

I left him to deal with the horses and went into the house. I didn't tell him what I now remembered – that Lillian had pushed me down the stairs. There was no point, because he wouldn't believe it and I was still trying to process it myself. Upstairs, I took off my clothes and brushed as much mud off them as I could before getting into the bath.

I stayed in the bath a long time, going over it all in my mind.

Had I deliberately suppressed the memory of what happened the evening I fell? It must have been an accident, I told myself. Lillian had cared enough about me to want to prevent me from finding out about her and James in such a horrible way. She hadn't meant to push me down the stairs. I had lost my balance. But maybe, at the time, I hadn't been able to believe that. Maybe I'd subconsciously chosen to remember nothing about her part in my fall so that our friendship would survive.

But they had both let me believe that I'd simply tripped, caught my foot on a loose piece of carpet, or that dizziness brought on by the flu virus had made me lose my balance so much that I fell backwards. They had both lied. And James – how could I believe anything he said now?

I started to put my clothes back on. They were still damp from the mud, which had somehow managed to cover almost every inch of fabric, and horribly uncomfortable. There wasn't much I could do about the jeans, but maybe I could borrow one of Aidan's jumpers. I called downstairs to him, but he didn't reply. He was probably doing something in the yard. Anyway, he wouldn't mind.

There were no pullovers hanging up in the wardrobe, so I went to the chest of drawers and opened the top drawer, which contained underwear and socks, all mixed up together. The second drawer turned out to be where he kept his woollens and T-shirts, which had all been flung in without any attempt at order. I selected the oldest-looking, most ragged-looking thing in the drawer and was starting to pull it out when I realised that there was something in the sleeve. It turned out to be a rolled-up magazine section from *The Sunday Times*. Curious, I leafed through it, wondering why Aidan had kept it. Of course, I thought, as I came to a profile of some photographer whose work had won first prize in a major competition. The profile was accompanied by a photograph that covered nearly half of the page. I was about to put it back when something about it caught my eye. Something familiar. I held it up and recoiled in shock.

The photograph was of a man and a woman embracing in the snow, a frozen canal behind them. The woman was Lillian, wearing the red coat she'd bought before she left London for Ardgreeney. She was wearing a fur hat. She had her hands on the man's chest and the look on her face was one of pure tenderness. The man had his arms around her and he was gazing at her as if she was the only thing in the world that mattered. The man was James.

I knew they'd had an affair, and I was suffering from that knowledge. But this, this photograph that showed such intimacy between them, was like a knife through my heart. I sank back on to my heels, staring at the paper. Phrases from the piece flew out at me, punching me again and again: *wrapped up in each other . . . looking into each other's eyes as if nothing and no one else existed.*

James had told me that Lillian had ended their affair when she met Aidan. But now I knew that was a lie, too. I remembered calling James after Lillian had left for the airport. His landline and mobile had rung unanswered. He had called me, hours later, from his mobile to say that he had been out visiting friends for the day and had forgotten to take his phone with him.

I remembered, too, that Lillian had told me not to call her for a couple of days because it might make her too sad. Better to wait for a few days, until she was a bit more settled, before talking on the phone.

Oh, the horrible deceit of it all. Just as Lillian and I had done, James and Lillian had walked by the canal. They had embraced, oblivious to the world around them. They were in love. The camera didn't lie. The photographer had captured it perfectly. She probably hadn't gone to Ireland that day, but had spent the night with James in some hotel. And it had taken ten years for the truth to come out in a photograph.

I thought of Aidan and the anguish he must have felt on seeing the photograph. I wanted to run down to the yard and put my arms around him. And then I looked at the date on the magazine and I felt myself go cold with fear. The magazine was years old. It was from September 2006 – two months before Lillian disappeared, in November. Aidan had known about her and James. He had known for two whole months. I had to get out. Still holding the magazine, I ran down the stairs and towards the front door, but, as I got there, it was already opening. Aidan. He stared at the jumper I was wearing and then at the magazine. He lunged at me, pushing me back inside.

I tried to fight my way past him, but he was too strong and he dragged me to the kitchen. He snatched the magazine from me and threw it behind him. He didn't look any different. He didn't look angry or dangerous. But I knew I had to get away from him.

'I . . . think I'd like to go home now,' I said.

'I'd much rather you stayed.'

His voice was calm. He even sounded reasonable. I tried not to show my panic.

'Fidelma knows I'm here. I told her I'd be back in time for dinner.'

'Well, you're going to tell her you won't be back, after all,' he said.

He went to my bag, which I'd left on the table, and took out my phone.

'What's the code to unlock the screen?'

'I don't remember.'

'Give me the code to unlock the phone, Orla.'

I had no choice. I gave him the code. He scrolled through my call lists and text messages, and then tapped out a message, which he showed me.

Bumped into old pal. Going to have dinner with her and catch up. Hope you don't mind. x

My heart sank as he pressed *send*.

'She'll know there's something wrong if I don't turn up later. She'll call the guards. She'll tell them I was here.'

'And I'll tell them you left as soon as we came back from the ride,' he said. 'They won't find you here, Orla. Believe me.'

He picked the magazine up from the floor and took it across to the big Belfast sink. Then, one by one, he tore the pages out and set them alight.

'I should have burned this years ago,' he said. 'But it has certainly kept me focused. You don't open the paper you read every Sunday, expecting to see the woman you're going to marry wrapped around another man. I worked out that the photo must have been taken on the same weekend she left to come here.

It hit me like a ton of bricks. But I did a lot of thinking. She was here and everything was great, and so I told myself that, if she'd uprooted herself to come and live with me, whatever she had going with him was over.'

'It *was* over,' I said quickly. 'It was you she loved. That night . . . she told me how well everything was going.'

'Are you really so naïve, Orla? I *saw* him here that night. My mother called while I was in the pub and I went outside so I could hear her, away from the noise. I saw him. He got out of his car and asked someone where he could fill up with petrol. I heard him speak. I recognised him. There was no one else it could have been. And the only place he could have been coming from was Oriel Cottage. That's when I knew it was still going on. She knew I'd be out for hours that night, so she invited him over for a quick fuck.'

'But he didn't see her, Aidan! He went away. He told me he realised there was no point.'

'Oh, yeah, *sure* he didn't see her. Give me some credit for intelligence.'

'But you didn't even give *her* a chance. Why couldn't you have just sat down and talked to her?'

'Don't use that tone, Orla. It doesn't suit you. You sound like a social worker. *Why couldn't you have just sat down and talked to her?*' He raised his voice to a falsetto, mimicking me. 'I'll tell you why I couldn't have sat down and talked to her. I went back home and I saw through the window that she was on that Skype thing, talking to you. I was hardly going to walk in and have it out with her in front of you, was I?'

I stared at him, aghast. 'So you knocked on the door to get

her away from the screen, so that I couldn't see what was happening. And you killed her.'

He was gripping my arm tightly now, but he was frighteningly calm. He leaned forward.

'I asked her if James had been there. She said no. She lied. I might have been able to deal with it, if she'd admitted it, but I couldn't handle a big lie like that. To tell you the truth, I didn't mean for her to die. I did hit her – I'll admit that. But I didn't kill her. She must have hit her head on one of the stones.'

'But you can tell the guards that! That it was an accident!' I cried, grasping at the possibility that I could convince him to let me leave the house. 'They'll believe you!'

He shook his head. 'I don't think they will. Too much time has gone by. They wouldn't be able to prove I killed her, but I wouldn't be able to prove to them that I didn't. So I don't think I'm going to be telling the guards anything.'

I thought suddenly of Patsy McLennan.

'That old man . . . Did you . . . ?'

'Ah. Patsy. He was, as the saying goes, in the wrong place at the wrong time. He saw me putting Lillian into the car. I didn't have much choice. I didn't kill him. Not technically. I just, shall we say, directed him.'

'What are you going . . .' I choked. I was so frightened now that I couldn't get the words out.

'What am I going to do with you?' he said, his eyes narrowing, his eyebrows coming together in a frown. 'That's a good question, Orla. It's bad luck you found that magazine. And it's bad luck you left London. How do you think I felt, seeing that boyfriend of yours strutting around the place? I had a really good plan with those letters – and it was working. The guards would eventually have arrested James and he would have gone to prison knowing that I'd sent him there and that I'd taken you from him. Unfortunately, things haven't quite worked out the way I planned. So, as to your question – I'll have to think about that. But I can't let you go, Orla. You have to understand that.'

Chapter Thirty-Eight

James Weston was almost certainly their man. They just had to prove it. But James was still denying that he had even spoken to Lillian Murray that night, let alone killed her, even if the anonymous letter-writer had pretty much accused him of her murder. And where was her body? Could James have put Lillian in the boot of his car and disposed of her somewhere in the north? The PSNI were going through their files on unidentified remains, to see if any might turn out to be a possible match for Lillian. They were also planning to check out a long-disused quarry, a few miles from the hotel where James had spent the night.

But the failure so far to identify the writer of the letters that had led them to James still troubled Ned. This person clearly had some knowledge of what had happened that night, but how much? And why had he or she waited nearly a decade to act?

Barney Kelleher had advised him to go back to the beginning, and Barney had been right, so Ned was spending a lot of time thinking about the night of Lillian's disappearance and the days and weeks following it.

He thought about Kathleen McManus and her reaction to him when he had visited her in the home. He thought about what Orla had told him, that Aidan and Lillian had planned to take over Eaglewood and turn it into a hotel. Aidan had told his mother of their plans the day Lillian vanished, Orla had said. She'd also said that, according to Lillian, Kathleen hadn't quite embraced the idea.

What, he wondered now, if Kathleen had seen Lillian not as a welcome future member of the family, but as a threat to everything she loved – her son, her home. Could she have lured Lillian out into the night, perhaps with a story that something had happened to Aidan? He lay awake for much of the night, tossing and turning, his mind exercised by the possibility that Kathleen McManus had played a role in Lillian's disappearance.

It had been seen as a tragic coincidence that Aidan McManus's mother had a stroke on the same night as his girlfriend vanished, never to be seen again. No one had questioned that coincidence. But what if Kathleen McManus's stroke had been caused by extreme exertion? She was a strong, tall woman. Lillian was smaller and hadn't spent her life performing the kind of manual, laborious tasks associated with looking after horses. But Lillian was decades younger, and, if she had fought to defend herself, Kathleen would have had to push herself to the limit and even beyond.

And what about Aidan? Had he gone to Eaglewood that night expecting to help his mother ensure the horses were safe, only to be faced with the body of his girlfriend and a demand from his mother that he help her dispose of it? Blood was thicker than water. No matter how appalled he might have been by what his mother had done, wasn't Aidan more likely to have helped her cover up her crime than to have seen her go to prison for the rest of her life?

For months after Lillian's disappearance, the guards had trawled Ardgreeney and the surrounding area, identifying possible sites where a body might have been buried, but finding nothing

But what if Lillian wasn't lying in some unmarked grave on the side of a hill or a mountain? What if her body was still hidden somewhere in the area? What if it was hidden at Eaglewood?

Through the long hours of wakefulness, Ned swung between dismissing his hypothesis and developing it further. By morning, he knew he couldn't ignore it. His first cup of coffee drunk, he called UCD and, despite the early hour, was put straight through to Professor Mac Aonghusa. Ned told him he had seen his television programme and wanted to pick his brains about priest holes and other secret hiding places.

'Is this in connection with a case you're working on?' Mac Aonghusa asked.

'Not, er, specifically – I'm just exploring some possibilities. Secret rooms, that sort of thing.'

'I see. So what do you want to know?'

'The cave at Ardgreeney –'

'That's fairly specific,' Mac Aonghusa said.

'Did you get down into it for your programme?'

'We did, albeit with great difficulty, across the rocks when the tide was well out. But you would have seen the shots we took inside, no?'

'Unfortunately, I must have just missed that bit. I don't suppose you found any priests' bones inside?'

'No. If there ever were any in there, they've long been washed out and away by the sea. There's been a lot of erosion over the centuries. Of course, we don't know for sure that the cave was a priest hole. It may just as easily have been used by smugglers.'

'Would you say the only way into the cave is across the rocks?'

'I would. You'd have to be insane to try to get down into it from the headland. But those rocks are treacherous, even in the best conditions.'

Ned mentally struck the cave off his list of possible places where a body might have been concealed. 'That's what I thought,' he said.

'You mentioned secret rooms in old houses,' Mac Aonghusa said. 'Have you any particular houses in mind?'

'Can I ask that you keep this conversation confidential?' Ned asked.

'Of course.'

'There's a house up here in Ardgreeney, close to the headland. You'll have seen it when you were making your programme. It's called Eaglewood.'

'Ah, yes. Early Georgian. I noticed the house, but we didn't visit.'

'What do you think would be the chances of there being a concealed room somewhere inside it?'

'Zero, if you're thinking in terms of rooms to hide priests on the run. The chances would be higher if it was a much older house or a castle. You'll have read about the discovery at Barberstown Castle, down in Straffan, in the nineties,' Mac Aonghusa said. 'Of course, people also built secret rooms for other reasons. Here in Dublin, for example, there's a house on Ailesbury Road that was built in 1920 and used as a safe house by republicans during the War of Independence and the Civil War. It has a secret room on the first floor, behind a wardrobe and a false wall.'

'Part of Eaglewood was burned down in the nineteen twenties,' Ned said. 'A local man who made a lot of money in America bought it and rebuilt it in the thirties.'

'A republican?'

'Apparently so. There are plenty of rumours suggesting it was used as a safe house in relatively recent times.'

'Well, there you are. If there wasn't a secret room in this house of yours in Ardgreeney before the fire, the subsequent rebuilding would have provided a perfect opportunity to install one.'

'Thanks for the chat. It's been very helpful,' Ned said. 'And, if you don't mind – '

'Don't worry. Our conversation is our secret. But if you have any other questions do come back to me.'

'I will. And thanks.'

Ned strode into Fergus's office and told him what he wanted to do. Fergus frowned and tapped his fingers on the desk.

'Christ, Ned; I don't know. You really think Kathleen McManus could have done something like that? A woman in her sixties? Okay, okay, I suppose the sequence makes some kind of sense. She drives over to the cottage, sees through the window that Lillian is talking to someone, knocks at the door to get her

317

outside, kills her, throws her into the car and drives back to Eaglewood. And then she calls Aidan and tells him to get over there. But all that would mean an awful lot of premeditation. And why kill Lillian, anyway? And why take the risk of assuming her son, who's in love with Lillian and probably going to marry her, is going to help her?'

'I don't know the answers to those questions,' Ned said. 'All I know is that we have to do something to move things on. In all likelihood, James Weston is our man. But, as you keep reminding me, we have no real evidence against him. So, if we're going to charge him, I'd like to think we've looked at every possible alternative.

'Do you remember,' he continued, 'I went to Kilfernagh that time, years ago, and got a very strange reaction from Kathleen McManus when I told her who I was? I've never been able to work that one out, and it may be that it was no more than her state of mind after the stroke. But the way she responded to me felt very strange. And, regarding her call to Aidan that night – I've just been going back through the file, and that call was from her mobile, not the landline. Which means she could have made the call from outside the cottage.'

Now Fergus was massaging his chin between his thumb and first finger, and looking uncomfortable.

'Look, Fergus,' Ned said. 'We don't have to go in guns blazing, but I really do think we have to do something. How about we turn up at Eaglewood, tell Aidan we're serious about getting back into the investigation and that we need to tick a few boxes on the way, one of the boxes being a cursory once-over of the house, because we never did it back in 2006?'

'You think he'll go along with that?'

'Who knows? But, if he objects ... well, it will make him look obstructive, won't it? And then we'll just get a warrant.'

'I still don't like it. But if you think you can do it that way, go ahead.'

'Grand. I'll take Brennan and a couple of the lads with me.'

'Okay. But go easy. Because, if you're wrong and he gets wind of what you're up to, there'll be wigs on the green. The last thing I want is for the papers to be comparing us to the Keystone Kops.'

Ned went back to his desk to grab his coat and his phone, which showed several missed calls from Eily. *Shite*. He must have inadvertently turned the sound off. She'd left a voicemail.

'Can you call me when you get this? It's about Tom.'

Not again, he thought. What was it now? He was beginning to sympathise with Tom. He would call Eily, but not until he had been to Eaglewood and checked out his hunch.

Aidan opened the door, a mug of tea in his hands. He was wearing jodhpurs and riding boots. His eyebrows lifted in surprise as he saw Ned and Brennan and the two uniformed guards standing there.

'Aidan,' Ned said. 'This is Detective Sergeant Joe Brennan. Do you mind if we come in?'

'Ned. No, of course not. Come in,' Aidan said. 'But –' he nodded towards the two guards – 'what's going on?'

Ned looked back over his shoulder, as if he had just remembered the presence of the guards. 'Oh, sorry. Garda Neelan and Garda O'Driscoll. Aidan, new information has come to light about the events of ten years ago. I'm afraid I can't talk to you about it, but you'll be glad to hear that we've decided it's definitely worth revisiting the case.'

Aidan exhaled loudly. He placed a hand on his stomach and was silent for a couple of seconds.

'Sorry; I'll be okay in a minute. It's great news, but ... I'm feeling quite emotional about it. I think I need to drink something. Can I offer you anything?'

'No, thanks, Aidan. Actually, we're here to look around the house. It's pro forma stuff, just to get all the boxes ticked, because we didn't search it back then.'

Aidan looked bewildered. 'But ... why would you want to search Eaglewood?'

'As I said, Aidan, it's pro forma stuff. And I've brought the lads so we can be in and out before you know it.'

'It seems a bit ... unnecessary,' Aidan said. 'But, fine, crack on. Go wherever you like.'

Ned had told Brennan, a good detective he had worked with for a few years, and the two uniformed guards that they were looking for any sign of a secret room or space, so they went around the house pressing walls, lifting rugs, and moving bookcases and paintings. He stayed with Aidan, who took him into a sitting room at the front of the house and said he'd be back shortly with mugs of coffee.

There were family photographs on the walls and mantelpiece, and, as he waited for Aidan to come back, he had a quick look at them. There was something oddly familiar about some of them, even though he hadn't known the McManuses well. Everything he had ever known about them had come from Eily and her parents. He had never met Aidan's father, and yet, as he looked at a photograph of a younger Malcolm, perhaps in his late thirties at the time, he had a feeling that he must have encountered him somewhere.

When Aidan returned to the room, Ned asked him how his mother was.

'The same. She seems to have all her marbles, but she's physically and emotionally fragile.'

'A tragedy for someone I'm told was a fine woman,' Ned said. 'I'm sorry to hear that. One of the reasons I'm asking about her is ... well, it's another thing we should really do: have a chat with her. Just to cross it off the list. If we do bring a case against –' he hesitated, as if he was about to come out with a name, and then continued – 'against anyone, we'll need to have all our ducks lined up.'

'And my mother would be one of your ducks?'

'Ideally, we'd get to talk to her and ask her what she remembered about that night. We'd do it sensitively.'

'I'd rather you didn't, but I suppose, if you have to, you have to.'

'Grand. We'll be in touch about that,' Ned said. He glanced at his watch and then towards the ceiling. 'I'll go and see what they're up to,' he said, adding, with a laugh, 'Make sure they're not creating a mess.'

'I'll wait down here,' Aidan said, taking the empty mugs and moving towards the kitchen as Ned climbed the stairs.

Brennan was in what must have been Aidan's room, judging by the big photograph of Lillian, which seemed out of place with the old-fashioned wallpaper and furniture. It gave Ned the creeps.

The man was still obsessed with her. But then, why wouldn't he be? There wasn't much else going on in his life, bar the riding school, and, despite what Aidan had told him not so long ago about business having improved, Ned doubted there was much money coming in from that.

'Anything?' Ned asked, quietly.

'Nope.' Brennan said. 'I think we're finished. Unless you think we should lift a few floorboards?'

'Better not, unless they're obviously loose. He seems to be taking this well, but if he gets it in his head to make a complaint, there'll be enough shit hitting the fan without lifted floorboards.'

'We're done, so,' Brennan said.

They trundled back downstairs and Aidan came out of the kitchen to meet them. He didn't look anxious. He didn't look anything, in particular. His face was blank, and, for a moment, Ned felt sorry for him again. But at least he had tested out his theory about Eaglewood, which appeared to have been not much of a theory, although there was still Kathleen McManus to talk to. He would try to set that up for sometime in the next day or two.

He held out his hand to Aidan.

'Thanks for your time, Aidan. I'm sorry we had to do this, but at least it's done. We'll leave you in peace,' he said.

He sent Brennan and the two uniformed guards back to the station, telling them he wanted to swing by the dry cleaner's to pick up some clothes he had left there weeks ago.

So it was all still pointing towards James Weston, Ned thought, as he drove along the Seapoint Road, back into town. James had been involved with Lillian. He had travelled to Ardgreeney the night she disappeared. He had admitted those things. The only thing James was denying was that he had harmed Lillian. And the funny thing was that Ned wanted to believe him. He realised he had been hoping that the writer of the anonymous letters would turn out to be the person responsible for Lillian Murray's disappearance and Patsy McLennan's terrible death. But, the way things were looking now, James was likely to be arrested, charged and put on trial. He might even be convicted.

Ned felt unutterably weary. This job was sucking the life out of him. It really was time to give it up. He drove slowly, because he needed to slow down in every way – most of all, in his mind. But his mind was racing.

He thought about Annie's looming trip, his mother, his father, Irene, Orla Breslin, Lillian Murray, Rose, Barney, Tom, the anonymous letters. And then, for no reason he could identify, a phrase from one of the letters came back him: *You didn't look in the right place*. Maybe the anonymous scribe hadn't intended to be literal. Maybe he had simply been building a series of hints that would lead Ned to James Weston. But maybe, just maybe, and without realising it, he was also laying a trail that would lead all the way to himself.

Ned thought of something else, too. He remembered now exactly when he had seen Malcolm McManus: he had been one of the men in the house the day his mother angered his father so much by singing the ditty about De Valera. He pulled over to the side of the road and called Brennan. Then he swung the car round and turned back towards Eaglewood.

Chapter Thirty-Nine

Orla

It was dark. I couldn't move. Why was I still on the landing? Why didn't someone turn on the light? What had Lillian done to my arms and my legs? The nightmare had come back and it seemed so real, but now Lillian was in it. And Aidan – he was in it too. Where was he now? Why had he . . . ?

Everything came back then, rushing into my mind like a gale-force wind, overwhelming me. Now I knew I wasn't asleep and in the old nightmare. I was awake – horribly, terrifyingly awake – and I could remember everything. I remembered Aidan dragging me out to the yard, me screaming and struggling, and him telling me to shut up, because no one would hear me except the horses. I remembered seeing the whites of Petra's eyes as he opened the door and started moving the straw to reveal the trapdoor. And then he lifted it and dropped me down into the darkness.

Oh, Jesus! Oh, God! Help me!

But I couldn't scream because there was tape around my mouth. My hands and ankles were bound, too. I didn't remember him doing those things to me. I must have hit my head and lost consciousness when he pushed me through the trapdoor.

I listened, trying to pick up the sounds outside, but all I could hear was the deafening beat of my heart and the rapid breaths I was taking through my nose. I couldn't hear Petra above me, even though I knew she was probably moving around the box, as she always did when she was nervous or upset. He must have spread the thick layers of straw back over the trapdoor.

Frantic and increasingly aware of a terrible pain in my head, I began to panic. But I couldn't make a noise, and I couldn't move. And then, suddenly, the trapdoor lifted again and, before I could make out what it was, something tumbled down and landed with a thud. For a moment, there was silence, and then I saw another shape come down through the trapdoor and stand in front of me in the gloom. It was Aidan. I tried to make sounds to make him look at me. My eyes begged him to take pity on me. But he ignored me and went to whatever he had pushed down through the trapdoor.

'Company for you, Orla,' Aidan said. 'Not that either of you will be capable of much conversation.'

That was when I realised the shape lying on the ground, trying to move, was a person. I moaned. Please don't let it be Fidelma lying there, I prayed. But it had to be Fidelma. Who else would have come looking for me?

Aidan climbed out, closing the trapdoor behind him. The

darkness was all enveloping. My body began to shake uncontrollably. I was in a dungeon with Fidelma, both of us tied up and unable to communicate with each other. This was where Aidan must have put Lillian. Perhaps her bones were still here, somewhere in this dark, cold space.

After a while, I stopped shaking. I had no energy left. I tried to hold on to a spark of hope that, because I was still alive, Aidan wasn't planning to kill me. But then a sickening wave of horror swept over me and I knew what was in store for me. Aidan didn't have to kill me. He didn't have to do anything. He could leave me here, keep the trapdoor shut, and, eventually, without food and water, I would die. Even if people began looking for me, no one would think of looking down here. Because no one knew it existed.

I prayed again, but I knew I couldn't hope for rescue.

Please, God, don't let it take too long.

Ned

This time, he didn't stop in front of the house, but drove straight to the stable yard. He grabbed a pitchfork that had been left propped up against a wall, opened the half-door of the first loose box and went in. The horse eyed him nervously as he shut the bolt behind him, but didn't object, even when he started lifting the straw bedding and moving it around with the pitchfork, which he scraped along the ground. Nothing. He went into each loose box, repeating the lifting and scraping. Nothing.

There was one box left, and when he slid the bolt and went inside, the animal threw its head up and pressed its ears back and he saw the whites of its eyes. He moved to the back of the box and waved his arm at the horse, driving it out through the open half-door.

He started raking through the straw, lifting and moving it to expose the concrete floor. And then the metal struck something that wasn't concrete – something that was more like wood. He scraped away the straw and there it was: the trapdoor that he knew he would find.

But, before he could lift it, Aidan was in the box, throwing himself at him, and Ned felt the weight of the former rugby player come down heavily on him, pinning him to the ground. He was no match for this kind of fury and, as Aidan's big hands closed around his neck, he started praying that Brennan and the two guards would arrive soon. The hands kept squeezing. His own hands were trying to prise Aidan's away, but it was getting harder to breathe. And then, *Deo gratias*, he heard the siren.

Aidan jumped away from him and ran out into the yard. Ned managed to get to his feet and staggered after him. It was mayhem outside. The guards had grabbed McManus and had him pinned against the gate. The horse was snorting and rearing, the sound of its hooves reverberating around the yard.

'Calm that thing down before it injures itself!' Ned shouted at Brennan.

'Not on your nelly!' Brennan shouted back, keeping well out of the horse's way.

Ned started to walk slowly towards the horse, speaking quietly to it all the time. Eventually, it stopped moving and allowed him to come closer.

'Easy, easy,' he said. And, in the same low tone, he told Brennan to bring him a head collar. Between them, Ned and Brennan closed in on the horse, soothing it to the point that Ned was able to slip the head collar on it and coax it into one of the empty loose boxes.

'I found a trapdoor,' Ned said when he managed to get his breath back. 'Haven't opened it yet. Aidan jumped me just as I got to it.'

'Let's get it open.'

They started to raise the trapdoor. Ned felt his heart beat faster. He held his breath. This was where Aidan had dumped Lillian. Maybe what was left of her was still down there. But, as his eyes got used to the darkness of the space below, he saw the terrified face of Orla Breslin. She was bound and gagged, propped against a wall. But she was alive.

He dropped down and rushed to her.

'It's all right, Orla. You're safe now,' he said.

She was crying and shaking. As gently as he could, he removed the tape from her mouth and freed her wrists and ankles.

'Do you think you can move, if I help you?' he asked.

She nodded. He thought she might be about to faint.

'I'm going to lift you up to a guard called Joe Brennan and he's going to pull you through the trapdoor. Are you all right with that?'

She nodded again, and now she was making sounds as well – the kind of sounds a small, frightened animal might make. He put his arms around her.

'It's all right; I've got you. No one's going to harm you now.'

He lifted her up to Brennan and, just as he took his hands away from her, she looked down at him and pointed beyond him. He turned around. The open trapdoor gave some light, but he had to strain through the gloom to make out a stack of old mattresses, fruit crates that were probably used as tables, piles of blankets. He had no doubt that, somewhere in this underground prison that once sheltered the paramilitary friends of Aidan McManus's father, somewhere among the damp blankets and mattresses, he would find either the remains of Lillian Murray or evidence to show that she had been put there at some point.

And then, to his horror, he heard another noise, a human noise, and it was coming from the piles of blankets, which were starting to move. He ran towards the sound and pulled the blankets away to see the shape of a young man lying face down, his hands tied behind his back. Ned's stomach turned as he realised there was something horribly familiar looking about the young man's dark hair and his long neck.

'Oh, no! Oh, sweet fucking Jesus!'

Orla

Detective Brennan took me to the house and made me a mug of tea. It was strong and there was too much sugar in it, but I gulped it down.

'The ambulance will be here in a few minutes,' he said.

'Fidelma – is she going to be all right?'

'Fidelma?'

'My sister. Aidan threw her down there, too.'

He looked at me as if I was talking nonsense. 'It wasn't your sister down there with you,' the detective said.

'Thank God!' I blurted out. 'But who . . . ?'

'You don't know who it was?' he asked.

'No.'

'Look, I don't know if I should tell you this, but it was Ned's son, Tom.'

'Ned's son? But . . .'

It didn't make sense. What had Inspector Moynihan's son got to do with Aidan? And then I understood.

'*Tom* is Ned's son?' I asked.

The detective nodded. 'I think that's the ambulance,' he said. 'Hold on here for a minute.'

He went out and I attempted to stand up. My legs were so weak and shaky that I had to sit down again.

'You're all right,' Detective Brennan said, coming back in. 'Take your time. There's another one on its way. We'll get you into that.'

'Does that mean Tom is badly hurt?'

'It just means that there's another one half a minute away and there'll be more space in that. Ned's going with Tom.'

'And . . . Aidan?'

'We've got him.'

I thought of Lillian.

'Was there anyone . . . anything else down there?'

'The forensics people are on their way.'

He didn't say any more than that, but I knew that Aidan must have put her down into that place. He had said her death was an accident, that she had hit her head outside the cottage. But maybe she had still been alive when he lowered her into that dark space below the stable. Maybe she had lain down there for days, or even longer, dying a slow, desperate death.

I turned my head away and heard myself moan. I could feel my eyes beginning to sting. I pinched them shut to try to stop the tears that were welling up. And, for just a little while, that was all I was able to think about – the need to stop the tears. Because, if I started crying, I might not be able to stop.

Ned

All the way to the hospital in the ambulance, Ned held Tom's hands, warming them in his own.

'Sorry, Dad,' Tom kept saying.

And Ned kept telling him he had nothing to be sorry about and that he didn't have to say anything at all now. The most important thing was to get him to the hospital and make sure he was all right.

But Tom wanted to talk.

'That's where I've been going with Andrea,' he said. 'I didn't want you or Ma to know . . . I wanted to show you that I was serious . . .'

'Serious about what?' Ned asked.

'About being a guard . . . a detective.'

'Hang on, Tom,' Ned said. 'Are you telling me that you were checking Aidan out?'

Tom nodded. 'Yeah.'

'But how . . . ?'

'Andrea and me . . . we were already going out, but mostly just after school. She was always at that place at weekends. So I started going there, too, just to see what I could find.'

'But why? What were you looking for?' Ned asked.

'I heard Ma and Garret talking, a few months back, about you having a bee in your bonnet about what happened to Aidan's girlfriend. So I looked it up on the internet, and it just seemed obvious that Aidan had murdered her. And I thought . . . I thought that, if I could prove it, you'd stand up for me wanting to join the guards.'

'Oh, Tom,' Ned said. It was all he was capable of saying at that moment, thanks to the lump that had formed in his throat. But he didn't have to say anything more because Tom was still talking.

'I always thought it was a bit odd that he wouldn't let anyone into Petra's box. He said she wouldn't let anyone in except him and that she could be dangerous. But I knew that was crap, because I went in a couple of times, just to see if she'd let me, and she did. I had a feeling . . . I just wanted to know why he was keeping everyone out of there. So I skipped school today and went over to the stables, because they're closed on Mondays. There was no one in the yard and everything was quiet when I got there, but then I saw him coming out of the house, and he was dragging Orla behind him. Dad, it was horrible. I thought he was going to kill her.'

He was, Ned thought. And he was going to kill you, too. He winced. He couldn't bear to have such thoughts in his head.

'What did you do then?' Ned asked.

'I hid in the tack room. I thought if I stayed there for a while, he wouldn't know. I was going to sneak out later and call you. But it was as if he had eyes in the back of his head. He caught me. Dad, I'm sorry. I'm really sorry.'

'You don't need to be sorry about anything, Tom. I'm the one who should be sorry. I should have been a better dad. And I should have listened to you instead of telling you what to do.'

'I fucked everything up.'

'You didn't fuck up anything,' Ned said. 'Your instincts are right. They're better than mine. You know what I think? I think you'll make a great guard. That's if you still want to be one. Do you?'

Tom beamed. He looked just like the little boy that Ned used to hoist on to his shoulders.

'Yeah. I do,' he said. 'Will you talk to Ma?'

Oh, Christ. Eily. He hadn't called her back and now he was going to have to tell her that her son had been in the gravest danger.

'I will. I'll call her once we get you inside the hospital,' he said. 'She'll be fine. She'll just be glad to know that you've come out of this in one piece.'

Telling Eily was almost as bad as finding Tom in that terrifying space. She screamed and wailed and, for a few minutes, he listened to her agony, holding the phone to his ear until Garret's voice came on the line.

'Ned, what happened?'

He told Garret what he knew, what he had been able to piece together from talking to Tom and Orla.

'He's going to be all right. He hit his head when Aidan pushed him down through the trapdoor, but there was no fracture. He's concussed, but he's going to be okay,' Ned said. 'Do you know why Eily called me earlier? She said it was about Tom, but I thought . . . I thought it was just Eily trying to get me to push him to do something or other.'

'He didn't go to school this morning. He said he was feeling ill and was staying in bed. But, when Eily went up later to see

333

how he was, the bed was empty and he wasn't in the house. She rang the school, but he hadn't turned up. So . . .'

Hours later, Ned was sitting with Eily in the hospital cafeteria. He wanted to hold her and comfort her, but he was afraid that, if he even touched her hand, she would jump up and walk away. He was still painfully conscious of how hostile she had been to him earlier, when she arrived at the hospital, brushing past him as he held out his arms to her.

'I should have listened to you that time, when you wanted me to follow him. I'm sorry about that,' he had told her. 'And I'm sorry I didn't call you back when I got your message. I was already on my way to Aidan's at that point. I thought it could wait.'

And she, her voice heavy with accusation, had spat out the words that had pierced him like a sword: 'It's your fault. If you'd followed him when I asked you to, you'd have known where he was going all that time.'

He had wanted to respond, to tell her that even if he had known about the weekends spent at Eaglewood, he couldn't have known that Tom was in danger, but his vocal cords wouldn't work.

Now they were sitting across a table from each other, speaking quietly for fear their voices would echo around the cold, clinical space.

'I'm sorry for what I said to you earlier. It wasn't your fault,' she said, looking away and adding, 'It was mine.'

'How could it be your fault? I'm his father. I should have been more concerned. I should have –'

She lowered her head and took a deep breath. 'It was my

fault,' she repeated, her voice dull, monotonous. 'That's what Tom told me, just now – that everything was my fault. I see that now. I turned him against you. I shouldn't have done that, but I did. I said things about you. I slagged you off. I said you were just like your father. If I hadn't been so against him joining the guards and turning out ... turning out like you, he wouldn't have gone anywhere near Eaglewood. I'm sorry.'

She was looking at him, imploringly. He saw that she wanted him to tell her that it was all right, that the most important thing now was that Tom was okay. But it wasn't all right. She shouldn't have involved Tom in their broken relationship. She shouldn't have deprived him of a good relationship with his son.

She reached out to touch him as he stood up. He had longed for this to happen, to feel Eily's hand on his skin. But it made him feel sick to his stomach.

'I'm going back up to see how Tom's getting on,' he said, and walked away.

Chapter Forty

Tom's brain scan showed no bleeding or swelling, but the hospital had kept him in for two nights to make sure that his concussion wasn't an indication of something more serious. He had refused to go back home to Eily and Garret, and had insisted on staying with Ned.

'Is that all right with you?' Ned asked Eily.

'No, it isn't. But if he won't come home, I can't make him.'

Ned liked having Tom around, getting to know him again. He was a good kid. A clever kid, too. It wasn't as if the pair of them sat around having deep, meaningful chats. It was more along the lines of quiet companionship in the evening, sometimes in front of the television, watching a football match, sometimes in the kitchen, stumbling through a jointly-prepared meal.

He wondered how long Tom would want to stay with him. With a slight twinge of guilt because of Eily, he hoped Tom would stay until it was time to go to university. He liked having him around for all sorts of reasons, the main one being the opportunity to bond with him. But he was also grateful that having Tom there, having to think about his needs, left less time to think about what his own father had done to his mother, and what, in the interests of justice, he needed to do about it.

He was thinking about how he would eventually broach the subject with Fergus, and ask for his advice, when the head of the forensics team called him from Eaglewood.

'Ned, we've got something down here. You might want to come and have a look.'

He arrived at Eaglewood, a few minutes later, to find Paddy Devine standing in the drizzle, puffing on a cigarette as if it was the last one he would ever smoke.

'I thought you'd given them up,' Ned said.

'I did. I just need the odd one every now and again.'

Ned nodded in the direction of the loose box. 'What have you found?'

'Bones,' Paddy said, drawing on the cigarette. 'Jaysus, Ned – there's a whole network down there. Goes right through all the stables from that trapdoor. We broke through a wall and . . . Well, go and see for yourself. Camp beds and all down there.'

'So the rumours were true,' Ned said.

'What rumours?'

'The word was that Aidan's father used to hide IRA men on the run. Anyway, I'll go and have a look.'

He put on the protective suit handed to him by one of the technicians and lowered himself down through the trapdoor, Paddy Devine behind him. Through the gap in the wall, where bricks had been removed, he saw another room, and another beyond it.

'Basically, there's a room under each stable, but the only entrance is through the trapdoor in the first one. At some point, the connecting doors were all blocked up.'

'Christ. You could hide a small army down here,' Ned gasped.

Paddy led him through the first gap in the wall. Ned saw stacks of all sorts of things – blankets, ancient-looking newspapers, tins – there were even cupboards. A couple of rooms on, Paddy stopped in front of a metal chest, the kind you might keep for storing tools. Ned remembered his father having such a chest in one of the outhouses.

'In there,' Paddy said.

The bones were all that remained of Lillian Murray. Mentally, Ned traced lines through the separate, ghostly off-white pieces that had once been held together by muscle and flesh. All this time, she had been here. He bowed his head and closed his eyes, offering the nearest thing to a prayer that he could manage.

He opened his eyes again, no longer prayerful, but in dispassionate detective mode. He gazed over the bones and around them. But then he saw that not everything in the box was what he had expected to find. His chest felt tight and heavy, as if a great weight was pressing against it. He was holding his breath, and that was making the tightness worse. He prayed that it was his imagination, that it wasn't what he thought it was. But he knew. *He knew.*

The button had long lost its sheen, but he knew that, if he picked it up in his hand and wiped it softly with a piece of silk, its iridescence would come back. He continued to stare down at the bones. But now, in his mind's eye, he was seeing his mother as she was on that last day – his beautiful mother, in her blue dress with the white mother-of-pearl buttons.

'It's not Lillian Murray,' he managed to say before his legs buckled under him.

He stayed with Rose and Barney for the two weeks he was signed off on medical leave, refusing Eily's offer to look after him. It was probably the medication he was on, but he was calmer than he had been for a long time. Or maybe it wasn't calm he was feeling, but emptiness. He wasn't feeling anything very much. His hatred for his father seemed to have moved to a place where he couldn't feel it.

Almost mechanically, he reconstructed the story of how his mother had come to lie in that terrible space under the stables at Eaglewood.

His father had killed his mother. Accidentally, Irene had said, but Ned would never know the truth about that.

His father had panicked and had taken his mother's body to his friend, his supporter in the party, Malcolm McManus, who had placed it in the rooms built by Phelim McManus, below the stable block.

Had his father left Eaglewood that day, not wanting to know what Malcolm had done with his wife's body? Or had he known all along where she lay, her flesh becoming dust in that metal chest, as her son grew up not understanding why his mother had gone away.

Ned hadn't wanted to think about his mother during those two weeks with Rose and Barney. Even with the medication dulling his heart and his brain, it would have been too much. But he thought about her now. He remembered her loveliness, her thick, dark hair, the brightness of her eyes and the creaminess of her skin. He remembered her laughing. He remembered her brimming with life and love.

It was only now that he started to cry, quietly at first. And, as the flow of tears that had begun as a trickle became a torrent, his quiet weeping turned into great sobs that shook his body to the core.

Chapter Forty-One

I was at Fidelma's. James was still at Quay Street, still running the café, which had now achieved a level of notoriety that was bringing in a lot of business. He came to see me a few times, begging me to give him one more chance. We could try to start again, now that everything was in the open, he said. We could make a go of the café and we could think about having children. Surely our years together counted? I did think about it, because it would mean something positive coming out of such a terrible sequence of events. But I knew it was impossible, and he knew it, too, even before I told him my final decision.

'What will you do?' he asked.

'Stay at Fidelma's for a while, and then I don't know. Maybe go back to London. Or move to Dublin. You can buy my share of the café when you're making enough profit.'

'I wanted to talk to you about that. The café ... I think we should sell it, once the trial is out of the way.'

'But it's what you've always wanted,' I said. 'And you've put so much work into it.'

'I don't have the stomach for it any more,' he said, adding, with an attempt at a smile, 'No pun intended.'

He was thinking of going back to Edinburgh, he said. He still had friends there. He knew it well.

It was probably for the best, Fidelma said, when I told her.

Christmas was just around the corner. The kids were home from school and the buzz they created was a welcome distraction from the horrible events of the previous month and a half, but it was hard to shut those memories out. All too often, even my most positive thoughts were interrupted by horrific images I would never be able to get out of my mind.

I found comfort in sudoku puzzles. There was a logic to them. The numbers were either right or wrong.

'I have something to tell you,' Fidelma said one day, breezing into the kitchen.

I looked up at my sister, who was dressed, as usual, in one of her expensive cashmere jumpers.

'I've made a decision. I'm going to sell this place – it's worth millions – and, if you're up for it, I'm going to buy James's share of the café.'

I stared at her. My first thought was how long those cashmere jumpers would last in the café's kitchen. Involuntarily, I heard myself giggle. This resulted in Fidelma putting her hands on her hips and demanding to know why I thought it was so funny.

'Sorry, Fidelma. I'm just imagining you dressed up as a chef,'

I said. 'But . . . are you sure? It's a huge thing to take on and it might fail miserably.'

'It won't fail. Not with me on board.'

'There's just one thing,' I said. 'I can do some basic cooking, but I'm not up to much. And, while you do some great meals, you have no café or restaurant experience. You've got to admit that James did set a high standard for the place.'

'My dear, we'll hire someone. We'll take on a young chef with ambition. What can possibly go wrong?'

I stared at her, imagining all the things that could go wrong, and then we both started laughing.

'A celebration is called for,' Fidelma said, taking a bottle of champagne from the fridge and popping it open.

'Cheers,' she said.

'Cheers.'

I couldn't have imagined this, just a few months earlier – my sister and I not only becoming friends, but making plans to work together.

We were on our second glass of champagne when my mobile rang. It was Ned Moynihan.

'Orla,' he said. 'Where are you at the moment?'

His voice sounded strange – heavy and anxious.

'I'm still at Fidelma's. Why?'

'Is she with you?'

'Yes. Why? What's going on?'

'Can you put the phone on speaker, so that she can hear this as well?'

I was beginning to be frightened of what he was going to tell us.

'Okay, it's on speaker.'

'I want you to hear this before the press get hold of it, which they will, any minute now. Aidan McManus is dead. He killed himself this morning.'

'Oh, Jesus!'

But it was Fidelma who had cried out, not me. I couldn't speak. I could hardly breathe. Aidan, dead. I had tried not to think too deeply or too often about what he had done, first to Lillian and then to me. I had tried not to remember the attraction I had felt for him, because the thought of it frightened and revolted me. But now everything was crashing inside and around me.

'Can we call you back later?' I heard Fidelma say.

'Is she all right?' Ned asked.

'She's . . . a bit upset, but she'll be fine. We'll get back to you.'

'No,' I said, managing to find my voice. 'It's okay; I want to know now. What happened?'

'He hanged himself. I've just heard the news myself. There's going to be a statement shortly,' Ned said. 'Look, Orla, I'm going to be up to my eyes for the next few hours, but I'd like to drop in on you this evening or tomorrow. Is that okay?'

'Are you going to ask me questions about Aidan?'

'No,' he said. 'I just want to see how you are. That's all. No questions about Aidan. We don't even have to mention him.'

'Okay. That will be . . . fine.'

That night, I lay in bed going over every moment of Ned Moynihan's visit.

I had tried hard to shut out the traumatic events. I had refused counselling. I had to deal with it all in my own way, and putting all my effort into refusing to allow Aidan McManus to invade my mind had been part of that way.

But Ned Moynihan had come to Fidelma's house and Fidelma had left us together, and, somehow, the two of us managed to talk about everything that had happened. Because Ned, too, was having to deal with trauma. It wasn't only Lillian who had lain hidden for years beneath the stables. His mother, he told me, had also been hidden down there.

'My mother died . . . in an accident at home, and my father – he had political ambitions – concealed it because he was afraid he would be suspected of having killed her,' he told me. 'I think my father went to Aidan's father, Malcolm, for advice. And I think Malcolm helped him by hiding my mother's body under the stables.'

'Did Aidan know?'

'Maybe, but I doubt it. I suspect he only knew about the space directly under that first stable. The other walls had been bricked up. And it's not the kind of thing a father tells his son,' Ned said. 'Or maybe it is. But his mother certainly must have –'

'She must have known about Lillian,' I gasped. 'Oh, God, it's horrible. To think that she knew and said nothing –'

'We don't know that for sure. The lads have been to see her a few times and she refuses to say a word. So we may never know. And Aidan, as you know, refused to talk. You're the only one he told about having killed Lillian.'

He was about to leave when I knew I had to tell him about what tortured me most, the worm of self-loathing that was eating away at me.

'Ned, can I tell you something?'

'Of course.'

'I became ... involved with Aidan for a while. Not when he was with Lillian, but ... recently. When things were going wrong with James. It makes me feel sick to my stomach. I hate myself for it. It's one of the worst things of all. It feels worse than thinking I was going to die down there. Sometimes I wish I *had* died.'

I had simply wanted him to know everything and I had hoped for a sympathetic nod in response. What I hadn't expected was that he would open his arms to me and that I would feel I had reached the safest place in the world.

Chapter Forty-Two

Ned

The first day of January. Ned was by himself in the house. He had spent New Year's Eve with Rose and Barney, and then had walked home in the early hours. He hadn't slept more than an hour or two, but had lain awake, thinking about the new year that was starting, and hoping that he could make it a year of going forward and not looking back.

He had sat up well into the night, reflecting on the past, trying to imagine the future and not getting very far. But he had promised himself that, whatever the future might hold, he would approach it with optimism and good will. He hoped his future would include Rose.

Right now, though, he wanted the first thing he did on the first day of this new year to be a positive one, one that would show his acceptance of the life Eily lived now and allow the two of them finally to become friends. And so, buoyed by a mug of strong coffee, he dialled her number and suggested that they meet in the next few days, whenever she liked, just for old time's sake.

'I can meet you today,' she said.

'But it's New Year's Day. Do you not have . . . well, guests and the like – things on?'

'Garret's gone to Fairyhouse. One of his pals has a horse running. Tom is at Andrea's and Annie's still in bed. I'm here by myself. But maybe you have things to do . . .'

'No, I have no plans. Where would you like to meet?'

'I can come over to you, if you like.'

'Are you sure?'

'I'm sure. What's a good time?'

'Why don't you come for lunch? I'll make us something. You won't be disappointed. I've improved in the cooking department.'

She laughed. 'I can't wait.'

That phone call was the most civilised, most ordinary conversation they had had since their split and since the business with Aidan McManus and Tom. It had been almost flirtatious. And now he was nervous. He was so nervous that he was tempted to go out and buy a packet of fags. It would be their first meeting alone, just the two of them, since Tom had left the hospital.

He tried to read the book that Annie had given him for Christmas, a beautiful edition of Bram Stoker's *Dracula*. But he was jittery, he couldn't focus and, when the doorbell eventually sounded, he jumped up and rushed to the front door. He had thought – no, he had agonised – about how he should greet her, telling himself that a handshake would be too cold, too removed, and that a kiss or a hug would be too forward. But

Eily, it turned out, had already made a decision on protocol. She leaned towards him and kissed him lightly on the cheek.

But he saw that she was nervous, too, as she stood in his house for the first time, looking around her at this place he had made his home without any input from her.

'Are you hungry?' he asked, breaking the silence that had lasted just a few seconds, but seemed to have gone on for much longer. 'I was thinking of making omelettes.'

'That would be perfect,' she said, a smile creeping into her face and spreading across it. This was the Eily he hadn't seen for a very long time – the Eily she had been before marriage to him made her angry and bitter.

He made the omelettes, throwing in ham, cheese and mushrooms, and, while the mixture was cooking in the pan, he put together a salad of lettuce and tomatoes, and made a dressing of olive oil and balsamic vinegar. Finally, he produced a bottle from which he added a few drops of a dark greenish-brownish oil.

'Austrian pumpkin-seed oil. My secret ingredient,' he said, waving the bottle at her, and he was pleased when she laughed and said he was turning into a foodie and wonders would never cease.

He had a bottle of champagne in the fridge, though now he was having second thoughts about opening it, because it might give Eily the wrong impression. But her presence in his house was something to be marked out as special, maybe the beginning of a new friendship between them, so he thought, Sod it, and opened the champagne as they sat down to eat. He noticed that Eily looked pleased.

'To Annie,' he said, lifting his glass. He was trying to feel, as well as sound, bright and nonchalant about Annie's impending departure for Australia.

'To Annie.'

'Won't you miss her, too?' he asked, as they began tucking into their food.

'Desperately,' Eily said. 'But it's what she wants.'

'She's so young, though.'

'I wasn't that much older when you and I got married.'

'And look what happened,' he said.

He was shocked by the bitter tone of his voice and the force with which he delivered the words, and by the way she winced. This wasn't how he wanted their meeting to go. He apologised.

'I'm sorry. I shouldn't have said that.'

But Eily shrugged, smiled and said it was all right. And then she put her hand over his, and he wasn't at all surprised to find himself thinking that this was what he had wanted her to do, but he was still a bit shocked that she was doing it.

'I know I gave you a lot of grief, Eily, even if I never meant to. I wasn't a great husband, and I didn't deserve you. I was immature and stupid. I put the job before you and the kids,' he said. 'I miss you every single day. No, don't get me wrong – I know it's over between us. I'm not trying to get you back. Not any more. Because I know there's no point. We've both moved on. All I want is for us to be friends.'

Eily nodded and Ned saw that her eyes were looking dangerously close to tears. She looked away and held out her glass, which was only half empty.

He went back to the fridge and retrieved the champagne.

When he returned to the table, her eyes were dry again. The break in the conversation had restored some equilibrium.

'Maybe you could come over every now and again, join us for Sunday lunch, or something like that,' Eily suggested, and Ned said that, yes, that was a good idea.

She asked him about his life, whether there was a woman in it.

'I've been seeing Rose, but I'm not sure it's going anywhere,' he said. And then, as if to emphasise to himself as well as to Eily that he wasn't still nurturing some vain hope that the old spark would reignite and bring the two of them together again, he said, 'But I'm working on it.'

'And work? Are you still thinking about the sabbatical?'

'Yeah. Haven't done anything about it, though.'

Eily looked at her watch. 'I think maybe I'd better get going.'

'I'm sorry,' Ned said, watching her gather her things.

'For what?' Her back was turned to him as she pulled her coat on.

'For everything. For not being up to scratch as a husband. Even as an ex-husband.'

'Oh, Ned, Ned,' she sighed, standing up straight and turning her head in his direction. 'You've said all that. We're beyond it now. But . . . well, I'm sorry, too, and – well, yeah – I wish, too, that it had all turned out differently.'

She put her arms around him and he put his around her, and they stood quietly together for a while. When she raised her head from his chest and looked up into his face, he was tempted to kiss her. She must have guessed at what was going through his mind because she pulled away just a fraction and smiled at him.

'We made a good pair once, didn't we?' She was laughing now, but her eyes were gleaming and he could tell she was close to tears. He didn't have to think twice again about kissing her. This time, he just did it. And she kissed him back.

'Pax?' he said, as they moved away from each other.

'Pax,' she said.

And then they both laughed and he walked her to the door.

Orla

I've never thought of myself as a religious person, but there was a comfort in lighting the candles on the first day of the new year. I put a few coins in the box for the money and took out three candles.

I lit one for James, holding it against one of the flames that already burned brightly. I mourned the end of our time together and hoped he would find a place for himself in the world beyond Ardgreeney. Sometimes I wished we had never left London, because then we might have stayed together and I would never have known anything of what had gone on between him and Lillian. But, if we hadn't gone to live in Ardgreeney, the truth about Lillian would probably have stayed hidden, because Aidan wouldn't have begun his campaign to destroy James. And Inspector Moynihan would never have discovered what had happened to his mother's body.

I lit a candle for Lillian. At first, the flame flickered weakly, and I was afraid that it would go out. My heart beat fast as I waited and prayed, willing the flame to take hold. And, when it did, I cried a little bit, remembering all the good and wonderful times, but also the betrayal that had cost her her life.

I hesitated before I lit the third candle, but I lit it, anyway. Wherever Aidan's soul was now, I hoped it was at peace.

As I walked out of the church, I felt as if a burden had been lifted – not taken away, just shifted to one side.

Fidelma was waiting for me.

'Okay?' she asked.

I nodded, smiled.

Was I okay? Not quite, but I was certainly getting better. I linked my arm in hers and we walked down towards the sea, the wind behind us and the winter sun low and dazzling on the waves in front of us.

Postscript

Letter found in Kathleen McManus's room at Kilfernagh Nursing Home, in an envelope marked for the attention of Inspector Ned Moynihan.

Dear Inspector Moynihan,

I have remained silent about what happened to Lillian Murray for over ten years, as much for my own sake as for that of my son. But now that my only child has taken his own life, I feel I am able finally to release myself from the burden I have carried for so long.

My son told me that Lillian's death was an accident. Whether he told me the truth is something I will never know. I chose to believe him, however, because I had no other option.

He brought her body to Eaglewood on the night of the storm. I helped him take it from the car and lower it into the secret place below the stable block. What choice did I have? You may argue that what I did was wrong. But he was my son. It was as simple as that.

I did not like Lillian Murray, but my son loved her. She meant everything to him. Had it come down to a choice between her and me, he would have chosen her. If I had been forced to choose between saving my own life and his, I would have saved his. What mother would betray her son?

This brings me to the matter of your own mother. I did not know my husband at the time of the sad events surrounding your mother's disappearance. Nor did I know, when I first met him, that he was anything other than the handsome, charming and charismatic man who swept me off my feet.

We had not been married for very long before I discovered that he was unscrupulous, possessive and violent, apt to fly into a rage at the slightest provocation from me. This provocation could be a greeting to one of his associates that he deemed too warm, or it could be a friendly exchange with the vet. I tried to leave him after the first time he attacked me. That was when I was pregnant with my first child, which I miscarried. It was also when he told me he had once hidden a woman's body in that terrible place beneath the stables to help his friend conceal her death. He threatened me with a similar fate every time I summoned the courage to pack a bag.

As I bring my life to an end, I offer you my heartfelt sorrow and sympathy for everything you have endured, and I earnestly hope that the rest of your life will be peaceful and happy. You are the product of what I am told was a less than happy marriage. My son was similarly cursed.

Yours sincerely,

Kathleen McManus

Acknowledgements

Special thanks to Nicola Barr, my agent, and Stef Bierwerth, my editor at Quercus, for their unstinting help and patience. They are absolutely fabulous! Thanks also to Rachel Neely, Alainna Hadjigeorgiou, Hannah Robinson and all at Quercus, to Penny Price for her excellent copy edit, and to Niki Dupin for her beautiful and atmospheric cover.